Tokens of the Liars

by

BETSY RANDOLPH

Shoppe Foreman Publishing

Guthrie, Oklahoma

Published by

Shoppe Foreman Publishing

Guthrie, Oklahoma

Printed in the United States

ISBN-13: 978-1478269465
ISBN-10: 1478269464

Dedication

To my Mom,

Joyce Elizabeth Byrd,
who bought me my first typewriter
when I was ten years old

Acknowledgements

*T*okens of the Liars was made possible with the advice and affirmation of my fellow Red Dirt Writers, Beth Stephenson and Larry Foreman. Much thanks to my publisher, Shoppe Foreman Publishing, for making my manuscript into a book.

I'd like to express my appreciation for my keen editing staff – Joyce Byrd, Susan Hartford, Carol Evans, and Larry Foreman. Technical advice was graciously given by my fellow gunslingers at the Guthrie Police Department, Oklahoma City Police Department, and Oklahoma Highway Patrol, as well as various members of the Oklahoma Department of Public Safety.

Thanks also to Paula and Darrell Burnett for sharing the beauty that is Rosa Bella Guest Rooms that was the inspiration for Cat's apartment. Kudos to Rick Buchanan for his photographic skills that captured the essence of Guthrie. Thanks also to my cover model, Tatyanna Neely, and her photographer-mother Melissa Neely.

I give God the glory for His unbelievable blessings and for giving me my patient spouse, George, and imaginative son, Bronson, both of whom have endured countless, long-winded story ideas.

Chapter 1

Juan Diaz' gold-toothed smile reflected his unmistakable happiness in the harsh Oklahoma sun. His last day on the planet would be his best. His brown-eyed princess had just celebrated her eighth birthday and he had been allowed to attend her party. Picking his daughter up, he swung her around the dandelion covered yard causing her pink-flowered dress to hop on the breeze while she squealed.

After six excruciating years behind the chalky white walls of Granite Reformatory, Juan was a free man. His wife, Maria, had divorced him while he was incarcerated, but she still brought his daughter, Rosalita, to visit him. Once a month, they would sit across the cool metal table from each other in the gray prison cafeteria. He'd studied her delicate features and tiny tan fingers as she sat on her mother's lap twirling strands of her shiny black hair. He would do anything for her. Anything. He smiled while watching her clutch the blond-haired dolly under her arm. It was the first birthday present he had given her in six years. He wasn't sure if she was too old for a doll, but wanting to make up for his absence, he had bought it anyway, plus a pink stroller, a change of baby clothes and a baby swing. He smiled as his eyes followed her at play, but the smile evaporated as he watched an old accomplice exit a blue Chevy El Camino and swagger across the yard toward him. Juan was already shaking his head no when Chaz Rodriguez stuck his tattooed hand out for a familiar handshake.

"Come on…just this one time, Juan," Chaz insisted.

"Man, I don't do that stuff no more," Juan argued, nervously wiping at sweat collecting on top of his smooth, bald head. "You know I can't go back to prison," Juan said as he used his chin to point at his daughter. A shiver of fright ran through him at the thought.

If he hadn't splurged on Rosalita's birthday he would have insisted that Chaz leave immediately. As it was, he listened to the plan and nearly sighed with defeat while he considered repeating his old offenses. Juan searched his former partner's pock marked face. He wanted Chaz to see that he had truly changed while he was locked up. But all Chaz knew or cared about was that Juan was the right guy for the job.

In the old days, Juan Diaz could get his thieving hands on anything. He was one of the sliest thieves Chaz Rodriguez had ever known. Besides, this would be an easy job. Chaz was counting on his long-time acquaintance to come through for them both again.

Juan was the right guy for the job, but before the night was over, "the job" would cost Juan Diaz more than he would be willing to pay. By morning, there would be an eight-year-old little girl with a broken heart, and she would have a liar to thank for it.

Chapter 2

Catherine "Cat" Carlyle, radio network news journalist, worked the evening shift for Sooner Broadcasting in Oklahoma City. At twenty-eight, Cat was an "old timer" in radio. She had worked at radio stations across the country but had come back to Oklahoma three years ago and established herself as a serious journalist.

Cat had grown up in and around radio. Her father owned and operated a small country radio station since before she was born. She hadn't been willing to fulfill his dreams and carry on the family business. Cat was a journalist, not a disc-jockey.

Philip Carlyle had devoted nearly half his life to the radio station he started in Oklahoma City. He considered it his legacy. Cat's mother, a delicately featured woman named Linda, played mediator between Cat and her father. They were so much alike: arguing had become the only way they could communicate. Sometimes, Cat's mom found it difficult to understand her only child.

Cat knew she had changed since she moved away to college. She also knew it wasn't for the better. Her hair was no longer brown – it was bleached blonde. She drank heavily, swore proficiently and lied a great deal. She considered the lying more of a courtesy, though. She would often confess to her best friend, Susan, that lying eased the pain of failure. Her failures. She'd say that she lied to protect herself or protect others. It wasn't malicious. She just hated controversy. The irony of her constant lying wasn't lost on Cat. Being a news journalist, she was supposed to report the truth. Instead she constantly lied. Shame filled her every time she opened her mouth to put her spin on a story. But no matter how shameful, she didn't or wouldn't change.

Susan understood. Susan Richmond had been Cat's best friend since sixth grade, and they tried never to lie to each other. Susan had been the one to ask Cat to be friends first. Cat liked Susan immediately, with her brilliant blue eyes and her short red hair. Best friends is what they had always been, would always be.

Cat was thinking of calling Susan as her tedious shift ended at the radio station that night. She faked a smile into her voice as she signed off the air and quickly gathered her things to leave.

Rick, her producer, had been especially critical and demeaning tonight, she thought, as she loaded her arms to go. She was hoping to get out of the building before she had another confrontation with Rick. She grabbed her purse, some CDs she needed to review and her favorite silver bracelet that Susan had given her on her last birthday.

"Yes, please don't forget your silver security blanket, Cat," Rick sneered.

She paused as if to say something, then turned and headed out the door. She didn't even look at him as she made her way out of the booth and out of the building. She stopped briefly to use the restroom before rushing to her car. She was running away, like a child from a bully.

Why am I so pathetic? Cat thought. All night long she hadn't responded to any of Rick's hateful comments. Maybe she was just weak, she mused as she trudged down the sidewalk. Her flats did little to cheer her as they made their usual clippedy-clomp melody on the concrete. Fine, she could admit that she hated confrontation. She sighed with disgruntled agreement. She knew she seldom retorted when any unpleasantness was directed toward her. She just took whatever from whomever, in silence. She hated herself for it. Making her way through the desolate parking lot, she berated herself, unaware of what lay ahead.

In a dimly lit corner of the sparsely used lot her Toyota waited patiently. As Cat searched her purse for her car keys, her mind replayed the night's controversial events. A deeply ridged frown grew across her forehead as she analyzed every hostile encounter with Rick. She wondered if he thought she had no self-esteem at all.

Rick Hurley was gorgeous with his blonde hair and sea green eyes, but he was also self-important, he couldn't have a conversation without saying, "me or I" half a dozen times. He never admitted being wrong, and he always brought up the fact that he was Cat's boss. Just the way he waltzed around the station like a demigod was enough to make Cat want to vomit. Rick had been an only child, born to wealthy parents who showered him with praise. Probably undeserved praise at that, Cat thought. She couldn't see why everyone thought he was such a great radio phenomenon. She had been in radio long enough to spot a phony when she saw one. And Rick Hurley was a phony. Not to mention a jackass.

Rick complained as usual about her bracelet at the beginning of her shift. "Why do you insist on wearing that thing?" He pointed at her wrist, his eyes big and questioning. "It's not like anyone can see it, besides it makes a lot of racket on air." He imitated her moving her arms around the control booth, his big arms flapping around carelessly, banging the imaginary bracelet on the Formica countertop.

"Lose the bracelet Cat, or else." He sliced a single tan finger across his throat, mimicking her demise as he smiled that wicked smile producing perfect white teeth.

"Whatever," Cat mouthed as she slipped the bracelet off her arm. She made a production of setting it close to the plexiglas window that separated them from each other.

Betsy Randolph

She couldn't explain why she wore the bracelet every day. Maybe it was just to irritate Rick. There was something about the guy that drove her crazy. Not a good crazy either, she thought with a deeper frown.

Cat fumed as she neared her car and fumbled with her keys. She would end up dropping everything she was carrying if she wasn't careful, she thought. As if on cue, her bracelet slipped out of her hand and hit the ground rolling. "Perfect!" she complained aloud as she laid her things on the ground to search for the object of her disdain.

"I should have just put the stupid thing on my wrist," she grumbled. She chided herself for rushing out of the studio without being prepared. She had taken some self-defense classes several months ago after a couple of local young women had been raped and murdered. At the class, she had learned to have her keys in her hand, prepared to unlock her car, and to get in quickly, then lock the doors. Now here she was on her hands and knees in the dark, alone and getting more pissed by the second. As she searched for the bracelet, she wondered if anything else could go wrong.

In the low light she had to comb the concrete with her hand for the bracelet. Kneeling down further she could see the bracelet had managed to land squarely underneath the center of the car that was parked next to hers. *It's a good thing I wasn't planning on going out after work*, she thought, as she slowly lowered her slender frame to the ground. She had barely touched her favorite blue blouse to the dirty pavement when she heard footsteps approaching quickly. She froze in place.

"Hand it over," she heard a man's voice say.

Was that Rick? she wondered and stretched her arm out to retrieve the silver bracelet.

"I didn't find it, man," she heard another man's voice say. He sounded unfamiliar and Hispanic.

"What do you mean you didn't find it?" the first man asked in a harsh questioning whisper.

No, that wasn't Rick, she thought. She laid her arm down and rested her chin on the back of her other hand and eavesdropped on their conversation.

"I'm telling you man, I honestly didn't find it. I searched her house and her car too, just like you said. I don't know where it is. I told Chaz the same thing."

She heard a scuffling sound then and profanity volleyed back and forth between the men. She feared they could hear her heart pounding against the cool concrete beneath her. She heard whispered threats as one man swore at the other.

"Tell me where it is, Diaz, or I'll cut you. Do you understand what I'm saying?" There was a slight pause, followed by a grunt from what Cat assumed was a punch to the gut followed by more grunts and groans.

"I would tell you if I knew...I swear!" Diaz wheezed. He sounded afraid. They couldn't have been more than six or seven feet away, she guessed.

They were standing between her car and a concrete wall that divided two separate parking areas. They were on the opposite side of her car, but she feared their violence would spill over onto her. How did she not hear or see them before she got on the ground, she wondered. Dreading the thought that they had seen her, she turned her head sideways and guided her cheek down to her hand. *Just breathe*, she coached herself. *Calm down.* She was attempting to soothe her rattled nerves when she allowed her eyes to search and find the two pairs of feet belonging to the men talking. She saw black western boots with shiny tips facing a pair of brown loafers with square toes. She noted the "S" on the side of the brown shoes and wondered which set of shoes belonged to whom, but she didn't have to wait long to find out.

"If you really don't know where it is," she heard the first guy growl, "then I guess I have no further use for you, do I?"

She wasn't positive, but his voice really did sound familiar. Before a response was spoken, she heard this sickening sucking sound of what would turn out to be a knife being thrust into the wheezing man's chest.

Suddenly, he dropped to the ground, and immediately Cat locked eyes with him. He stared at her pleadingly while clutching his bloody chest. His eyes remained fixed on hers as he took his last ragged breath. Cat watched as the life in his dark brown eyes drifted. She couldn't make herself look away as his pupils enlarged and froze in place.

"It was the most horrifying thing to see," she would say later, "looking into a man's eyes as he dies."

She didn't know how long she lay there trying to figure out what had just happened before she reacted? She heard a voice screaming hysterically, not realizing it was her own. Her mind was racing, her thoughts banging into one another so violently that she wasn't sure if she had sustained a brain injury somehow. The terror that had seized her body thrust her into a catatonic state at first. It caused her to be unable to move or speak, as if she were paralyzed, but for how long she didn't know. All she could remember was the horror of hearing the stabbing, then time stood still. Then the screaming and crying, that was her. Someone had heard her. Someone had come, but she didn't know who. She didn't remember anything else until she lifted her head off the stainless steel table at the Metro Police Station.

Chapter 3

She looked around the room in a daze until a wicked thought came to her. *If I hadn't dropped my brace-let, would he still be alive?* The question played over and over again in Cat's head as she sat slumped in the hard, metal chair in the police interview room. Her hazel eyes burned from hours of crying and lack of sleep. *Maybe I would have been killed, too.* That thought pierced her brain with a jolt. She sat up abruptly and lifted the sleeve of her blue shirt to view the silver bracelet on her arm. Maybe the bracelet had saved her life, but her silver hero was missing. Then she remembered she never picked it up off the ground.

Cat didn't know how long she had been there, but she was weary of sitting alone at the table in a staunch white room with a scratchy wool blanket around her shoulders. She peered into the paper cup in front of her. It appeared to be cold coffee. *What time is it?* She wondered. She had been there for hours it seemed. Her arms felt lifeless, folded across her chest. She was about to scream when the door swung open and in walked a tall, dark-headed man in a grey suit jacket and jeans. His unbuttoned collar and loosened tie indicated that he too had been up a long time.

"How ya doing, kid?" he asked casually as he pulled a chair out from the metal table and sat down, allowing his long legs to stretch out beneath it. "Remember me? I'm Detective Thomas Sullivan, Homicide. You can call me, Tom. Are you feeling any better?" His light brown eyes showed true concern she thought. "Ready to talk to me now?"

Had she met him before? Yes, she remembered. He was the one who brought her the gaud-awful coffee and the blanket. She had been shivering and crying when he tried questioning her before. She couldn't quit shaking, and her voice had failed her. The smell of Pine Sol cleaner and vomit had assaulted her nostrils when they showed her into this small, cold room with mirrored windows. She looked at Thomas Sullivan for a few silent moments mulling over the words, "Homicide Detective."

Thomas Sullivan had been with the Oklahoma City Police Department for eighteen years. He had been in Traffic Patrol, the Gang Task Force, Narcotics and finally Homicide. Of all the specialized fields, homicide fit him best. A single man with no immediate family living close by, his lifestyle was ideal for the job. Often he would get called away from home in the middle of the night on a murder case and wouldn't come home for days. He was forced to work weekends, holidays and many overtime hours. Sullivan didn't mind. In fact, he loved it. The best part of his job was the knowledge that people counted on him. He needed

Betsy Randolph

to be needed. Of course, the down side to his job was when murders went unsolved. Those cases haunted his dreams. His eyes traveled over Cat's face, resting on her full mouth, willing her to speak.

The blanket hadn't eased the icy ache Cat felt deep within her bones. Finally she looked Sullivan in the eyes, "Yes, I remember you. You read me my rights. Why did you do that?" Her tear-streaked face frowned as she stared searchingly into his eyes.

"Well, there was a stabbing last night outside your place of employment. I'm trying to figure out your involvement." He searched her face for any reaction. What he got was a blank stare.

"My involvement?" she demanded. "What the hell are you talking about? I am not involved." She practically spat the last word at him.

"Then how did you come to have what appears to be the victim's blood all over you?" Detective Sullivan asked. His brown eyes no longer seemed kind. They were steely and accusing.

"How did I what?" Cat gasped. Suddenly she was no longer cold. She shrugged the blanket off, not even wondering why she felt hot all over so fast. "No, that is not correct, I was under my car. I wasn't even close to that man. I didn't even know that guy."

Her palms went sweaty, and the need to swallow nearly choked her. Cat felt the room spinning – she was certain she had a brain injury now. Either the lights were flickering on and off or she was about to pass out.

She had to get out of there. Her lungs were screaming for oxygen. She was certain she was drowning while staring into the eyes of the handsome, seasoned cop. She lunged to her feet, deciding it was time to leave. That was the last thought she had before she toppled over the table and onto the cold concrete floor.

Cat awoke in what she thought must have been heaven. I guess I made it after all, she thought. She closed her eyes again, enjoying her effortless reward for what she was certain some would call, "a life not well spent." Wait a second. Suddenly she realized where she was and why she was there, and the dizziness returned.

"Miss, how are you feeling?" A young, Hispanic man in scrubs was checking an IV on her arm. He tapped her shoulder lightly and repeated himself. "Miss?" he began.

Cat cut him off with a curt, "I'm fine. Where are my clothes?" But before he responded, he leaned to Cat's left and motioned for someone behind her to come to him.

Detective Sullivan came around where he could see her. "We needed your clothes for evidence. The lab has them. They will be returned to you eventually. I can arrange to have some more clothes brought to you."

"Don't bother. I don't need your help," Cat declared. She thrust her chin out a little further and turned her face away from him, exposing her injured cheek.

"Ouch! That looks painful." Sullivan said as he gave a dismissive nod to the nurse. He didn't touch her, but he was close enough to see the swelling and the blue patches of bruising around her cheek and under her eye.

Cat turned her head slightly and caught the look of concern and feeling on Sullivan's face and in his eyes. "I'm fine. It doesn't hurt that much," she confessed.

She watched as Sullivan seemed to relax a little and gave her a half-smile. His hands seemed restless as she watched him cross his arms, then put his hands on his hips and finally stick them into his pockets where they stayed for at least a few minutes as she talked.

"What happened? Did I faint?" Cat asked while gently touching her cheek. From the feel of her wound, she had gotten several stitches. Six, to be exact.

"Yes, you briefly passed out." Sullivan admitted. "Maybe you stood up too fast. They don't really know yet. The doctor has decided you need to stay the night in the hospital for observation."

He asked how he could reach her next of kin. Cat gave him her parent's information and considered warning him that they might overreact. But then she realized she didn't know how they would react.

Chapter 4

"I told you this kind of thing was going to happen," Linda Carlyle was saying to Cat's father. They still stood in the entryway of their luxurious house in a gated community in the northwest part of Oklahoma City. A uniformed police officer had just left after informing them of Cat's plight and her current status at the University's hospital downtown.

"Your daughter has always been so reckless and impulsive." Linda stated to Phillip. She was furious. "She will likely go to prison over this, won't she? God help her." Linda nearly sobbed into her hands as Phillip took her into his arms. "My baby! My baby girl! What has she done?" Linda broke down then. They held to each other while the news of the early morning's events sank in.

"Come on. Let's get dressed and go see her. Maybe I should call an attorney. It sounds like she'll need one," Phillip suggested. He could not make any sense of what he heard himself saying. His beautiful, sweet, little girl, a killer? No, it wasn't true. Sure, she was rebellious, stubborn and even stretched the truth from time to time, but a killer? No, she was several things he disapproved of, but a cold-blooded killer, she was not.

Betsy Randolph

After meeting with the nurse and then the doctor attending Cat, Phillip and Linda Carlyle entered her room. They had been informed that Cat had just drifted off to sleep. She looked so peaceful and sweet that neither had the heart to wake her. So they made themselves comfortable and waited for whatever was to come next.

"Hello, you must be Mr. and Mrs. Carlyle. I'm Detective Sullivan," the detective introduced himself as he entered Cat's hospital room about an hour later. He held out his wallet badge and identification for them to see. He had already spoken with the charge nurse and knew they were there. Sullivan was hoping they could shed some light on this interesting young woman who was at the center of his investigation.

"Phillip Carlyle. This is my wife, Linda," Philip offered as he stood and held a hand out to Sullivan. Linda nodded her head and smiled slightly. She remained seated, but looked intently at Sullivan.

"How is Catherine feeling? Did she tell you what happened?" Sullivan asked as he looked from Phillip to Linda. They both looked at each other and then at Cat before responding.

Linda spoke first, "We really don't know." She stood quickly as if someone had poked her and then continued, "She has been asleep since we arrived, and we hated to wake her. She looks so pale and exhausted." Linda moved from her seat and took what appeared to be a protective stance between Sullivan and Cat's hospital bed. Feeling the tension and reading the body language, Sullivan changed tactics. He needed them on his side.

"I was about to get a cup of coffee," Sullivan said as he turned toward the door. "Would you care to join me, Mr. Carlyle? We'll let Catherine sleep a little while longer," he finished in a near whisper.

"I suppose so," Phillip agreed. He needed a reprieve from the stale room anyway. "We'll bring you back some coffee, too." Sullivan said to Linda, who still stood rigid with her arms crossed stiffly in front of her.

She nodded at his comment but didn't speak. As soon as the door shut behind them, Linda began smoothing her shirt hem with her hands. The western shirt she wore was curling up on the end making her feel self-conscious. She wished she could have spent more time putting herself together before they rushed down to the hospital. She would take this opportunity to freshen up while the men were gone and Cat was still asleep. She stood just inside the open door in the tiny restroom of Cat's hospital room. She stared at her haggard appearance in the mirror.

"How can this be happening?" Linda wondered aloud as she pulled the lid off her lipstick and began applying it.

"Mom, is that you?" Cat asked groggily from her bed.

With only the top lip colored, Linda rushed to Cat's side. "Oh, sugar, how are you feeling? Your dad and I have been so worried. Why didn't you call us immediately? What happened? Are you alright? Who was that man that was killed? Did he hurt you? Did he give you this cut on your cheek?" Linda peppered Cat with questions and would have continued had Cat not stopped her by holding up her hands in protest.

"Mom, take it easy. I have this all under control," Cat said as she raised herself up in bed. She started to get out of the bed and then thought better of it. "Trust me," Cat assured her mom. "There is no reason to worry. I am just fine. I am..."

"Catherine Elise Carlyle, don't you dare say another word." Linda snapped. "You are in so much trouble, young woman. Do you have any idea what has happened and what you are accused of doing?" Linda stopped her tirade just as Detective Sullivan and Phillip came through the door.

"She's awake!" Phillip exclaimed as he handed the coffees to Linda and strode to Cat's side. He squeezed her in a hug that nearly crushed her ribs.

"Hi, Daddy. Like I was just telling Mom here, I am fine," Cat assured him as she smiled weakly.

Phillip relaxed his arms and grabbed both of Cat's shoulders. He looked intently into her face and took up where her mother had just left off. "What have you gotten yourself into this time, Girl? Who did this to your cheek?" Phillip gently grazed her cheek with his lips.

"Oh, Daddy, it's just a huge misunderstanding," Cat began. "I'll tell you what happened, just let me explain. But first, will you hand me my cell phone? It should be there in my purse.

Phillip rifled through the bag and found her phone. He handed it to her as she raked her fingers through her frizzy hair, which she seldom styled. She thought she probably looked pretty rough considering all she had been through. Because she didn't consider herself very pretty, she usually didn't waste much time or money painting herself up. She usually wore a little mascara and some lip color and called it good. While she tried to slick her hair down, she turned on her phone and let her eyes scan her mother's beautiful face. Linda was the epitome of style and femininity. It was hard being her daughter most of the time Cat thought, but looking at her mom now she smiled and pointed to her lips.

"Mom, what's with your lipstick?"

Cat had barely gotten the words out of her mouth when Linda flew from the room, horrified. Sullivan chuckled to himself as he approached Cat's bed and asked if she needed anything.

"Yeah, my clothes and a decent night's sleep. When can I leave?" she asked impatiently.

"Not until tomorrow morning, I'm told." Sullivan said, noting her discomfort.

He liked how child-like she looked in the gown and how vulnerable it made her seem. For some unknown reason he suddenly wanted to protect her. He felt an urge to take care of her. It had to be because of the smudged mascara stains under her beautiful hazel eyes, he thought. Or the stitches she wore like a medal on her cheek. Whatever the cause, the effect was undeniable. He had to remind himself that at the moment she was his only suspect in a murder investigation. He couldn't deny those facts either. Sullivan was grateful that the nurses had cleaned her up before her parents had arrived. It was hard enough for him to see her covered in dried blood, and he didn't even know her.

When he first saw Cat she had blood caked in her blonde hair. A large clump of it had congealed. Had Cat's mother seen that, she might have fainted, also.

"I have a few more questions for you if you're feeling up to it?" Sullivan asked.

"Actually, I would like for you to wait until our attorney arrives, Detective," Phillip intervened.

He stood by Cat's side holding her hand. Linda rejoined them, lipstick repaired. She went to the other side of Cat's bed and took her other hand. Her parents' presence made Cat feel more confident, but also more dependent.

"I don't mind, Dad," Cat said, letting go of both of their hands after giving each parent an affectionate squeeze. "I don't need an attorney. I didn't do anything wrong. I was trying to explain earlier to Detective Sullivan here...,"

"Tom, please call me Tom," Sullivan interrupted.

Cat continued without acknowledging his request. "I was explaining...that I was merely a witness to the murder." She stressed the word "witness" by staring at Sullivan and drawing air quotes around the word as she said it. Her voice quivered just a little then, as her mind flashed the dead man's face front and center. Those cold, dead eyes would haunt her for the rest of her life.

Cat squeezed her eyes shut as she continued. "I didn't kill anybody." She put her hands on either side of her head as if to keep it on her neck. It felt like her head was going to explode.

"Can I have a glass of water please?"

Linda found a plastic cup, unsealed it and poured water from a pitcher that was on a nearby bedside table. As she handed the cup of water to Cat their eyes caught, and Cat saw the worry and fear in them. It wrenched her heart.

"Better?" Sullivan asked. "Let's just go over a few things shall we?"

With Cat's permission he launched ahead with his questioning. He took out a notebook and flipped through several pages, selected the one he wanted and pulled a pen from inside a breast pocket of his jacket. Cat watched him with keen eyes. She hadn't noticed before how tall he was. Standing beside her hospital bed he appeared to tower over her parents.

"I need you to think back to the beginning of your day, Cat," he began. "But before you say anything I want to remind you of your rights." He hesitated long enough to turn a mini-tape recorder on and lay it beside Cat on her bedside table. "This will help me with my report later," he said, pointing his pen towards the recorder.

"Wait a minute," Phillip interrupted hurriedly. "I really think we should wait for our attorney to arrive. He'll be here shortly."

Cat shifted her weight on the hospital bed and pulled the covers higher. Maybe her dad was right, this didn't feel right. It angered her that this cop sounded accusatory.

"The murder happened after my shift at work," Cat protested. "What difference does it make what I did earlier in the day? What is it you're after, Detective?"

Sullivan opened his mouth to speak and closed it again. His chance of an informal interview was dwindling. "Well, I want to go back twelve hours from the crime and work forward. It's standard procedure I assure you."

He paused with his pen hovering above his notebook, waiting for a reply. Cat was old enough to make the decision to speak with him without representation. He hoped she chose to do so. He doubted her attorney would allow him to interview her today once he showed up. He changed gears, without waiting for a response.

"What time did your shift end at the station?" he asked, without looking up.

"Midnight."

"And what time did you start the shift?"

"Four p.m., but I got to the station early yesterday because I had some promos to cut."

"Promos?" Sullivan asked.

"Promotional advertisements. Lindsey, one of our sales reps, sent me a message earlier in the day and asked me to cut them. The customers had requested my voice for the ads."

"What's Lindsey's last name?" Sullivan asked, while scratching away furiously with his pen.

"Byrd. Lindsey Byrd," Cat replied.

Phillip stepped out to the hallway to place a phone call. Reaching the answering service for the second time that day, he asked about his attorney as he walked down the lonely corridor. He was wondering where their attorney was and how soon he would arrive. He was afraid that Cat had made the wrong decision. He wished she had chosen not to speak to the police detective without legal counsel first. After being placed on hold for several minutes, a woman came back on the line.

"Mr. Neal is on his way," the young receptionist said into the phone. "He was delayed for just a few minutes."

"Fine, if you have a way to contact him, please tell him we are in room 515 and there is a detective from Homicide already here." As he disconnected, Phillip frowned. He realized he was beginning to feel the strain from the emotions and lack of sleep. He knew Linda would be feeling much worse. Her health really wasn't the best, and problems with Cat usually brought on a migraine headache.

When Phillip stepped back into Cat's room his heart sank. Linda sat on the edge of Cat's bed, and the two of them were hugging. He could hear Cat crying softly and sniffling. He searched around for a box of tissues and began asking what was going on and where the police detective had gone.

"Detective Sullivan informed me that I'm their only suspect and that I cannot leave town without letting them know where I'm going," Cat sniffed.

"Did he already leave?" Phillip asked. "I was only gone for a minute. What happened?"

"Well, your daughter didn't like his tone and told him to get out," Linda said. "It must have made him mad because without another word he slapped his notebook shut and grabbed his recorder and left."

"Cat!" Phillip started.

"Dad, the guy is bipolar, one minute he is all looking gooey-eyed at me, and the next he is insulting my integrity and calling me a murderer!"

Exasperated, she fell back to the pillow and draped an arm over her face. *Why is all this happening to me?* she wondered. Her face had begun to ache from the injury to her cheek, and she silently acknowledged the throbbing headache it had given her. She would likely have a hideous scar on her face. Not that it mattered, she thought. No one cared to look at her anyway. She had nothing and no one, she told herself. No, she *was* nothing and no one, she corrected herself. Everyone would be better off if she were dead.

"I wish he had just killed me, too." She sobbed, as her tears ran down either side of her head. As she lay on her back, the tears began filling her ears.

"Stop it! Don't talk that way," Phillip said. "We'll get this all straightened out. You're just exhausted. You've been through a lot." He patted Cat's shoulder to reassure her.

Cat continued to cry and didn't respond, but drained her tear-filled ears by sitting up. She could feel the warm tears turning cold quickly as they dripped off her earlobes and onto the front of her thin gown. She wiped her face with the sheet that covered her and rolled over in the bed, turning her back to her parents. Linda turned a tear-streaked face to Phillip and shrugged her shoulders sadly. She dabbed at the corners of her eyes with the tissue Phillip had handed her. He could tell by the way her right eyelid was sagging, that a migraine would be forthcoming. It was going to be a long day for all of them.

****

Poking the knife into the tires of the little white car felt good, too good to be true, in fact, almost orgasmic. The quickly escaping air made hissing sounds as he

27

moved around the car and sliced every tire. His heart was racing, and his hands were slick with sweat. His excitement grew with each stab of the knife. He could only imagine what it would feel like to slide his blade between Cat's ribs and watch her eyes fill with horror.

Under the cover of darkness he slid the knife back into its sheath inside his boot. Pulling the dark hoodie over his head, he squatted in silence planning his getaway. Stunts like this made him feel more like the man he knew he was inside. He felt strong and power-ful. Carefully, he looked around for any witnesses before leaving the security of the shaded hiding spot where he knelt.

In the same parking lot a car door slammed shut. It was close by, startling him so that he almost bolted like a deer. Fortunately, he had the presence of mind to plaster himself against the now vandalized car and lower his body to the ground instead. He peered under the cars and saw someone walking away from a vehicle not fifty yards away. He wondered if they had seen him, but they weren't coming in his direction and they weren't in any hurry. He reassured himself that his dirty deed had gone undetected for now. He started to push himself up when something caught his eye. Under the car lay a slightly oval, silver object.

He knew exactly what was engraved on its smooth, silvery edges. His spirit soared as he stretched out his tattooed arm and his long, thin fingers closed around Cat's bracelet. Could this night get any better?

Chapter 5

Rex Neal, attorney-at-law was a quiet, albeit ferocious man. He wasn't good-looking; he could admit that. But that had helped him in law school. While his counterparts were "hooking up" and partying, he was studying. The thirty-year-old had graduated from the University of Oklahoma Law School near the top of his class. His greasy-looking brown hair was slicked over to one side, and his disheveled tan suit hid his lumpy frame.

He wandered the halls of the hospital texting on his Blackberry. "Room 515. Ah, here we are," he said out loud as he knocked twice on the closed door.

"Come in," said a female voice from inside.

"Miss Carlyle?" he said, as he opened the door and stuck his head in the room.

"Yes, please come in. We've been expecting you," Linda said. She wanted to say, "You're late!" But she refrained.

One of the Carlyle women should act civil, and Cat certainly was not going to do it. She had begged Cat to calm down and allow the system to work "for" her not "against" her. Cat acted like she hadn't heard anything either of her parents had said, but why should today be any different than any other day?

Rex set his briefcase down and opened it while making the Carlyle's introductions. His office had already given him the basic information on the case, but he was anxious to hear from Cat herself about what had transpired. He was particularly interested in exactly what she had already said to the police.

"Have you given any statements to the police?" Rex asked politely while settling his notepad on the bedside table. He pirated the little table away from Cat as soon as he reached her side.

"May I?" he asked and began moving the table without waiting for a response.

Cat looked at him with eyebrows raised and turned to scowl at both her parents. The first thing that griped Cat was that if Rex had been there a half hour ago like he should have been, then he wouldn't have to ask these stupid questions now. She just stared at Rex, her frown only deepening. Rex laid his pen on top of the notepad and gazed at her over his grimy looking glasses. He could tell by the expression on Cat's face that she was less than impressed with him. It never dawned on him though that his personal hygiene and appearance disgusted her and made her question her father's decision on retaining him in the first place.

"Look, Ms. Carlyle..." he began. "I am here to help you. So help me, help you by answering each question honestly and to the best of your ability." His demeaning tone had Cat sitting straight up on the bed and pointing a thin almost delicate finger in his face.

"No, you look, Bozo! You are here at my father's request. He is the one who thinks I need an attorney. I haven't done anything wrong and I refuse to sit here and be talked down to by some....some...." Her parent's presence had saved him from getting the tongue lashing she thought he deserved. Her respect for them had her biting her tongue, literally. Her anger was just about to the boiling point. She was exhausted, injured, traumatized, wrongly implicated and now insulted.

"Just get out." She said.

Her anger heated her up. It colored her face and neck a deep red. She admitted to herself that it felt good to speak her mind.

"Let's step out into the hallway a moment, shall we?" Phillip suggested while holding one hand out towards the door and placing the other on Rex's shoulder.

Rex and Phillip exited the hospital room without another word being spoken. When Phillip reentered the room, Cat had settled back on the bed and her mother was standing looking out the window with the palm of her hand pressed against her right eye. Phillip knew that meant Linda's migraine had settled in for the long haul.

"Rex is going to call us tomorrow. He'll come by the house and visit once you have had some rest. How does that sound?" Phillip said wearily.

31

Without a word, Cat bobbed her head up and down slightly and closed her eyes. She had no intention of ever seeing or speaking to Rex whatever-his-name-was again. She would tell her father just that the next day. For now, all she wished for was to be in her apartment, tucked away in her own bed with Hannah. Suddenly, she remembered Hannah.

Cat shared an apartment above a posh antique store with an old family friend named, Hannah. The two of them lived in Guthrie, a small Victorian town just north of the Oklahoma City metropolitan area where the red brick cobbled streets rumbled as cars drove atop them. The town was known for its beautiful two-story houses with laced window dressings and white picket fences. Hannah was well-known in Guthrie. Cat and Hannah spent a great deal of time walking the downtown streets and parks together. Her rust-colored face had turned white several years ago and she moved a bit slower these days, but she was a great listener. Cat and Hannah had been through a lot together and managed their friendship with love and understanding.

"Mom, I just remembered Hannah is still in her crate!" Cat threw the covers off and started peeling the tape off her arm that held the IV catheter in her vein.

"Stop! Don't do that!" Linda yelled. "Phillip, help me, call the nurse." She shouted as she put her hands on Cat's arms to keep her from disconnecting herself from the only water she figured her daughter had consumed in days. Phillip sprang into action by pushing the call nurse button on the controller by Cat's leg.

"That poor baby dog has been in her crate since yesterday at one o'clock mom. I have to go," Cat pleaded.

"Your dad and I will go take care of her right now. I promise," Linda assured her while still holding both of Cat's arms.

"There isn't any reason for me to stay here. I am perfectly fine and I am going home to Hannah," Cat pleaded, tears in her eyes.

"I think you should do what the doctor says, Cat," Phillip said. "You don't have any idea why he wants you to stay overnight, and the Doctor told us that he was waiting on some lab results to come back before he could conclusively say why he thinks you passed out."

Cat absorbed what her dad said and finally conceded with an, "Okay, okay."

"Yes, can I help you?" A delayed response came through on the speaker on the controller.

"No, thank you. Please disregard the call," Phillip huffed as he looked back at Cat.

Linda released her grip on Cat's arms, but remained by her side as she reassured her they would take care of Hannah and get her a clean change of clothes to replace the ones seized as evidence.

"We'll go over there right now and take care of her," Linda continued. "I have my key. We'll check on everything and lock up when we're through. I can bring your clothes and anything else you might need, if you want me to," Linda added quickly.

She wanted out of the hospital nearly as badly as Cat did, if not more.

"No, I don't need anything else. Just take care of Hannah, please," Cat pleaded.

Phillip and Linda were gone when the doctor arrived to discuss Cat's lab results and check on her. With him were several young people dressed in medical scrubs. He introduced them as medical students and asked permission for them to remain in the room while he discussed the results with her. Cat acknowledged their presence with a slight smile and nodded her head in approval.

"Your test results indicate that you are dehydrated and slightly anemic. I'm also concerned about your low potassium level and have ordered a potassium drip for your IV. We will have to hook you up to a heart monitor for that because we need to observe you and your vitals while you receive the potassium. The potassium drip can cause some heart arrhythmias so I will I want you to stay overnight for observation. Tomorrow morning we will do another blood draw. If everything looks good, I will discharge you then." Without waiting for a response, he continued, "Your cheek was stitched up by Dr. Peterson, our on-call plastic surgeon. It looks like it should heal nicely." He said, while gently touching a gloved hand to Cat's cheek.

One of the medical students chimed in then, "Does the patient have any other complaints, Doctor?" The doctor looked at her with an inquiring expression. Cat thought of that for a moment. By now she was feeling almost giddy from lack of sleep. I have a long list of complaints she thought, with a goofy grin.

"None that you guys would care to hear about," Cat said, causing the group to chuckle.

"Any questions before I go?" The doctor asked.

"Should I be concerned about the anemia?"

"No, it is not uncommon for women to be anemic. Let's start you on an over the counter iron pill taken once daily for a month and see if that helps." He patted her blanketed leg and told her to get some rest, and the group shuffled out of the room.

Cat had just about dozed off when her cell phone startled her awake. She answered on the second ring and sounded dazed and sleepy.

"Cat, its Mom. Hannah is just fine. Believe it or not she didn't make any messes in her crate. We didn't have the heart to make her stay there alone cooped up though, so we brought her on home with us," Linda explained. "After you get released tomorrow we'll just swing by here, pick her up and drop you girls off at your apartment together. Does that sound good?"

No, it sounds terrible, Cat thought. But she knew she didn't have any choice, and being hateful to the people who cared for her wasn't right. "Yes, Ma'am, that sounds good." She paused and then said, "Hey,

Mom, I know you have a migraine, and I know I caused it."

"Oh, Honey…," Linda started to protest, but Cat cut her off quickly.

"I really am sorry for all of this. You and Dad have been great. I'm sorry for being so grouchy earlier."

"It's okay, Babe. We'll get this all worked out," Linda said as she held her hand over her right eyeball. It felt like a hot dagger had been plunged into her eye socket. Her nausea was threatening to take her to her knees as she spoke.

"Please take your migraine shot and go to bed. I'll feel better knowing you are taking care of that headache."

"Alright, I will. Your father has already been griping at me to do that very thing. Now quit worrying about me and get some rest. I love you, Honey."

"I will. Thanks again, Mom, I love you, too."

After hanging up the phone, Cat sent a message to Susan telling her to call when she could. She hadn't talked to her best friend in two days, and she had to tell her about the craziness that surrounded her now. When Cat's phone rang she jumped. She hadn't expected Susan to respond so quickly.

"Where are you?" Susan demanded. "I have been calling your house, and I was beginning to think you turned your cell phone off. What is going on?" Cat quickly brought her up to speed and asked when Susan was going to be back in town. Susan had flown to Colorado to see her boyfriend and was sitting in the Denver airport waiting for her return flight to Oklahoma City. "I'll come by as soon as I get into town,"

Susan said. "Now, do what your mother said and get some rest."

Cat lay quietly for several moments after hanging up the phone. She was thinking about everything that had happened. Something was gnawing away at her subconscious. *There was something familiar about either the dead man or his killer. What was it?*

Chapter 6

R ick Hurley sent another message to Cat's phone. If she didn't show up in the next few minutes, he would have to fill her time slot with music. He threw the roster, clipboard included, on the desk and made a big production out of sorting through CD's as if he were searching for something.

Pat Gilbraithe, a part-time college intern, was running the sound board as commercials cycled through at the top of the hour. He looked through the Plexiglas at Rick and asked, "What can I do to help?" through the control room intercom.

"Crap Cat, so she can do her job, for starters!" Rick shouted. He loved that expression, "Crap Cat."

Rick detested Cat, there wasn't any hiding it. So he didn't even try. He thought she was dimwitted, egotistical, and arrogant. He didn't even like her voice. In radio, that's everything. She might be easy on the eyes, but that was as much credit as he gave her. He couldn't explain to anyone, not that anyone had asked, why he hated her so much. He just did. Maybe it was her condescending attitude or the way she tossed her head back when she laughed. Whatever the reason, he loathed her.

When Cat's shift began and she still hadn't shown up, Rick instructed Craig to play music and fill any extra time with Public Service Announcements as necessary. It amazed him that anyone would listen to Cat Carlyle anyway. If it were in his power, he would have fired her long ago. If things went the way he planned, he wouldn't have to worry about Cat "no-show" Carlyle much longer. The thought brought a smile to his face. He sat down at his desk whistling a happy tune and pulled up an Employee Discipline and Acknowledgement form on his desktop. He would enjoy filing this out. As he entered all of Cat's information on the form, he could almost picture her face as she read it. It would take all he had not to laugh in her face as she was forced to acknowledge her unexcused absence from work.

Across town Cat lay sleeping. At nearly six in the evening the hospital was quite calm. She might have continued to sleep all through the night if a bad dream hadn't awakened her. In the dream, a masked man held a knife to her throat as he raped her repeatedly. Her naked, bruised body trembled as she begged for death in a hoarse voice that didn't sound like her own. When she felt the cold steel slice her skin, she screamed. She woke with her hospital gown clinging to her still shaking, sweaty frame.

****

If there had been time to run, Detective Sullivan would have done so. As it was, he stood stock still and waited for Cat's response to his presence. He was pretty sure she was going to be mad about catching him watching her sleep. It took a second for Cat to realize that Sullivan had been there while she was sleeping. Without knowing how long he had been there or what she might have said in her sleep, she allowed herself to wake a little more before she spoke. In the awkward silence that stretched between them, Sullivan began to consider his approach.

"I came back to check on you. I'm sorry we got off on the wrong foot earlier." He paused, but then continued when she remained silent. "You looked peaceful, so I didn't wake you. I decided to hang around and see if you wanted to talk after you woke up." He paused again, but again she didn't speak. "You know, you went through something pretty traumatic last night. Bad dreams often accompany that."

This time, while he spoke she raised her eyes to his. He didn't seem like the enemy. He looked friendly. She realized that she must have done something in her sleep to convince him she was having a bad dream. The thought of him watching her sleeping made her blush all over. She felt very feminine and exposed lying there with the flimsy gown and hospital bedcovers on her. Sullivan was saying something about post-traumatic stress and its symptoms, but Cat was thinking how nice he looked after obviously getting some rest and cleaning up. She noticed he had changed into a pull-over, red polo shirt, jeans and loafers.

"Loafers, brown loafers!" she blurted out.

Where had that come from? She wondered. But Sullivan knew. He inched closer to the bed. "The killer wore brown loafers?" he asked excitedly.

"Yes, they had square toes and had an, "S" on the side of them."

She traced the letter "S" in the air with her finger and then starred off into space trying to recall more. Sullivan didn't say a word. He held his breath waiting for whatever else she could remember.

"That's really all I can remember," she concluded at last. Both of them had hoped she could share more, but at the moment, that was it.

"Don't rush it. Your memory of even the tiniest details will come to you in time."

He smiled at her then as he touched her arm to reassure her. The small gesture had her heart fluttering. She chided herself for being a hopeless romantic and hoped her warm, flushed cheeks were not giving her away. Sullivan would have stayed longer and pressed her for more had her parents not knocked on the door and come in without waiting for a response. Cat and Sullivan froze in place like a couple of teenagers caught doing something they shouldn't. Phillip and Linda didn't know what to think of it when they popped into the room. The four of them looked at each other a moment before Cat finally spoke.

"Detective Sullivan came by to check on me. Wasn't that nice?" she began awkwardly. "You'll be happy to know that we've made amends for this morning," Cat continued while waiting for her parents to respond. They were acting odd.

"Good, very good," Phillip stammered.

"Oh, okay," Linda said. She walked to Cat and handed her a magazine and some fuzzy socks she had retrieved from Cat's apartment. "I thought you might like a few comforts from home."

41

"Thanks, Mom. You are the best! How's your headache?" Cat asked nervously as she pulled the covers aside so she could slide her toes inside the warm, blue socks. "Delicious!" Cat exclaimed.

Linda told Cat that after taking the migraine shot and falling asleep, she had awakened pain-free.

"I'm glad, Mom. Hey, while you were gone, I remembered something." Her parents seemed to come closer to her while she spoke, and she watched with disappointment as Sullivan began easing away from them towards the door. "I remembered the killer's shoes and something else."

"Something else?" Sullivan asked quickly, his eyes intent and alert.

"Yes, I remembered that I dropped my bracelet last night, and when I was at the police station, it wasn't on my arm." As Cat spoke, her mind replayed the events, and she began telling the story. When she finished, she mentioned the missing bracelet again and wondered if one of them would go look for it. She hated to ask, but hated to lose the bracelet also.

"I tell you what," Sullivan said. "Why don't I go take a look for the bracelet?"

"Would you? Please?" Cat asked, thrilled that he would do it without her asking.

"Sure, no problem. I wanted to put my eyeballs on the scene again anyway." *And see if our forensic folks missed anything...else,* he thought to himself. "I didn't see the bracelet listed on the evidence sheet. Are you sure it was under the car the last time you saw it?" Sullivan asked.

"Yes, I'm positive. That's why I was lying on the ground. I was trying to reach it," Cat added.

Sullivan said he'd let her know when he found it. After a brief exchange with Phillip and Linda, he left to search for the bracelet.

"Well, what do you make of that?" Phillip commented to Linda before the door had completely shut behind Sullivan. Linda smiled at him before turning her smile on Cat.

"Interesting, very interesting."

"It's not what you think," Cat said defensively. She nervously ran her fingers through her hair and wiped invisible crustiness from her eyes.

"What do we think?" Linda asked. She was still smiling as she wrapped her arm around Phillips waist and pulled him next to her. Cat began to blush again and quickly changed the subject.

"I had a bad dream, and when I woke up Detective Sullivan was here," she told them. "Something about the dream or seeing him right after waking up, reminded me about the killer's shoes. It was really weird." She paused to see if they were listening. "That's when you guys came in, so there was nothing to it. I just thought I should explain."

"That's fine, Honey. We are just glad you got some rest and seem to be in better spirits." Linda assured her.

"Has the doctor come back to visit with you yet?" Phillip asked.

Cat told them what the doctor had said and what the plan was for the next day. After promising to get some rest, Cat encouraged her parents to do the same, and they left shortly after. Cat turned her cell phone back on and repositioned herself in the bed. She had turned the phone off to get some rest earlier and thought she better check for any missed calls or texts. It never occurred to her to ask if anyone had contacted the radio station about her shift. She hadn't thought of it at all before now. From the number of missed calls and the tone of Rick's text messages, no one had contacted the station for her. The sense of impending doom sickened her stomach as she dialed the station's number. This was going to be bad.

Pat Gilbraithe answered cheerily on the first ring. "Good evening, Sooner Broadcasting. This is Pat." Cat smiled as she silently acknowledged and applauded his eagerness.

"Hey, Pat, it's Cat!"

"Cat! Where are you? Rick is royally pissed at you!"

"That figures. I'm in the hospital, but I'm okay." Cat said. She could just picture Rick making everybody miserable at the station because he was mad at her. "Are you covering for me?" Cat asked.

"Yes, I have it all under control. Several people have called asking where you are though. You have quite a following." Pat said.

The news made Cat happy. She apologized for him having to deal with Rick and for any unnecessary stress her absence had created.

"Don't worry. I'm happy to do it. I love this." Then Pat told her how he had played a Lynyrd Skynyrd song that lasted long enough for him to relieve himself and get a drink of water before it ended. He told her how he had congratulated himself on his timing. Cat knew that Pat had once cut himself short on time between songs. He never wanted to repeat that mistake. That had only been a few months ago, but the wound was fresh enough to make Pat wince at the thought of repeating it. Cat had assured him that every disk jockey makes that error at least once in their career. Cat reminded him that being an on-air personality was often stressful and "live" mistakes were hard to avoid and overcome, even for seasoned disk jockeys and journalists.

Pat lowered his voice to a whisper as he looked around like a thief for witnesses before committing a crime. When he thought the coast was clear, he continued, "I have to warn you. Rick is up to something."

"What do you mean?"

Pat told her how he had walked by Rick's office on his way to the water fountain earlier and how he had heard Rick whistling while it sounded like his fingers were attacking the keyboard. Pat was certain the furious typing had something to do with her.

"Don't worry. His bark is worse than his bite," Cat replied.

"Just be prepared, that's all I'm saying," Pat said. "By the way, he's still here if you want to talk to him."

"No, I don't really, but I guess I should," Cat admitted.

She sighed at the thought of having to speak to Rick at all. At least she could do it by phone and not have to endure his accusing stare while she attempted to explain her absence. After being placed on hold for what seemed like an eternity, Rick finally picked up. He sounded calm and only slightly irritated.

"Well, well, well. I knew you would eventually resurface." His menacing voice slithered into her ear piece. "You must have had too much fun last night, huh? Or are you still hung over?" Rick asked in his fake radio voice with added inflection and near perfect enunciation.

Cat took a deep breath before she began. It wouldn't help her any to be pissy with Rick, regardless of how much she wanted to or how much he deserved it. She explained the best she could about what had happened. Rick denied knowing anything about the incident and didn't show much interest in her side of the story. She asked how he managed to have missed all the excitement in the parking lot.

"You're telling me that I'm the first person to tell you about the murder from last night?" she asked.

It amazed her that he could be so isolated from current events and work as a producer and assistant network manager in a medium size market. The guy shouldn't even have a Ham radio license, she thought bitterly.

"I told you, this is the first I have heard about it." Rick assured her again. "Are you telling the truth Cat? No offense, but this sounds kind of like the time your car broke down, or the time you had the medical emergency with your dog?"

"Those things really did happen, Rick, and yes, I am telling the truth."

"Fine. You saw a murder, you passed out, you're in the hospital and they won't let you leave. That's your excuse for not showing up or letting us know you weren't coming in?" He sounded more irritated the longer he talked.

Cat began chewing the inside of her cheek. She was dying to get off the phone. She was thinking he sounded more like a liar than she did. He expected her to believe that he somehow left the station after the murder happened, and he neither saw nor heard any emergency vehicles?

She mustered all her nerve and finally said, "Well, obviously I won't be in today. I don't know about tomorrow either. I'll call after I talk to the doctor tomorrow."

Rick ended the call rather abruptly after that. He alluded to the fact that Cat's unexcused absence would cost her. Before she could respond, he had slammed down the phone.

She sat in silence for a long time, fuming over the arrogance and ignorance of the pig she called a boss. She couldn't stand the guy. She knew him well enough to know he would try to cause her big problems with the network manager Frederick Davidson. Mr. Davidson seldom took her side of anything. What Rick wanted, Rick usually got. Sometimes she thought the only reason Davidson didn't fire her was because he was afraid she would sue him. Cat also had the sneaking suspicion that her difference in genitalia was the main source of contention between them. She lowered the head of her hospital bed and tried to relax. This line of thinking wasn't helping. She had to get some rest. She'd be needing it tomorrow.

Chapter 7

In a gourmet coffeehouse in downtown Guthrie, a man sat looking out the large plate glass window, pretending to examine the historic architecture of the sandstone buildings across the street. The buildings were over a hundred years old according to the date that was chiseled in stone at the top of one of the buildings. Although the buildings were connected, they each had individual store fronts with various patterns of brick or sandstone etchings. The man watched as the sunset cast warm shadows against the front of Cat's building. His eyes drifted to the door that led up to her apartment on the second floor. His mouth began to water at the thought of her fumbling with the keys hurrying to get inside to safety only to find him already there, waiting. He raised his cup to his lips while his eyes scanned the large, rectangular windows of her apartment above the overpriced antique shop below.

He could almost taste her, Cat Carlyle, radio news reporter, liar and whore. He was thinking about how easy it was going to be to gain access to her apartment again. Interrupting his dark thoughts, a chubby faced woman running the coffee bar announced that they would be closing in about ten minutes.

"Can I freshen up your coffee one last time?" she asked and held up the carafe of the hot, black liquid and smiled.

"No, thank you, Ma'am." He placed a hand over the cup's mouth.

She cocked her fat face to the side and stared at him inquisitively.

"I've notice you staring at the apartments across the street. Are you thinking of moving to Guthrie?" He watched her fat jowl move in cadence to her words.

Clenching his fists, he stood and took a step toward the counter she rested her heavy body against. Anger rose violently inside of him. His lips formed a tight smile, as he forced himself to stop thinking of twisting the barista's head off her body. He could almost taste the familiar flavor of death floating in the air between them. It cheered him. Smiling, he toasted her with his Styrofoam cup and swallowed its contents in one last gulp. He made his way to the front door, and after depositing the cup in the trash can, paused with his hand on the door handle. He needed to squash any suspicions she might have.

"If I were looking to rent, do you know of any apartments that are available?" he asked with the friendliest smile he could force on his face.

"I don't know of any right off the bat," she stuttered. He could see the fear in her eyes. Maybe he should deal with her now. "But you might check with Darrell Burchett over at Dia Bella Rosa. It's an upscale antique shop over on the next block." She pointed in the direction behind the apartment he intended to enter illegally. "If there are any available, Darrell will know about them," She said as she hid her rotund frame behind the large wooden bar.

He watched her hands nervously wiping at invisible crumbs on the quartz countertop. He raised his hand in a farewell wave and showed her his perfect teeth in a sinister smile, then pulled his black, leather jacket together in the front as he zipped it up. He stepped out onto the Herringbone patterned sidewalk and began walking toward his target. He wanted to look back to see if the coffee lady was watching him, but he knew she was. He raised the collar of his jacket and cussed her under his breath.

It had turned cold while he sat in the coffee shop. There was a wickedly cold wind forging through the breezeway made by the tall buildings. He was grateful for it. No one would think it suspicious that the collar of his jacket shielded his face. Hopefully no one would recognize him as he rounded the corner and ducked into the alley that separated two buildings. He quickly made his way to the back entrance of Cat's apartment. Quietly he crept up the old metal stairs in the nearly darkness, looking back every few steps to ensure that no one had followed him. Having reached the top of the steps, he paused and listened for any sounds while slipping his leather gloves on his hands. On the rickety old landing outside of Cat's apartment building, he hesitated. Taking slow, deep breaths to calm his nerves, he fished for his lock picks in his jacket pocket. He listened for any sounds before trying the lock. When he felt sure he was safe, he turned and went to work.

Once he got the door unlocked, he pushed it open with a squeak and quickly stepped inside, shutting the heavy wooden door behind him. Leaning against the door, he listened for any possible threats down the long wood-planked hallway. Cat's apartment was one of six on the second floor of the old building. What once had been a hotel at the turn of the century had been refurbished into upscale apartments above the exclusive European antique store. Quietly he crept down the entire length of the hall with the creaking floor defying him every few steps. He strained an ear towards each door as he made his way to Cat's apartment. He thought he heard someone moving around in the apartment next door to Cat's, so he quickly unlocked her door with his own personal key and slipped inside.

His eyes scanned the familiar room with satisfaction. Seeing Cat's running shoes by the door, he frowned. She was so unorganized and sloppy. When he was satisfied that his presence had gone unnoticed, he began his search. He would find it, since Diaz had failed. He should never have sent an amateur to retrieve his token of affection from the slut. He searched room to room doing his best not to disturb anything. He didn't want to tip his hat too soon. When he did not locate what he was searching for, his head began to ache.

Thoughts of setting her apartment on fire with her in it tickled his brain. He cautioned himself not to get too worked up. He had a plan, and he had to stick to it. Making Cat suffer was his intent, and he always thought his plans through carefully. He could not allow his emotions to rule him. Standing in the center of her kitchen he closed his eyes and counted to ten slowly. When he felt his breathing return to normal, he opened her refrigerator and retrieved a cold beer. He twisted the top off, took a long swig and walked through the tall doorway leading to her library. He knew where Cat was, so he wasn't in any hurry to leave. He plopped down into an oversized chair and crossed his legs at the ankles, resting his boots on the matching ottoman in front of the brown leather chair. He looked around the room while enjoying his drink. Cat's collection of books had always puzzled him. She didn't have a green thumb, but she had numerous volumes of gardening books crammed onto two dusty shelves. Stacks of cheap paperback romance books lined one shelf and various murder mysteries filled the remaining four shelves. *Did she really read this junk?*

He nearly jumped out of his skin when someone knocked on the front door. He waited for what seemed like ten minutes, before it stopped. Tiptoeing to the door, he looked out the peep hole, but no one was there. Crouching down he stole across the living room to the large windows overlooking the street. Without moving the curtains, he peered out. He didn't see anyone on the street below. He took a final look around the unkempt apartment and sighed. Since she was hiding something from him, maybe he should send her a little message. He wanted her to know he had been there, but he didn't want it to be too obvious. He retreated to the tiny bathroom where he huffed and blew his hot breath onto the mirror. With his gloved finger he traced a heart with an arrow through it and stood back to admire his work. She would love that, he decided with a smirk. Then he made his way out the door, down the stairs and safely away.

****

When Sullivan arrived at Sooner Broadcasting it was nearly 6:45 p.m. The early fall night had turned cool, so he slipped on a jacket before making his way on foot through the parking lot. He took his department camera with him to capture any evidence on film before handling it. He had loaded his pockets with evidence bags, tape and a marker should he need them. When he spotted Cat's car in the back corner of the lot a thought crossed his mind. *Why would a young lady who worked late at night, park so far away from the building?* The question was bugging him as he took a picture of the car sitting alone in the far corner of the lot. He took pictures of the lights that illuminated the lot, the entrance, the exit, tire marks and the other cars that were there. He hoped his forensic team had captured all of this already and that they had gotten all the tag numbers off all of the cars that were parked there last night.

As he approached Cat's car, he saw the tires on the driver's side were flat. On closer inspection he saw that all the tires were flat. Not just flat either – slashed!

He studied the puncture and slash marks on each tire and photographed each. He was certain the tires had not been like this the previous night. He looked again at the blood stains on the concrete. No one had bothered to clean anything. He could tell where someone had brushed up against Cat's car, leaving a partial bloody hand print on the concrete wall next to it. He captured all of this on film before he walked around to the other side and knelt down to look for the bracelet. He didn't immediately see it, so he retrieved a mini-mag light, about the size of a pen, out of his jacket. He shone the light under the car, but failed to find the bracelet.

After looking the entire lot over and not finding it, he returned to his car, recorded in his notebook what he had seen and logged the date and time. He drove out of the lot just as a blonde-headed man exited the radio station and quickly made his way to a black pickup truck that was parked near the building. Something about the guy made Sullivan want to visit with him, but he decided it would have to wait.

He pushed the Crown Victoria to nearly ten miles an hour over the speed limit as he headed to his office. He needed to call Cat. He knew he was going to have to give her the bad news about her tires and the bracelet. He had to update his murder book first and review all the evidence his team had collected the night before. Maybe he had missed seeing the bracelet on the evidence log sheet. So far, the clues were not forthcoming, and he didn't want to entertain the idea of a killer on the loose who could strike again at any moment. Without a motive, murder weapon or suspects, this was going to be a long night and a tough case.

****

After leaving the airport parking, Susan made her way through traffic across town to the hospital. She parked her car in the hospital parking lot and made her way to the building grumbling to herself about her traveling experience. It had been a long day, and she was exhausted. But she had said she would come, and here she was.

She saw the familiar looking man get on the elevator ahead of her so she quickened her step to catch the elevator before the doors closed. She frowned when the doors slid shut in her face. She was thinking that he had to have pushed the button to make the doors close.

"People can be so rude sometimes," she exclaimed as she waited for the elevator to return. She exited on the fifth floor, made her way to Cat's room and nearly shouted, "Wake up, Sister!" when she saw Cat. After receiving a warm hug, Cat sat up in bed and asked about Susan's trip and about her new boyfriend, Jackson Wright.

Susan conceded with a sigh and sat on the edge of Cat's bed after examining Cat's cheek. When she was convinced that Cat was okay, she told about her trip and about her new love.

"The traveling was hectic as usual, but Jackson was fantastic. He is so sweet. Let me show you what he bought me."

"Is it a ring?" Cat asked excitedly.

"No, goose! It's a necklace." Susan dug around the neck of her shirt and produced a gorgeous gold chain with a heart-shaped diamond pendant.

"It's beautiful! Too bad it wasn't a ring," Cat added, smiling. "That would have been nicer."

"Bite your tongue, woman," Susan replied, while she put the chain back under her shirt and laid the pendant against her warm golden skin. They both laughed, they knew that Susan wasn't in any hurry to put a gold ring on her finger. For nearly an hour, there was talk of murder, romance, and the mysteries that involved both. Finally a nurse entered the room with a scowl and ran Susan off, telling her that visiting hours had ended long ago. Before Susan left, she made Cat promise to call her as soon as she talked to the doctor the next morning.

Cat faded in and out of consciousness for several hours before finally giving up and turning on the light. Looking at the time on her cell phone, she saw that it was closing in on two o'clock in the morning. Sighing, she unhooked her IV bag from its hanger and carried it with her as she shuffled her way into the tiny sterile bathroom. She hadn't bothered with turning on the bathroom light or shutting the door, but just as she sat on the stool she heard the outer door open and someone enter her room. She was about to say something when she heard a man's voice swear.

Fear choked her. She remained quiet, holding her breath and covering her mouth with one hand. She didn't trust herself not to scream. Several terrifying minutes passes as she sat, frozen in fear, unable to swallow, unable to move. Then she heard the hospital room door open and close again, and after several seconds of unbearable suspense, she allowed herself to breathe.

She reentered the room by first peeking through the crack in the open door above the hinge. When she was certain her uninvited guest was gone, she raced across the room, IV bag in hand, to where her phone was lying on the bed and speed-dialed her parents. When Phillip answered the phone out of a dead sleep he always sounded the same – wide awake and alert. Although nothing could have been further from the truth, he was pretty convincing.

"Dad, someone was just in my room!" Cat whispered, breathing heavily into the mouthpiece.

"Okay, Honey, who was it?" Phillip replied. He hadn't even sat up or turned on the bedside lamp. He thought he was dreaming the conversation.

"Dad, Dad! I need you to wake up! Someone snuck into my room while I was in the bathroom. I think it was the killer!" Cat was now in full blown panic mode. She had retreated back to the tiny bathroom and had locked the door. With her cell phone in her hand, she hung her IV bag up on a hook on the wall and sat on the stool, waiting for her Dad to come to his senses.

"Did you understand what I said, Dad?" she asked a little louder. "Just give the phone to Mom." Cat demanded. She waited as Phillip handed the phone over to Linda.

"Cat, Honey, what's wrong?" Linda asked as she sat up in bed. Phillip began snuggling back under the covers until Linda's fear-filled voice had him springing to life.

"What? You think it was the killer? Why do you think that? Where are you now? Should I call the police?"

As Cat explained what had happened and what she heard and felt, Phillip was dressing and telling Linda to do the same. He leaned across the bed without waiting for a reply and took the phone out of Linda's hands.

"Get dressed," he instructed Linda. "We're on our way. Notify the nurse and have her get security up there," he ordered.

After disconnecting, Cat wrestled with the idea of just staying hidden in the bathroom until they arrived. She debated with herself for several minutes before finally unlocking the door, carrying her IV bag back to her bed and pushing the call button for the nurse. It seemed to take a very long time for the nurse to respond. When she did, Cat tried to sound sane as she explained that someone had been in her room and she needed security, immediately! When the security guard arrived he seemed uninterested in Cat's story. He listened intently to what she said had happened and then tried to reassure her that someone had probably just entered her room by mistake.

"What did he look like?" he finally asked her when she would not abandon her story.

"I don't know. I was sitting on the toilet. I just heard him. I didn't see him."

The young security guard could tell that Cat was frightened so he agreed to stay with her until her parents arrived. When they did, he said he would write up a report about the incident. The nurse settled Cat back in bed, hung her IV bag back up and encouraged her to get some rest.

Phillip and Linda decided to take turns staying with Cat until she got released later that morning. Phillip said he would stay first and practically had to shove Linda out the door. She finally consented and went back home for a few more hours of sleep.

Phillip pulled the pastel colored recliner next to Cat's bed and eased himself into the chair watching Cat carefully. He raised his feet, leaned back and told her to relax. If anyone came in the room, they would meet him first. Phillip tucked the blanket around her shoulders and kissed her forehead before he sat down.

"Thanks for doing this, Dad." Cat murmured as she closed her eyes. Cat hadn't been asleep any time at all when a nightmare made her scream and she set up in bed.

"It's okay, Honey, I'm right here. Everything is alright," Phillip reassured her.

He had watched her tossing and turning and heard her moaning in her sleep. He knew she was having a nightmare, but hoped it would end without her waking up. While he was trying to get her back to sleep, they heard something in the hallway. They exchanged worried glances and Phillip quietly got out of the recliner and jerked open the door. Right outside the door, a startled janitor was kneeling. Phillip later described him as a dark-haired man with a large, new tattoo of a sun with rays stretching out in all four directions on his right forearm. He said he thought it was a new tattoo because it was so red and had what looked like Neosporin smeared all over it. Phillip said it appeared the man was mopping the floor. He had knocked his mop bucket into the wall with his shoe as he knelt to clean a scuff mark off the tile next to Cat's door. In the janitor's hand was a short wooden handle from what might have been a mop, with a tennis ball attached to the end. The janitor was using the tennis ball to remove the scuff mark off of the tile. Without a word, Phillip shut the door and returned to the recliner. He told Cat it was just the janitor, and they settled back in for a few more hours of rest.

Promptly at 6:00 a.m. the shift change at the nursing station began. After being briefed about the patients on the floor, the day shift nurses began their rounds. Before entering Cat's room, one of the day shift nurses froze outside of Cat's door. Crude words had been written in what looked like blood across the door. Whitney, the young nurse on duty, nearly dropped her tray full of pharmaceuticals. She rushed back to the nurse's station and phoned security. By 6:15 a.m. the entire floor was abuzz with the news.

Chapter 8

When Sullivan entered his office the next morning, he had two messages on his voice mail. One was from the Medical Examiner's office regarding the current homicide victim, and the second one was from Phillip Carlyle. Sullivan listened intently to the messages, then pounded the desk with his fist. He immediately hung up and redialed the number Phillip had left. When the phone was answered in the hospital room across town, Sullivan could hear the strain in Phillip's voice.

"Detective, we are at a loss. What is going on? We believe Cat is in danger, and we don't know how to protect her or what to do next."

Sullivan told him to stay put and grabbed his jacket to leave. As he drove across town he assembled a list of to-do's in his mind. The first one was to interview the security guard at the hospital and get to the bottom of the threat that was written on Cat's hospital door. He wondered if Cat had somehow written the message herself and had invented the story of someone coming into her room to throw the investigation off track. She's intelligent enough to pull that off, he thought sourly. He didn't want to believe that she would lie to him, but he knew she could have done so.

Betsy Randolph

Positive identification had been made on the stabbing victim by his next of kin. Sullivan had researched the victim's background and was trying to make a connection to Catherine Carlyle. So far nothing was panning out in this case. He pulled into the hospital parking lot and shifted his black unmarked patrol car into park. He flipped the sun visor down and stared at his reflection in the little mirror. He ran his fingers through his wavy brown hair and attempted to smooth down the multiple silver streaks that poked out wildly from each temple.

"You need a haircut and a good night's sleep," he admonished his reflection. The dark circles under his eyes didn't lie. He hadn't been sleeping well lately. With a sigh, he flipped the visor back up, grabbed his notebook that lay on the passenger seat and headed for the hospital security office. He was thinking about Cat as he weaved his way through parked vehicles and made his way to the large sliding glass doors. From the sound of it, Cat hadn't gotten any rest either. He felt himself feeling anxious to see her. He reassured himself that it was a purely professional draw that he felt. He needed to question her about the victim and their possible relationship. And he needed to see the so-called threat left on her hospital door. That was all.

Sullivan was so lost in thought that he did not notice the man who stood smoking outside the hospital entrance. His dark sunglasses hid his eyes, but he didn't try to hide his smile as he blew smoke into the path of the homicide detective who breezed past him and into the building. *Not much of a cop*, the man with the sunglasses thought as he lifted his foot off the ground and braced it against the outside wall. He was standing by a sign that said smokers had to be twenty-five feet away from the building. He continued to pollute his lungs until his flavored cigar burned down to the wooden tip. Crushing out the embers, he pocketed the wooden tip and slowly made his way to his truck parked on the street.

After stopping in the security office and visiting with a heavy set, older security guard with layers of dandruff on his shoulders, Sullivan headed for the stairs. He decided that his lack of physical exercise the last few days had contributed to his poor sleep. Taking two stairs at a time he reached the fifth floor, slightly winded. He congratulated himself for the exertion but chided himself for the underlying reason: Cat.

As he rounded the corner to where her room was located, he saw the door to her room had been covered with a large plastic bag. He stopped at the nurse's station and asked about the door and about the log from the overnight nurse. Quickly he scanned the report, asked for a copy and made his way to Cat's room. He decided to see the message before speaking to Cat or her family. He peeled the tape off the door that held the plastic in place. Scrawled across the door in what appeared to be dried blood, by the brown crusty appearance, was the phrase, "The only good cat is a dead Cat."

Sullivan could feel the anger welling up inside him. *She wouldn't do this*, he thought. This is the real deal. Sullivan resealed the tape and pulled his cell phone from his pocket. He dialed the homicide unit and asked the forensic team to come process the door. Then he pocketed his phone and tapped on the door with his knuckles.

Phillip, Linda and Cat all appeared shaken and withdrawn. Sullivan couldn't hide his concern for them as he entered the room and shut the door behind him. Phillip had given Linda the recliner and had been standing, looking out the window. He greeted Sullivan with a handshake and began telling him about the events that had occurred overnight. It was apparent that Phillip was fired up. His breathing was hurried to the point that Sullivan thought he might hyperventilate. Sullivan noticed how just hearing the story being repeated had Linda wringing her hands and Cat sinking down beneath the flimsy covers.

This is what the messenger wanted, for them to be afraid. It was working and it angered Sullivan more. He told them about the vandalized tires and about the missing bracelet.

"Catherine, can you think of anyone who is mad at you or who would intentionally do this?" Sullivan asked.

"No, not really." Cat said. Her eyes were large with fear and misty with tears.

"Has anyone made any threats to you before or made you feel threatened?"

"Ummm. I don't think so." She seemed to hesitate and looked off toward the left as she answered.

"Think hard. This is important," Sullivan urged. He could tell she was holding something back. He wanted to grab her thin arms and shake her. He hated to be lied to, especially if someone's life was at stake. He believed hers was.

"Nope, can't think of anyone that has threatened me recently," she finally said.

"Okay, who has threatened you in the past?" He inquired again.

"No one."

"But you said 'Recently.' 'No one had threatened you recently.' That's what you just said."

Cat looked like she had been slapped. She glanced at her parents and then to Sullivan. "I guess I didn't mean it that way. I meant to say that no one has threatened me," she sighed. *This police questioning is tricky business*, she thought.

There were few things in life that Sullivan despised, but none more than a liar. This gal was lying to him, and he didn't know why. But he intended to find out. He thought about shaking her until her teeth chattered. Instead he gritted his own teeth until his jaw ached.

He needed a drink. Coincidently, that is the exact thought that Cat was having. Except his version was a strong, black coffee and hers was a strong, cool whiskey.

Later that morning, after having her car towed from the station parking lot to a tire store for repairs, Cat's parents dropped her off at her apartment as promised. Cat had said she wanted to get cleaned up in her own shower and then planned to meet her parents for lunch at a restaurant in downtown Guthrie. Her father had insisted on checking the apartment first for any sign of an intruder. After he cleared the apartment, he and Linda left Cat and Hannah alone, unwillingly. Phillip had tried to persuade Cat that she shouldn't be alone, but she said she couldn't stand another minute of being hovered over and babied. Linda and Phillip decided to walk around downtown while Cat got ready for lunch.

As soon as Cat shut the door, she turned to look at Hannah who sat patiently with eyes shining, her cropped tail wiggling back and forth furiously. "Come here, baby dog," Cat said as she scooped her up and twirled the dog around the room. Hannah's wet little nose pressed against Cat's neck as the two got reacquainted after their brief separation.

"Want to go for a walk? Get your leash. Where's your leash?" Cat asked over and over as Hannah danced around in a circle. She snatched the leash in her teeth and raced for the door. Looking back over her shoulder, Hannah whimpered and half-heartedly growled at Cat as Cat slipped a light jacket on and finally made her way to the door. Cat picked up the end of the leash that wasn't slobber-ridden and slipped it on her wrist, then snapped the clasp into the D-ring on Hannah's red collar.

"Let's go!" Cat said enthusiastically.

Hannah pranced and pulled, straining against the leash until she choked herself. "Take it easy, sister. I can only walk so fast." Cat laughed at her goofy little roommate as she was pulled down the hallway and out the back of the building where a fenced in courtyard awaited them. While Hannah searched for a place to relieve herself, Cat seemed to zone out. Her mind was reliving the past twenty-four hours. Suddenly, she snapped out of it.

"Come on, we have to hurry. I have to jump in the shower. Not all of us live the life of luxury."

Cat rubbed her furry friend's belly after Hannah rolled over on her back. Hannah began kicking one leg in a seizure type reflex as Cat scratched her favorite spot. When they were back in the apartment, Cat put Hannah back in her kennel and shut the door. She made kissing noises as she walked out of the room, but Hannah didn't seem to notice. Hannah was already burrowing under her covers and settling in for an early nap.

Finally! Cat thought, as she stood in the bathroom and peeled off her clothes. She dropped them into the wicker basket she used as a dirty-clothes hamper. She couldn't remember ever feeling so disgusting in her life. Even though she had taken a shower at the hospital and had put on fresh clothes, she still felt nasty. The stench of antiseptics from the hospital lingered on her clothes and skin.

As she waited for the shower to warm up, she turned on the radio that sat on the counter and brushed out her hair. She suppressed the desire to analyze all the recent events. She needed to turn her brain off for awhile, she reasoned. She began singing with the song that was playing and stepped into the tub. She hiked up the heat and stuck her head under the simulated rain shower.

For nearly half an hour she scrubbed herself, shaved her legs and stood under the hot water trying not to think. She let the nearly scalding water wash over her skin as she envisioned it washing away the filth that she couldn't scrub off. Finally she turned the water off and wrung her hair out.

Betsy Randolph

She stepped out of the shower, into the steamy room, wrapped a towel around her and started planning the rest of her day.

There wasn't any reason not to go on into work tonight she decided, except that she really didn't want to face Rick. She toweled off her hair and ran her fingers through it when her eyes saw the heart and the arrow. It took a second for her brain to decide what it was that she was seeing and what it meant.

"He's been here!" she whispered, before the screaming began.

Chapter 9

Sullivan typed reports, thought of Cat and created a murder board, which consisted of photos of the victim, his personal information, crime scene evidence and any tips or leads they were following which weren't much. He had drunk a pot of coffee and started on another pot by 9:30 a.m., all while thinking of Cat. He could feel his anger rising as he rehashed their last conversation. *She was a liar. Why had she lied to him? What was she hiding and why?* He sat at his desk with his teeth clenched when his partner interrupted his brood.

"Hey, Sully," Clint Bronson began. "Where you taking me for lunch?"

"It's your turn and you know it, cheapskate," Sullivan retorted. He looked over at Bronson and frowned. It seemed like Sullivan always ended up paying.

When Bronson was first assigned as his partner, the kid was barely making it on a cop's salary. Now he had three babies and a stay-at-home wife. The kid was not only nuts, he was broke.

"Why are you always mooching off me, man?" Sullivan asked, only half joking.

Clint Bronson had joined the force seven years before and from all accounts was one of the sharpest men in the agency. He was well educated, physically fit, handsome and respected by his peers and superiors. Sullivan had joked to him on several occasions that if he were gay, Bronson would be his type.

"Well, old man, you wouldn't be my type," Bronson had joked back.

There wasn't any denying that Bronson's looks had helped him his entire life. Was it his fault his thick, dark hair curled across his forehead and his square jaw framed a perfect face with deep dimples in each cheek? He would say he was just blessed with good looks. Those looks had helped him with most female witnesses and his partner Sullivan didn't mind that. Most of the time Sullivan wouldn't even try to question a woman younger than thirty. They wouldn't even hear anything that was being said if Bronson was around.

"Why don't we take your car, and you can buy today, sweetheart," Sullivan jeered as he slid his arm in his jacket sleeve. "Besides, I want to read you some notes on this Diaz case, and you never like me multitasking while I drive."

"Only because I want to live to see my kids grow up. You're dangerous without distractions, Sully," said Bronson.

They headed out the door and climbed into Bronson's white unmarked Dodge Charger. Sullivan was a good five inches taller than Bronson and hated the cramped feeling of the Dodge. Bronson always told him the leg room was the same, but he never fully convinced Sullivan of that fact.

"I forgot how much I hate your mini police car."

"I'm telling you, it's your imagination. This car is as big as yours. Wait till you get one, you'll see," Bronson laughed.

Sullivan slugged his partner's arm. "They don't give midget cars to grown-ups. Besides, I'll retire before I get a new car."

They both laughed as they headed south on Classen Boulevard and made a right on Northwest Fourth.

"Where are we going?" Sullivan asked.

"Mexican sound okay?" Bronson suggested. "It's been awhile since we had El Flamenco."

"You're not fooling anyone, kid. That girl in there gives you a discount every time."

Bronson gave a sideways glance at Sullivan, and the pitiful look in his eyes had Sullivan grabbing his folder to read the case notes. Bronson had been off duty and out of town on the night of the murder, so he needed to be brought up to speed. He had seen the reports and looked over the evidence that morning, but Sullivan continued to harp about the witness. Bronson thought he seemed overly preoccupied with her, and he was trying to figure out why. Bronson and Sullivan worked well together because they often disagreed on the direction of the investigation.

This investigation was no exception. Sullivan was obsessing about their witness, and Bronson was fairly certain that was a dead end. He held his tongue as he allowed Sullivan to repeat part of his theory from this morning.

"Why does an attractive young woman, who obviously has some self-confidence issues, park in the back corner of a dimly lit lot, knowing she is going to have to walk out there alone after midnight every night?" Sullivan said. "It doesn't make sense. How does she miss seeing the murder, but gets covered in the guy's blood and doesn't know how it happened. I'm not buying it, her story is weak."

Before Bronson could say anything, Sullivan continued. If Bronson weren't mistaken, Sullivan seemed angry at their only witness.

"So if we are to believe her story, which I don't," he said with a sigh. "She has no idea who the victim is or who murderer was, who came into her room at the hospital or who left the message on her hospital door, if anyone did at all. Her story is crap." Hearing no reply, he asked, "Why are you so quiet? What are you thinking?" Sullivan stared at Bronson who was smiling, looking forward.

Bronson kept his eyes on the road and his hands on the wheel and simply smiled while his partner ranted about the girl. *That's it,* Bronson thought. *This is about a girl. Finally!* It had been a dry spell for Sullivan. He had taken the breakup with his wife really hard. But that was three years ago. What looked like a happily-ever-after turned into an overnight nightmare for Sullivan after he spotted his wife of eight years with another man. She never would admit her full involvement with the man, but Sullivan knew. "Some things you just know," he had told Bronson.

So Sullivan threw himself into his work, dated sporadically and never let himself get too close to anyone. Bronson had hoped his partner would find someone like he had. Someone that would make him laugh, cry and love more than anyone before.

His own girl made him feel that way. He found himself wanting to rush home and throw his arms around her every day. A woman like that lifted your spirits and drove you mad with just a single look. Sullivan needed that. Bronson finally glanced to his right to find Sullivan with his head leaned back against the head rest with his eyes closed.

"What's her name again?" Bronson finally asked.

Sullivan turned his head slightly and opened his left eye but didn't respond for a few seconds. "Catherine Carlyle. She goes by Cat though," Sullivan said and closed his eye again.

"Cat Carlyle? As in the radio news reporter, Cat Carlyle?" Bronson asked excitedly.

"You know Cat?" Sullivan asked, surprised, as he lifted his head and turned questioning eyes towards his partner.

"Sure I do. We use to go out," Bronson said matter of fact. He could see Sullivan's countenance fall. Bronson thought he actually looked injured. "Oh, my gosh! You have got it bad for this girl," Bronson declared as he began to laugh.

Sullivan sat stiffly in his seat, his mouth gaping open. "What are you talking about? She's a witness or a suspect to a murder. I have yet to determine which. There isn't anything between us, especially now since I know you have dated her," Sullivan said flatly.

He ran both hands through his hair and straightened his tie. He brushed off the shoulders of his jacket and placed the file he was holding into the back seat. Bronson laughed for nearly a full minute before he relented and conceded the truth.

"Seriously, I was just pulling your leg. I never dated her. I hear her on the radio all the time. I don't even know what she looks like."

"Really?" Sullivan asked, turning towards him in his seat.

"Really." Bronson assured him.

"Wow, that's a relief. I have to admit, I was feeling sorta ill there for a second," Sullivan replied as he backhanded the younger Bronson across the chest.

Immediately, Sullivan felt his mood improve. A smile snuck upon his face and stayed there. Bronson intended to get a lot of mileage out of this one. It wasn't very often that Sullivan left himself wide open for insults or irritations. This girl had gotten under the thick, bronzed skin of his pal, and he was going to ride this like a stick horse.

"Looks like you will be buying lunch after all, Romeo," Bronson commented with a sneer.

"What? Why?" Sullivan demanded.

"Cause I found the chink in your armor," Bronson said as he cut his eyes at Sullivan and raised his eyebrows a couple of times in rapid succession.

"I have no idea what you are referring to," Sullivan began, but stopped short of an all out lie when Bronson started meowing loudly. Sullivan grabbed Bronson's knee and squeezed causing Bronson to nearly rear-end the car they were behind at the stop light.

When they finally pulled to a stop at the fast food restaurant, Sullivan turned a serious face to Bronson and made a single threat. "Stay away from Cat Carlyle, or I will seriously hurt you. Got it?"

Chapter 10

The Carlyle family of three had chosen to eat lunch at a small cafe in downtown Guthrie. Granny's Table was one of the oldest restaurants in Guthrie and was one of their favorites. Tea-colored crocheted doilies adorned the refinished tops of antique end tables that nuzzled between the Victorian sofas in the lobby.

Linda rubbed her hand across the floral upholstery covering of the love seat and studied its intricately carved wooden legs. She was thinking how sad it is that furniture isn't made as nicely nowadays. They waited in the little seating area for Cat to join them and watched as the wood burning fireplace pumped out waves of heat into the otherwise unheated dining room.

Glancing around the room, she studied the antique bar along the back dining room wall. It was made of rich mahogany and marble and was beautifully restored. Its shelves held antique bottles of all kinds. Cobalt blue, emerald green and pale yellow bottles lined the wooden shelves. Patrons sat on barstools along the gleaming bar and at individual wooden tables covered in white linen tablecloths. The original, wood-planked floors had also been restored and were complete with squeaks, moans and a high polyurethane sheen.

When Cat joined them, they each ordered their lunch then slipped into a quiet almost reflective mood. The cozy atmosphere appeared lost on the three as they ate their lunch in silence. Linda stared at her daughter as they ate, wondering what she was thinking. Linda watched as Cat's brows scrunched together across her forehead giving her a vertical frown between her eyebrows, identical to Phillip's.

"How are you feeling, Sugar?" Linda asked her timidly.

"I don't know. Tired, I guess," Cat said behind her napkin.

She patted her mouth with her linen napkin and laid it gently back on her lap. She took a nervous glance around the room and picked up her glass of iced tea.

"Anything else bugging you?" Linda asked in almost a whisper.

She too took a quick look around the room. She could sense Cat's unease, but Cat held her tongue. Cat couldn't decide if telling her parents about the drawing on her bathroom mirror was a good idea or not. They would only worry and probably insist that she stay at their house. She wasn't about to move back in with her parents, she thought sourly. So she only partially lied.

"No. I'm just dreading going in to work tonight."

She sat her tea glass down and rested her arms on the table. Then she told them about her conversation with Rick and how Pat had warned her that Rick was up to something. Linda and Phillip looked at each other and both silently worried that Cat was thinking of quitting her job. Linda's silent sigh went unnoticed while listening to Cat ramble on and on about Rick. She wondered when her daughter was going to grow up and stay with a job longer than a few years. She had lost count of how many jobs Cat had held and how many times Cat had picked up and relocated since she moved away from home for the first time. It seemed to Linda that whenever things got rough, Cat would just quit. If the sky wasn't always blue in Cat's world, then she would turn tail and run. Where had she gotten that from? Cat was saying something to Phillip about a programming problem Phillip mentioned at his radio station when Linda mentally rejoined the conversation. Linda patted her mouth with her napkin and laid it across her half-eaten sandwich.

"Why don't you try telling the truth for a change, Cat? We are your parents and we know when something is wrong. Tell us what is going on."

Cat stopped chewing and swallowed hard. She pulled her tea glass to her lips with shaking hands and sat it back on the table nearly tipping it over as it caught the edge of her salad plate. She sat speechless looking at her mother, her face and neck turned red and splotchy. When Cat didn't answer Phillip announced that they needed to get a move on. He claimed he had to have his engineer take a look at the satellite at the radio station. If the programming problem wasn't fixed it was going cost the station thousands of dollars. He raised his hand to gain the attention of the young waitress, and she hurried over, carrying a pitcher of freshly brewed peach tea.

"Would you care for a refill or a to-go cup?" she asked sweetly.

"No, thank you, just the check please," Phillip replied as he fished in his back pocket for his wallet. He handed his credit card to the girl before she handed him the check.

She got the message that they were in a hurry and scurried away. When she returned, the silence at the table of three was deafening. No one spoke as Phillip signed the bill, added a nice tip, stood and placed a hand on the back of both the women's chairs. It was a clear sign to stand, so they did. Cat had chosen to walk the three cobblestone blocks to lunch from her apartment, and she intended to do the same on her return trip. Her parents had tried to discourage it, but since the tension was high they said their goodbyes and watched sadly as she began walking away.

Cat accepted the temperature change outside with a shiver and quickened her pace. She was not looking forward to winter. She hated the cold, and she hated the ice and snow even more. She rubbed her hands on her arms to warm herself as she walked through the alley to her apartment entrance. She couldn't help but feel like someone was watching her. She looked around nervously as she climbed the old metal stairs and entered the outside door. She hurried down the hall to her door. Key in hand, she stuck the key in the lock. Just as she was turning the key and the knob, a hand touched her shoulder causing her to jump and shriek loudly.

"Oh, my goodness, Honey. I didn't mean to startle you. I'm so sorry!" It was Miriam Thornton, Cat's silver-haired neighbor.

She had lived in the apartment across the hall since her husband had died seventeen years ago. At seventy-three, life had just begun, she had told Cat once. She claimed the stairs kept her in shape, and she loved living downtown, watching people coming and going all the time. She and Cat would visit occasionally and sometimes even share a cup of coffee or tea when Cat made time for her, which wasn't often enough for Miriam. She was lonely, and she thought the world of Cat.

"Oh, that's alright, Miriam. I am sorry to be so jumpy. I never heard you, that's all."

She decided not to tell Miriam about what had happened the night before. She would only worry.

"Well, maybe I am getting sneakier in my old age," Miriam joked. "If you have time, I would love to show you a quilt I'm working on for the Apples and Quilts Festival. It's supposed to look like a Gaillardia flower, the State Flower of Oklahoma." Miriam's eyes sparkled as she described the quilt and how many hours she had put into it so far. Cat started to decline and say how busy she was, but she was always busy. She hated to disappoint her kind old friend and neighbor.

"Sure, I'd love to see it," Cat said with a grin. "I have to get ready for work, but I have a little bit of time still. Let me take Hannah out, and then I'll come right over."

Miriam was delighted and hurried home to put on some coffee and slice up some coffee cake she had made just that morning. She had been hoping to run into Cat before she ate it all herself. Her timing couldn't have been better. She was placing a matching cup and saucer next to the plate of coffee cake when Cat tapped on the door.

"Come on in," Miriam called out.

Cat opened the door and stepped back in time. It always amazed her how Miriam's spotless apartment looked like an upscale antique shop. Miriam had nothing but antiques in every room. Except for the overwhelming aroma of mothballs seeping from the closets, Cat loved the place. The golden walls held black and white photos of departed ancestors and a few originals that Miriam's husband had painted some thirty years earlier.

"Come on over and have a seat," Miriam invited as she patted the cushioned chair next to hers. "I made some coffee cake this morning and took the liberty of dishing you up a slice."

"Oh, you shouldn't have gone to any trouble," Cat said, more out of habit than manners.

She knew that Miriam wouldn't allow a guest in her home without offering food and drink. Cat had found it was easier to just accept Miriam's hospitalities. Besides, Miriam was a wonderful cook and whatever was served was always delicious.

"Umm, it's wonderful," Cat remarked after the first bite. "When are you going to teach me to cook like this?"

"Anytime you are ready, I am willing. You know that," Miriam replied as she beamed from the compliment. She poured a hot cup of coffee into a ceramic cup with blue forget-me-nots painted on the side. Cat took a sip and set the cup down gingerly onto the matching saucer as Miriam quizzed her about any potential beaus.

It was almost a ritual, Cat thought. Miriam the match-maker had tried to set her up several times, but Cat had always refused. Cat usually tried to steer the conversation another direction. Today she could use the quilt as the distraction.

"No, Ma'am. I'm afraid all the good ones are already taken," Cat quipped.

Before Miriam could propose any romantic possibilities, Cat asked about the Gaillardia quilt, and Miriam seemed to forget momentarily about playing cupid.

"Well, it is coming along nicely," Miriam beamed. "I have almost got it completely laid out. When you're done with your dessert, I'll show you."

Miriam had the quilt pieces laid out on top of a paper pattern on top of the guest bed in her second bedroom. Cat listened intently to Miriam's explanation of the quilting process and complimented her on her tedious work numerous times. Miriam seemed tickled by the attention.

"Thank you so much for the delicious cake and coffee, Miriam," Cat said as she hugged her dear friend. "If you're going to be free on Saturday, I was thinking of going over to the Bluegrass Festival. Would you care to join me?"

"Oh, Honey, I'd love to. That would be great!" Miriam exclaimed.

Cat thought she looked like she was near tears. Miriam laced her arm through Cat's as they walked to the front door together. Miriam reminded Cat of her own grandmother who had died several years before. As Cat walked across the hallway to her apartment, she was thinking how grateful she was to have Miriam as a neighbor. Good neighbors were a rarity, she thought. Cat grabbed her mail from the mailbox by the door and then stepped into the apartment. Immediately Hannah began bouncing around and rubbing against Cat's leg like she hadn't seen her in a week.

"Did you forget I saw you half an hour ago, silly dog?" She rubbed Hannah's fur and squeezed her tight. Hannah acknowledged Cat's attention by wiggling her stubby tail furiously. She pranced around in circles and followed Cat through the apartment. Taking the mail to the couch, Cat flopped down and began sorting it out. "Junk, bills, junk, more junk, another bill," Cat commented with fake enthusiasm. Talking pleasantly out loud made Hannah happy, or so it seemed to Cat. Her little black and rust-colored miniature pincher was a good companion. Cat did whatever she could to return the favor to her favorite furry friend. Hannah's rust spots had turned white with age, but she still had the disposition of a sweet little puppy.

A white envelope with no return address didn't appear ominous to Cat. She tore it open without a thought of who had sent it, never realizing that the envelope was missing postage until after the fact. When she pulled out the note, she froze, staring at the one word printed over and over across a single white piece of notebook paper: "Die."

Cat immediately dropped the paper like it was on fire. She jumped from the couch and ran to the phone on the kitchen wall. She was halfway through dialing her parent's number when she disconnected. She hung the phone back on the wall and slowly looked around the apartment for other ominous threats as she crouched down beside the counter. There was no way she could tell her parents about this, she thought miserably. She would have to figure this out on her own. Cat slid down the wall until she was sitting on the tiled kitchen floor. She called Hannah to her.

"Come here, baby. Good girl, that's my good girl Hannah. What am I going to do, huh?"

Hannah responded by snuggling up against Cat, comforting her by wagging her tail and licking her face over and over. Cat sat there with her dog in her lap for nearly half an hour and cried. She chided herself for not knowing what else to do. It crossed her mind to phone the police, but convinced herself that nothing could be done. Then it hit her. "Sullivan!" Cat shouted, she picked up Hannah and headed for her room where she had deposited her purse before going to Miriam's.

She searched her wallet for Sullivan's business card. Once she found it, she used her cell phone, dialed his number and pushed send. She sat on the edge of the bed and waited while his phone rang.

"Detective Sullivan,"

"Detective, this is Catherine Carlyle. Do you have a minute?"

"Absolutely, Miss Carlyle. How can I help you?"

He put a finger across his lips to hush his partner. Sullivan pictured her in her hospital gown again and smiled. "You are hopeless," Bronson whispered and then muffled a laugh. The two homicide detectives had just gotten back into

Bronson's Charger and were winding through traffic when Sullivan's phone had rung.

"I feel foolish for calling." She paused, trying to formulate what she wanted to say.

"Don't. Is everything okay?" He knew he sounded too eager, so he slowed his breathing and waited for her response.

"Well, I don't know," she began slowly. She suddenly wished she hadn't called at all. Desperate for a way to get off the phone without telling him about the note or the mirror in her bathroom, she finally asked if he would meet her at her office at three p.m. Sullivan agreed without a second thought. After disconnecting he looked at Bronson, who gave him two thumbs up.

"She wants me to meet her at her work at three. What do you make of that?"

"She digs you, too, man, that's great! Or maybe she wants to sign a confession. No offense, but that would be even better."

Bronson was right, Sullivan thought. He needed to get serious. He wasn't acting like himself. They rode back to police headquarters in silence. Both men, lost in their own thoughts, formulating plans for the meeting at three o'clock with one, Cat Carlyle.

Chapter 11

R ick sat in his office and edited an advertisement proof that a salesperson had put into his box. It irritated him that the station's advertising staff got commissions for selling ads, but weren't required to write or produce said advertisements. A few of the sales staff did their own work, but some were so lazy and ignorant that Rick had to carry them. He had been working on this particular ad for over an hour and was getting frustrated. It was supposed to be a thirty-second ad. But the salesperson had gotten wordy and the client was not satisfied. He was trying to trim it down without having to rewrite it altogether.

He stood up to take a break. His neck felt stiff and sore. He rolled his head around to ease the headache that had begun at the base of his skull and was gnawing up and over the back of his head. Just then, Cat walked by his windowed door and smiled at him. Once she was out of sight, he balled his fist and punched the wall of his office. Raging, he picked up the ad and tore it to shreds. He threw the pieces towards the trash can and swore when the majority of the tiny confetti littered the floor.

He stared at the mess and added a few extra expletives. Rick thought he was losing control of himself. It was like someone else had taken over his body and he was forced to watch. He stood there for several minutes with his fists clinched and his entire body shaking with anger. He had to calm down. He walked to the wooden filing cabinet against the far wall and pulled the bottom drawer all the way open and knelt down beside it. Before grabbing the shoe box from the very back of the drawer, Rick looked over his shoulder. What had been a gag gift, the year before, had turned into a great hiding spot for Rick's current bottle of comfort.

The shoe box had been wrapped in Christmas paper and the top was wrapped separately so that it could come off without looking like the box had been opened. Rick took the plastic cup from inside the box, along with the bottle of Crown and sat them on his desk. With shaky hands he slowly poured the amber liquid into the cup and resealed the lid. Quickly glancing over his shoulder again, he went back to the filing cabinet, placed the bottle back in the box and shut the drawer.

He held the cup under his nose and inhaled. He would feel better soon, he told himself. He carried the half-filled whiskey cup to his office door and looked through the window out into the hall. Hoping to go unseen, he opened the door and quickly made his way to the ice machine in the break room down the hall. There, he plopped a few ice cubes into his cup and turned to the vending machine, put three quarters in, selected a Coke and bent over to retrieve it from the bottom of the machine

"Hey, there you are," Cat greeted him as she leaned against the door jam.

"God, don't scare me like that!" Rick shouted. He nearly threw his precious drink in the air.

"I'm sorry. I didn't mean to scare you."

"Why are you looking for me?" Rick snapped. He wrapped his hand around the plastic cup and held it and the coke close to his chest like prized possessions.

Cat just stared at him. "I just wanted to let you know that …," she hesitated.

"What?" he said impatiently.

"Nothing, uhhh….I just wanted to make sure you knew I was here…in case you wanted to talk. Is everything okay?" she asked.

She didn't get a reply. Instead, Rick walked briskly by her and went into his office. He slammed the door while she stood there trying to figure out what had just happened. She had wanted to get anything unpleasant out of the way before Sullivan arrived. It crossed her mind to show Rick her bracelet free arm, but he was acting so odd. She assumed it was because she had been absent the day before. So she shrugged her shoulders and retreated to the main entrance. *He is one strange duck*, she thought.

She glanced at her watch and walked to the front door to wait for Detective Sullivan. She realized she had a few minutes before his expected arrival, so she stepped into the ladies room to check herself over. She had taken extra time to paint her eyes and lips and style her wind-blown hair for a change. As she looked at herself in the mirror, she wondered why she didn't dress up more often. She had chosen a cobalt blue cashmere sweater that she wore over a white silk blouse. She liked how the sweater pressed the silk blouse against her skin. It not only looked good, it felt great, she admitted to herself. Her favorite black slacks made her thin frame appear even thinner. She smiled when she looked down at her feet. Right before walking out the door she changed out of her black flats and put on some sexy black heels. She hoped it didn't look like she was trying too hard. Was she trying too hard, she wondered, and if so, why?

She didn't have long to mull it over. Sullivan pulled in front of the building promptly at three o'clock.

"This is my partner, Detective Clint Bronson," Sullivan said as Cat ushered them into the building.

"Hello, nice to meet you." Cat shook Bronson's hand and asked them to follow her. She led the way to the conference room where she asked if either man would care for something to drink.

"No, thank you. We know you have limited time to visit, so let's get started."

"Please sit down then," Cat invited. She pulled a wooden chair away from the table and sat down. She hadn't thought to shut the door and started to get up to do it, when Bronson pulled it shut and produced a brilliant smile. She decided she wasn't the only one trying hard.

This guy is full of himself, Cat thought. She smiled nervously. Before telling them the reason why she had asked to see them, she mentioned that on her drive into work she thought she had remembered something about the killer.

"I know this will probably sound ridiculous, but there was something about the killer's voice that sounded familiar.

I can't put my finger on it just yet. I just thought I better mention it."

Sullivan appeared to take an interest as Cat watched him writing something down in his notebook. Then he looked at her intently, as if he could see right through her.

"You sounded really upset earlier when you called. Has something else happened?" Sullivan asked. He continued staring unblinking.

When she hesitated he laid his notebook and pen down on the table. She wasn't convinced that he believed anything she had said so far, and she wasn't sure how much of the truth to tell him. She didn't know if she could trust him.

"There was something I wanted to tell you at the hospital, but chose not to because of my parents."

"Go on," Sullivan encouraged.

She began slowly. Her eyes darted nervously between Sullivan and Bronson. She wiped her hands on the thighs of her black slacks as she told them about a man that had worked at the station a few months back. He had gotten fired for stealing from the station and had not taken the termination well. He had threatened revenge as he was escorted out of the building by security.

"I should have said something the other day when you asked, but I was afraid," Cat admitted.

She told the detectives that her parents hadn't known that she had been dating him, and she didn't want them to hear about the things he had said and done to her when he was angry.

"His name is Warren Garrison, but on the air he went by the name of Wren Garrison. He was a pretty decent disk jockey, great on-air voice. He could probably even be a comedian because he has a talent for voice impersonations."

"I wondered what happened to Wren," Bronson interrupted. "I used to hear him in the morning while I was getting ready for work. I really liked him. So he got fired, huh?" Bronson asked while Sullivan glared at him.

Cat continued by nodding her head, "Yes, like I said, he got caught stealing. Our network manager caught him loading his truck with some promotional items one weekend."

"What kind of promotional items are we talking about?" Sullivan asked.

"Nothing of much value. I think it was a box of cup cozies, music CD's and t-shirts. You'd have to ask the manager to be sure. His name is Frederick Davidson."

Sullivan wrote the information down in his notebook then flipped a few pages back. He scanned his notes with his finger and then looked back up at Cat.

"Are you suggesting that this Mister Garrison might have had something to do with the murder of Mister Diaz?" Sullivan asked with a frown.

"Oh, no, nothing like that," Cat said quickly. "I thought he could possibly be the one who wrote that horrible message on my hospital door."

"So you think the message on your door had nothing to do with the murder from the night before?" Sullivan asked. He wasn't following her line of reasoning. He still felt like she was holding something back. He laid his arms on the wooden table top and leaned across the table toward her. She immediately leaned back in her chair and fidgeted with a silver chain that hung around her neck.

"No, I don't think it had anything to do with the murder, but I can't be certain. I just know that Warren was really angry when we broke up. He tore up a book I had given him and dumped it and some of my things I had left at his house on my doorstep. He kept harassing me to give him this necklace back." She held the silver chain out for them to see. "He made a huge deal out of it. He insisted I give it back, but I wouldn't. I really liked it."

"How long ago was that?" Sullivan asked.

"About three weeks ago."

"What else makes you think it was Garrison that left the message?"

"Well…" She swallowed hard and forced herself to go on. Her voice quivered a little as she said the next part. She could feel her heart pounding and tried to calm herself as she recalled her last encounter with Warren. He had hurt her and told her there was more to come. She hadn't seen or heard from him since.

"I was here working one night about three weeks ago. Pat and I were the only ones here." Sullivan interrupted her by asking for Pat's last name and then went silent so Cat would continue. "Warren showed up around ten that night. He was in a foul mood. I told him he couldn't come by the station anymore. I could lose my job for letting him back in the building. We fought, and I broke up with him. Then he yanked my hair and pushed me against the wall just outside the studio booth. He put his hand around my throat and was choking me. He told me that I would be sorry for breaking up with him. I thought he was going to rape me because he tried to undo the front of my pants." She paused and crossed her arms across her chest. She felt herself flush and hurried through the last part to get it over with. "We struggled there in the hallway." Cat pointed towards the outside wall and both men turned their heads as if they could see back in time and see the two of them in the hallway.

"Warren said he was going to teach me to respect him. He was tearing at my clothes and squeezing my neck really hard. Pat heard me screaming and ran up here to see what was going on. Luckily he was just coming out of the sound proof production room after recording a sound bite. Warren didn't know he was here."

"So this Pat guy stopped Garrison?" Bronson asked. He leaned forward on the table too and had fisted both of his hands while she talked. Sullivan looked at Bronson with a scowl and jotted down something in his notebook, while Cat took several deep breaths and steadied herself to continue.

"Yes, Pat stopped him. They didn't fight though. Pat asked if I wanted him to call the cops and I said no. I just wanted Warren to leave. Warren only laughed and jerked me toward him. I tried pushing him away but his teeth hit my lips and busted the lower lip open. Then before Pat or I could do anything he shoved my head toward the wall, called me a few ugly names, said something like, 'This will be continued' and then left. I wish now that I had reported it then," she added thoughtfully. She watched as Sullivan's pen scribbled quickly on the paper.

"What are you leaving out?" Sullivan asked as he lifted his keen eyes to hers. She bit the inside of her cheek and raised her shoulders a little.

"I haven't left anything out." She crossed her legs and hugged her arms tighter.

"Sure you have. Tell me everything." He narrowed his eyes at her, dropped the pen and formed a little pyramid with his hands on the table between them. She watched as his index fingers began tapping together to some silent rhythm. The silence lingered between them as she studied his hands. They looked strong and capable. She noted his nails were trimmed and clean. She also noticed that he wasn't wearing any jewelry.

Then suddenly he slammed both hands, palms down onto the table, startling her and making her jump.

"Tell me!" he shouted.

Cat began stuttering and stammering. She covered her mouth with both of her hands, as her eyes filled with tears. "He raped me." She choked on the words.

She had never admitted it to anyone before. She couldn't look at Sullivan for a long time. The room was silent except for the soft crying noises she made. The detectives waited for her to continue, not bothering to offer her sympathy. When she continued, her throat burned with embarrassment and shame as she explained how and where the attack had taken place.

Warren had followed her home that night. Just as she was opening her apartment door, he had appeared out of no-where. He shoved his way in the door and threw her on the floor. She stopped then and left the unspoken horror hanging between them.

"Was that so hard?" Sullivan asked. He didn't expect a reply. He was telling himself how infuriating this woman was when he realized he was really just angry because she had been assaulted and didn't report it. He wanted to lecture her, to scream, but instead he laid a hand over her shaking ones on the table.

She pulled her hands away and wiped the tears off her cheeks then and told them about the drawing on her bathroom mirror and about the note that she had received before coming to work. Her eyes welled with tears again as she remembered how scared and helpless she felt when she opened the note.

"Where is the note now?" Sullivan asked, his anger rising again.

"I left it lying where I dropped it. I thought about bringing it to you when we decided to meet, but I couldn't make myself touch it again. I'm sorry."

She dropped her head then as tears streamed out of her eyes. She began inspecting her own hands, turning them over and over in her lap. She stopped only when Sullivan got up and walked around the table. She looked up at him fearfully as he pulled the chair beside her out from under the table and sat down in it. He placed his hands on top of hers again and reassured her that he and his partner were on her side.

Betsy Randolph

"Please, don't hold anything back from now on. I can't help you if I don't know everything."

Her heart felt like it was flopping over and over in her chest. She tried to reason with herself about her reaction to this stranger's touch. She could feel herself compelled to trust him. Sullivan kept his hands on hers a moment longer than was necessary and before he finally withdrew them, he squeezed her fingers gently.

Something about the tenderness in which he touched her gripped her heart like a vise.

Chapter 12

Cat had agreed to call Sullivan when her shift was over at midnight. The plan was for him to come to the station, and together they would go to her apartment where she would give him the note. As Bronson and Sullivan left the conference room, Sullivan saw Rick's blonde head dart behind a door quickly as if he had been peeking through the window at them. Sullivan walked straight towards the door and rapped on it, so Bronson and Cat followed him. Rick pulled the door open and stood in the doorway with a quizzical look on his face.

"Yes?" Rick asked snootily. "Can I help you?"

"I hope so," Sullivan began. "My name is Detective Sullivan, Homicide Division, Oklahoma City Police Department. I have a few questions for you, if you have a minute."

"Actually, I don't," Rick said. He started to close the door in their faces when Sullivan put a hand out and stopped it.

"You can speak to us here or you can come downtown with us Mister…?"

"Hurley, Rick Hurley," Rick answered indignantly. "I will be happy to look at my schedule and see when we can set up a time."

Sullivan laughed and turned to look at Bronson who had moved closer to the open door. They both chuckled as they pushed their way into the office, forcing Rick to back up.

"Excuse us, Miss Carlyle," Sullivan called over his shoulder.

"It was a pleasure meeting you," Bronson added. He turned and flashed another smile that was completely lost on Cat. She smiled back, though, and quietly left, leaving Rick to fend for himself. She thought it felt pretty good seeing Rick treated with as much decorum as he often treated others.

"You can't just barge in here like some kind of...thugs," Rick stuttered.

"What? You think you can just shut the door in our faces, and we are just going to leave, Mister Hurley?" asked Sullivan. He leaned closer to Rick and sniffed. "Been hitting the bottle a little early in the day, haven't you?"

"I don't know what you're talking about," Rick said defensively. He put his hands on his hips, flexing his chest and neck muscles.

"Don't hurt yourself there, Hulk," Bronson laughed. He was thinking to himself that Rick looked more like a playground bully than an "Assistant Network Manager" like the nameplate on his desk suggested. Bronson picked the nameplate up and showed it to Sullivan who only raised his eyebrows and rolled his eyes.

"Look," Sullivan said, "I just have a few questions for you and then we will let you get back to whatever you were drinking...I mean, doing."

Tokens of the Liars

Rick's face reddened and his lips formed a thin tight line. Sullivan and Bronson watched as his chest rose and fell quickly. Tiny little specks of sweat appeared above his upper lip and across his forehead. Rick worked his fingers through his thick blonde hair, combing it over to the side. He didn't think either of them would notice that he let his palm wipe his forehead off or his forearm brush across his sweaty lip as he returned his hand to his hip. Sullivan enjoyed watching the effects of Rick's discomfort.

"Would you care to sit down or would you like to stand?" Sullivan gestured toward Rick's chair.

Completely flustered and stuttering, Rick demanded, "What is it that you want to know?" He tried to appear relaxed by allowing his arms to hang by his sides, but it felt unnatural and stiff. So he crossed one arm over his chest and held the elbow of the other arm while that hand rubbed his chin with his fingers and thumb.

Both detectives noticed the fresh bruises on Ricks knuckles. Sullivan asked him how he had gotten injured.

"Oh, that's nothing," Rick tried to assure them as he looked at the back of his hand. "I accidently hit the wall earlier today, that's all. I'm fine."

Bronson shook his head and exchanged glances with Sullivan. Sullivan asked Rick about his whereabouts the night of the murder, about what kind of vehicle he drove and where he usually parked. He asked where he was parked the night of the murder. He asked whether or not he knew or had ever met the victim, Juan Diaz. Sullivan asked him about Cat and what her demeanor was like the night of the murder. He

99

asked if he remembered what time she left the building and when was the next time Rick talked to her. He asked Rick about the condition in which he found Cat's car the next day. Sullivan jotted notes down while Rick answered the questions. Bronson roamed the room.

Rick appeared to keep a close eye on Bronson's movements. Occasionally Sullivan had to repeat the question because Rick was so distracted by Bronson's close examination of Rick's personal items on display. Bronson smiled while looking at Rick's wall decorated with numerous broadcasting awards. Bronson thought it was odd that a guy would have so many pictures of himself in his own office. Many of the photos were of Rick with famous rock bands, but still Bronson thought it was weird. He looked around but didn't find any photos of a wife or kids, not even any photos of girlfriends. Then Bronson sniffed at the plastic cup that sat on a coaster next to the keyboard and identified Rick's drink of choice as a Crown and Coke.

"That's not mine," Rick declared.

Bronson replied, "Yah, whatever," and continued looking around.

Bronson saw what appeared to be a hand-shredded piece of paper scattered all over the floor by the trash can. He moved it around with the toe of his boot, but didn't ask about it. Sullivan wrote Rick's answers in his notebook and noted his odd behavior. He was hiding something. Sullivan could sense it. While Bronson continued his examination of the room, Sullivan dug deeper and asked Rick personal questions. Was he married, was he seeing someone and if so what was his or her name? That last remark must have hit a nerve, because Rick's eyes instantly flashed something akin to anger.

"That is all the time I have for you gentlemen, if you would please excuse me." Rick's voice had also changed instantly, Sullivan noticed. If he wasn't mistaken, it sounded like Rick turned his radio voice on for that last sentence. That struck Sullivan as very odd, and he scratched out what he thought about it on paper. He enjoyed his charade of note taking. His mini-recorder had been recording since they got out of the patrol car.

"We will be in touch," Sullivan said as he gave the nod to Bronson to indicate he was ready to leave.

"Nice office," Bronson commented to Rick as he followed Sullivan out and into the front entrance where they had entered an hour or so earlier.

"Nice fella."

"Yeah, right. Hey, I'd like to see if we can catch the network's station manager before we leave and maybe visit with this Pat Gilbraithe. What do you think?" Sullivan asked Bronson.

"Sounds good. You're the boss. Whatever you say."

"Right. Come on." He followed Sullivan across the foyer to the receptionist's desk. A teenage girl sat behind a large wooden desk that had a beautiful finished surface. She was chewing gum and texting on her cell phone. She slid the phone under the desk as the men approached.

"How can I help you?" she asked. She was staring at Bronson and smiling. Bronson, taking his cue, stepped around Sullivan and up to the desk. He asked to speak to the station manager and then rewarded the girl with a dimpled cheek smile and sealed the deal with a compliment about the color of her shirt.

"You are pathetic, son," Sullivan whispered as the girl scurried down the hall to go speak with the station manager.

"I'm just trying to help out, Sully. Don't judge me," Bronson responded with a sly smile.

Before they left, they had spoken to Frederick Davidson, the network's station manager; Brooke, the teenage receptionist; the intern, Pat Gilbraithe; and the sales representative named Lindsey Byrd.

Sullivan mentioned on the way back to headquarters that he didn't think they had gained any new or relevant information out of the last few people they talked to. He was curious to hear what his partner thought of Cat Carlyle.

"Well, what was your take on Cat?" Sullivan asked Bronson.

"I thought she was adorable, and I loved her outfit," Bronson commented with a fake lisp.

"Be serious, man. What did you think about her story?"

"I think she might have a stalker. I wouldn't put it past that Rick guy to be it either. Or maybe she has two stalkers. She's credible, but skittish."

"I agree," Sullivan added. "Let's take a closer look at Rick and this Warren character."

"Tell you what," Bronson said with a grin. "Since you're going to be putting in some long hours today, I'll run down Warren Garrison and get a statement from him."

"Sounds good," Sullivan agreed. "I need to do a little more digging on our victim Diaz and visit with his ex-wife again. I have his Department of Corrections file on my desk. I thumbed through it this morning. It looks like he has stayed clean the last few months. He checked in regularly with his probation officer and was looking for full-time work. His ex seemed pretty torn up over the killing and couldn't think of anyone who would want to harm him. Who knows? Maybe the killing had nothing to do with Cat. Maybe it was payback or a drug deal gone wrong. I didn't see any drug convictions in Diaz' file, but as you know, that doesn't really mean he wasn't involved with them."

"Yeah, it's possible your smokin' hot' girl was just in the wrong place at the wrong time. She seems perfectly innocent to me," Bronson added glibly. He poked Sullivan in the ribs producing a yelp and a jerk of the steering wheel.

"One of these days…" Sullivan began, but didn't finish as he lowered his elbow against his side to prevent further attacks.

When they parted ways at the police station, Sullivan agreed to contact Bronson, if necessary, after he picked up the note from Cat's place. "It won't be necessary," Sullivan assured his partner.

"Enjoy your evening and kiss your beautiful wife for me."

"Never gonna happen," Bronson declared as he walked away.

Sullivan went to his desk, draped his blue wool blazer over the back of the chair and loosened his favorite striped tie. He unbuttoned his shirt sleeves and rolled them up as he walked to the refrigerator. God, he was tired. He opened the door, picked out a cold can of Dr. Pepper, popped the top open and drank half the can. As he was shutting the refrigerator door, something came to him. He stood there drinking and staring off into space. Something was bugging him. That little voice inside his head was trying to get him to remember something he had seen or heard today. What was it?

Chapter 13

Susan pulled up in front of the station just as Sullivan and Bronson were leaving. She sat in her car and whistled while she watched them exit the building and get in the unmarked police cruiser. Smiling, she entered the radio station and made her way back to where Cat was printing off news stories for her top of the hour broadcast. Her show was starting in a few minutes, and she was still putting the first hour's news and weather together.

"Who were the two delicious specimens that just left?" Susan asked as she pointed back over her shoulder.

"That was the detective I told you about and his sidekick."

"Wow, which one was which?" Susan smiled.

"The tall one in the blue jacket was Tom Sullivan. The other guy I can't remember his first name, but his last name was Branson something or another."

"Are they single? Which one do you have your eye on?"

Cat frowned and shrugged her shoulders. "I couldn't tell you about their status, and I couldn't care less," Cat responded with a cross look on her face. To which Susan started laughing, full belly laughing. She laughed so hard she had to hold her belly with both of her hands.

"What is wrong with you, Susan? I'm serious. Quit laughing and get out of the way. I have work to do." Cat piled CD's in a tray, copies of news stories and walked past Susan into the sound booth to set up.

Rick was already in the control room and tapped on the Plexiglas. He motioned to his wrist watch as she walked in.

"I know, I know. I'm ready...take it easy."

He frowned at her and took another sip of his second drink of the day. He put his headset on and began preparing for the telephone calls by placing call sheets on a clipboard and placing a marker next to it. Part of Cat's shift was dedicated to listener requests and comments. The sheer volume of incoming calls required assistance. Without someone to screen the callers, the show couldn't be sold to advertisers as live radio. There were just too many weirdoes that called in to live radio shows for Cat to put them directly on the air. There had to be a controller or screener who could be blamed when a caller got disconnected. Anyone could do it, but the network's station manager had made Rick perform that function since a lunatic slipped by a young disk jockey named Ted Holcomb two months ago. The station had received nasty letters from the FCC, and one listener even threatened litigation. So on top of everything else Rick was responsible for, he had to babysit Cat and her precious radio program.

Rick fantasized daily about tightening his fingers around Cat's throat until she quit thrashing around. It wasn't bad enough to have to do this, now Cat had a little friend over to play, Rick thought, as he glared at Susan through the plexiglas. Susan had followed Cat into the sound booth and was just about to leave to head back to work when she caught a glimpse of Rick staring at her.

"What is his problem?" Susan asked Cat. Cat glanced at Rick then back to her stack of papers.

"Same one as usual. I told you, he hates me, hates being made to produce the show and obviously hates you because you are my friend."

"Nice working environment," Susan chimed in.

"I tried to tell you. The guy is a ticking time bomb."

Susan hadn't been to the station since Rick had taken over Ted's position. She thought Cat had been exaggerating about how Rick treated her.

"Believe it or not, I am actually getting used to his hate-fulness," Cat sighed as she placed a CD in the player. She had cue cards for live promotional ads lined up and neatly stacked in front of her for easy access during the show. She tapped them on the desk as Susan sat on an extra seat in the booth and slid quietly to the edge of the desk.

"Back to our conversation," Susan said, but was hushed by a slap from Cat.

Without saying anything, Cat picked up a pen and some scrap paper and quickly scribbled out a note of warning. "He can hear everything we say in here!"

"Oh, sorry. I forgot," Susan scribbled back.

"We'll talk about it later, okay?" Cat wrote.

"Bet your sweet bee-hind we will. The tall one, huh?" Susan wrote and pushed the pad toward Cat.

"What?" Cat asked with scribbled question marks.

"The tall detective, Tom." Susan smiled knowingly.

"Who? Sullivan?" Cat broke her rules and said aloud. "I call him Sullivan."

Susan lifted her finger to her lips and drew one word on the note pad, "Why?"

"Cause he wants me to call him Tom," Cat wrote and then drew a big smiley face beside it.

"Whatever!" Susan wrote. Then she leaned closer and whispered, "I'm getting out of here before you start. I love you. Call me after work."

She darted out the door while the lead-in music began playing for the beginning of Cat's daily show. The show went remarkably well, and the night passed quickly. There weren't any occasions where Rick said something hateful, and Cat thought he actually appeared calm and almost lethargic at times. She didn't give it much thought. She was just grateful for the reprieve.

After her shift ended, the overnight DJ came in and began setting up. Cat put her music away, logged her cd's in, filed her news reports and picked up her things to leave.

"What's your rush, Cat?" Rick said from behind her as she was making her way to the door. The hair on the back of her neck stood on end as she slowly turned to look at him.

Something was different in the way he said her name. It made her skin crawl. He stood in the doorway to his office with one arm draped against the door frame and the other casually on his hip. He was trying really hard to look like a male model, Cat thought. Granted he was good looking, but he was such a jerk that his looks did not compensate for his personality. It almost seemed like he was coming on to her. Cat wondered if he could be hitting on her.

"No rush, just ready to get out of here," Cat replied as she moved her purse nervously from one shoulder to the other.

"You are forgetting something," Rick said as he moved from the doorway and slid closer to her.

She held her purse in front of her now with both arms, like a shield. "I am?" she asked curiously.

"Yes, you are." He took a step beside her and slid his hand down her back. Resting it in the small of her back, he used it to guide her towards his office.

She didn't want to go, but for some reason her legs refused to comply and continued carrying her towards his open office door.

"You have forgotten that I need to visit with you. Since you missed work yesterday without notice, I had to write you up. I need you to sign the disciplinary form. It should only take a moment."

"But I called you, and I explained what happened and..." Cat fumbled with words as Rick pushed her the last few feet and closed his office door behind them.

Cat smelled the alcohol on Rick's breath as the door closed behind them, and she heard the click of the lock as Rick turned it. Her panic didn't set in though until Rick pushed her down into a chair across from his desk and began rubbing her shoulders. His hands brushed her hair off her shoulders and he leaned down and sniffed her blonde hair and whispered in her ear that she had been a bad girl and needed to be disciplined.

"Listen, Rick, I need to go." She started to stand up, but he held her in place.

"Like I said, this won't take long. You just keep your pants on...or don't." He began laughing at his own joke and continued rubbing Cat's shoulders as he moved to her neck. His clammy fingers circled her neck and began caressing her skin. She stiffened beneath his touch and began to shift in the chair as she attempted to stand up again. His grip tightened around her neck and held her tightly in place.

"I am meeting someone. I have to go."

It thrilled him to hear the fear in her voice. Cat's mind was racing as she wracked her brain for a non-violent solution. Finally she asked, "Where is this discipline form you were talking about?" Her voice quivered.

He laughed and said, "It's there on the desk, under the crystal paper weight."

Since he didn't move to get the single sheet of paper that was face down on the desk and held securely in place by the paper weight, Cat did. She quickly lunged forward, stood, then spun around and readied herself for combat. She took a fighting stance and braced for the worst. Rick's only response was to laugh. He hadn't tried to keep her from escaping his grasp. He put his hands on his hips and just laughed at her. He grabbed the paper and turned it over slapping it down on the desk with a thud.

Cat didn't move. Her stomach was still queasy from the physical contact. She didn't dare approach Rick. She never wanted to feel his hands on any part of her body again. She remained in her combat stance looking like a ninja ready for sparring. Rick finally walked around the desk and sat down. He leaned back in his chair, threw his feet up on the desk and crossed his ankles. He laced his fingers together behind his head and finally said, "Go on, sign the damn form and get out. I have places to be, too."

His sudden change of personality was frightening. Cat took a short step towards the desk and reached out her hand to grab the sheet while she kept her eye on Rick. She imagined him lunging across the desk towards her.

"I'll need to read this before I sign it."

"Get after it, then," he said with a grunt.

Cat briefly scanned the document. She wasn't pleased, but she desperately wanted out of there. She would follow this up with Mr. Davidson tomorrow, she vowed to herself. She signed the form and without another word turned and rushed towards the door.

Rick was upon her before the lock surrendered in her hand.

"What is wrong with you? Why are you doing this?" Cat screamed.

Rick had encircled Cat with his arms and had pressed his body hard against her back as she struggled with the lock. Her anger was only surpassed by her fear and just as she pictured herself crumbling to the floor in a heap, someone knocked on the door. She and Rick looked up at the same time to see Tom Sullivan glaring back at them through the window of the door.

"Help me!" she screamed. "Help!"

"Shut up and move out of the way." Rick said as he shoved her away and unlocked the door. Then he retreated a few steps into the office. Cat rushed out the door and into Sullivan's arms. She began crying and pointing at Rick.

"He wouldn't let me out. He's crazy. He assaulted me."

"You wish, sweetheart. I was trying to unlock the door. Besides, you didn't have a problem with it last time." Rick stepped towards Cat as he spoke. He pumped his pointed finger at her with each word.

Sullivan could feel Cat shaking with terror. With every word and step closer to them Rick came, Sullivan could feel Cat shrinking behind him. Sullivan blocked Cat with his muscled arm and intercepted Rick with a one-handed closed fist over Rick's pointed finger, making Rick squeal in pain.

"Ouch, let go! You're hurting me. You are hurting me!"

Sullivan got as close to Rick's face as he could and breathed a threat that Rick wouldn't forget. "Don't you ever touch her again. Do you hear me?" Sullivan demanded and tightened his grip around Rick's fingers. He wanted to break the weasel-like fingers that had danced on the skin of this petrified woman who hid behind him now.

When Sullivan finally let go of Rick, he did so with a shove. He gathered Cat and her things, and they made their way outside the station. Sullivan unlocked his patrol car and ushered Cat into the front passenger seat. He helped her buckle her seatbelt and pulled a couple of tissues out of the box he stored in his passenger side door pocket and handed them to her. He was still frowning as he shut the door and walked around the car to get in. Once inside the car he took a deep breath and let it out as if he was expelling all the anger he felt along with it.

"Are you okay?" He asked slowly as he looked over at Cat. He didn't dare touch her again, but he wanted to. He wanted to brush the stray hair back away from her flushed face and tuck it behind her pretty little ear. He wanted to see her face, her eyes. Those hazel eyes that appeared bluer tonight. When he first saw them through the window tonight and saw the fear and panic in them, he wanted to beat the door down and kill Rick with his bare hands.

Cat said nothing, but blew her nose and nodded her head at his question. They sat there in silence for a few moments. Sullivan gripped the steering wheel with both hands to keep them occupied. Without turning towards her, he finally said.

"You need to tell me everything he said and did. I think you need to press charges against him."

Cat sighed and leaned her head against the headrest. "Oh please, Detective. I'll lose my job. I can't." Sullivan stared hard at her and didn't even try to hide the disgust in his voice.

"You will not lose your job. He is in a supervisory position. He will lose his job. Trust me. Besides, he might spend some time in jail depending on how many laws he just broke in there."

When Cat didn't respond, he let go of the steering wheel and turned in his seat to face her. She refused to look at him. The longer they sat like that the angrier and more uncomfortable Sullivan got.

"Are you going to tell me what happened?" Silence.

"Well?" More silence. "Cat, I am here to help you. What would have happened if I hadn't planned to meet you here tonight?"

Still she said nothing. By now Sullivan was furious, tired and sick of games. This gal was acting like a kid and he didn't have the time, or the inclination, to play along.

"Fine, don't tell me. Hell, you probably enjoy men treating you like that. I am sorry I interrupted your fun."

She spun on him then, venom in her words and in her eyes. "You jerk! Don't you dare talk to me that way. I don't have to sit here and listen to you or your crap."

She unsnapped her seatbelt, pushed open the door and slammed it hard as she strode around the building towards her car in the back lot. Sullivan jumped out of the car and raced after her. Why had he said that? What had gotten in to him? He jogged to catch up to the quickly moving female figure.

"I'm sorry, Cat. Please wait."

Without so much as an acknowledgement, she unlocked her car and got in, slamming her own door. Sullivan began asking loudly through the glass for her to stop and then finally banging on the window with his hand as she started the engine.

"Please stop. Cat. Please!"

She was crying again, she wouldn't look at him at all as she put the car in gear and jammed on the gas. Sullivan had to jump back from the car to keep his toes intact as she sped out of the parking lot. He yelled at her to stop as she drove away and then suddenly he remembered who he was. He was a law enforcement officer. He could make her stop. He ran full speed across the lot and around the building to his car. He could see her tail lights ahead and mashed on the accelerator to catch up to her.

She had gotten on Interstate 35 headed north before he got behind her vehicle and activated his emergency lights to initiate a traffic stop. At first he didn't think she was going to pull over. She continued northbound swerving in her lane like a drunk driver. He ran her license plate through his dispatch to insure he was stopping the correct vehicle. When the tag came back to Catherine Carlyle of Guthrie, he knew for certain. He advised his dispatchers he would be out on traffic when he saw that she was finally yielding and pulling to the right of the roadway.

Sullivan approached the vehicle with caution, like every other traffic stop. He knew the state of mind of this particular driver already. An emotional driver was a dangerous driver and this emotional driver had nearly taken his feet off. He walked up along the passenger side and banged on the window. He instructed the driver to turn the car off, which she did. "Driver, roll down your window," he instructed as he tapped on the front passenger window with a knuckle. He shone a flashlight in her face, blinding her as he instructed her to hand him her license and insurance.

"I'm sorry, Officer. I just got off work and am on my way home."

"Uh huh, Miss. I need you to exit your vehicle."

She still didn't realize it was Sullivan as she opened the door and carefully looked back to ensure a car wasn't driving by before she stepped out. Once out of the car she saw Sullivan and stood there shivering in the night air, trying to decide what to do and what to say.

"Please step over here away from the vehicles, Ma'am."

He and Cat moved from between the vehicles and stood on the grassy shoulder. Looking serious, he glanced over her driver license and insurance form.

"Your license is expired."

"What? When?" She acted like she was going to take it back from him when he pulled his arm away from her and shook his head no.

"Operating a motor vehicle without a valid license is a jail-able offense in Oklahoma. Did you know that, Miss…?" He looked at her license again as if he had already forgotten her name. "Carlyle."

"You have got to be kidding, right?" Cat asked, but refrained from letting her anger show. She wasn't sure what Sullivan would do. He was acting so official and detached.

"Do you have any weapons on you? Gun, knife, bomb …?"

"No! You know I don't, I…"

"Come have a seat in my patrol car then."

He walked her back to his car, opened the passenger door and had her get in. He shut the door, walked around to his side and got in. After shutting his door he cleared his throat.

"Now, where were we?" He asked her as he pulled a brown leather binder from his door pocket. He unsnapped it and opened it up as Cat watched him anxiously. She realized it was a ticket book and watched as he slid her license into place under the stapled paper headings of previous citations. He picked up a pen that had been tucked inside the ticket book and started writing on a little form.

"Are you really going to write me a ticket, Sullivan?"

Now she didn't care if he could tell she was angry. This man was infuriating, she thought. "Stop writing and talk to me," She demanded as she gently touched his arm.

Before jerking away he immediately felt his insides go mushy. He stopped writing and closed his ticket book. He took a few deep breaths and let them silently out. Then he reached over and opened a little hidden compartment under his cup holder. He pulled out a package of peppermint gum and gestured for her to take one. She pulled a stick of gum out for herself and began unwrapping it, never taking her eyes off his. After getting his own piece of gum, he replaced his stash in its hiding place, unwrapped his gum and popped it into his mouth.

Cat's mind was trying to understand what this little dance they were doing meant. She was silently evaluating her feelings towards this man with the coffee-colored eyes when he finally spoke. His voice was husky.

"I'm sorry for what I said earlier. I believe you were victimized tonight. You shouldn't have to put up with that guy, and I for one would love to slam his head into a wall. If you will sign a complaint, I will put him in jail tonight. It's your decision though."

He looked into her beautiful hazel eyes as he spoke. He didn't allow himself to pressure her to talk, even though he wanted to know everything that had happened. Patiently, he sat there staring at her, trying hard not to look at her heart-shaped lips as she chewed her gum.

"Can we please just go to my place? I want you to see the letter. I'll make coffee if you want." The look she gave him made his heart hurt. He would do anything she asked. They both knew it.

"Okay, but your license really is expired. I can't allow you to drive."

"Are you kidding?" He just shook his head no again and smiled.

"Come on," she said, "I'll take care of it tomorrow, or today I guess. I promise, Officer."

She gave him a big smile and clasped her hands together like she were praying or begging. She figured a little flirting wouldn't hurt.

"Fine, I'll let you go with a warning, this time. I was actually already writing it out."

He retrieved his ticket book and finished the warning, he pointed to where she needed to sign and tore out her copy and handed it to her. She reached out to take it, and he pulled it back a little with a sly smile. A little flirting wouldn't hurt, he figured.

Chapter 14

He followed her north out of Oklahoma City to down-town Guthrie where they parked on the red brick street in front of an antique mall with large glass windows. The two-story, red sandstone building had been well taken care of since its construction in 1902. The date was carved into the stone at the highest peak of the building and just below it were tall windows with wavy glass. Cat pointed up to the windows.

"That's my place up there. Come on."

He followed her through an antique outer wooden door that had been painted brilliant blue, up a flight of steep wooden steps that seemed just a little too tall and into a long hallway with parallel wooden planked floors that appeared to have been recently polished. It reminded him of an old western film he had seen on TNT. His nose was detecting new paint, varnish, maybe even some mold as he walked down the hallway. The floors creaked and moaned under his feet. Cat paused at the first door they came to and put her key in the lock of apartment number 5 and unlocked the door. Hannah began to yip and whimper as soon as they entered the apartment. Hannah had never been a typical barking dog. It was one of the things that Cat loved about her pet. She only barked when she was frightened or was being protective.

"Please make yourself comfortable. I'm going to take Hannah out real quick. You're welcome to come with us or, if you'd rather, you can stay here."

She walked to the dog's crate just around the corner in the living room and began cooing and talking baby talk. "How's my Hannah-baby? Come on sweetie. Let's go pot-ty."

Hannah rushed from the kennel and barked once at Sullivan to prove she was guarding the place. "It's okay, baby. He's a friend. See, Hannah, friend."

Cat reassured her as she patted Sullivan's arm and then bent down to pat his shin so that Hannah would smell him. Cat smiled as Hannah sniffed and inspected Sullivan's pant leg.

Cat was thinking how good he smelt earlier in the car when she was close to him and when he had held her at the station. She was thinking to herself how delicious and manly he smelt. She was sure Hannah thought the same now. Without asking again if he wanted to join them, Cat opened the door and took Hannah out.

"We will be right back. Make yourself at home."

Sullivan stood in the entryway and looked around. He marveled at the twelve-foot high ceilings and the intricate crown molding throughout the apartment. The place open and airy and old, he thought. He walked on the Berber carpeted floors and entered an open living room. He walked to the tall windows, which he guessed had to be at least eight feet tall. He could see down the block and into the buildings across the street. Turning around he took in the furnishings and breathed in a decidedly female scent. He figured it was a combination of cinnamon, vanilla and something else kind of girly or flowery. Whatever it was, it was nice. It was very Cat, he thought. He was admiring her rustic-looking coffee table and southwestern décor when he saw the letter on the floor, just as she had described.

Squatting down he examined it without touching it. Seeing the one word threat written over and over made his blood boil. He left it lying there and stood up. He remembered what she had told him about the heart drawing in the bathroom. He made his way through her bedroom without stopping to look around. He felt a little uneasy being this close to her personal space. He flipped on the bathroom light with a pen that he retrieved from his jacket pocket. Huffing on the mirror in various places, he finally spotted the drawing. He would need a picture of this and was considering calling the evidence team out when he heard the front door open and close.

"Are you doing okay?" Cat called out as she led the dog into the kitchen. He could hear her running water in the sink, so he retraced his steps and joined her.

"I've looked at the note and the message. I'd like to get my evidence team in here to document everything and collect the evidence." Cat frowned and cocked her head to the side.

"Do they have to do it tonight? I'm exhausted."

Sullivan sighed and crossed his arms in front of his large chest. "If we want it done correctly and preserved for prosecution, we do."

Cat crossed her arms then uncrossed them. She rolled her shoulders and rubbed at the back of her neck.

"Can't you just bag up the letter and take a picture of the heart on the mirror. I really don't want a bunch of people in here rummaging through my stuff and making messes for me to clean up. I've seen how they do that stuff on TV. It's ridiculous."

He caved into her then and agreed to collect the evidence himself, but told her he wouldn't be able to dust for prints. He asked her if she were sure she didn't want it processed. She just flashed her hazel eyes at him and shook her head no as she filled Hannah's bowl with fresh water and measured out a little cup of dry dog food and placed the bowls on the floor.

"She doesn't like to be watched while she eats. Come on."

Cat walked to the living room with Sullivan following her. She hoped he was checking her out. She admitted to herself that it felt good to have a man under her roof.

"Tell you what. I'll get my bag from the car and collect what I can tonight. If it looks like I'll need the team, I'll get them out here later in the day. Deal?"

He held out his hand to make a pact with her. She looked at his large, strong hand sticking out there between them and then with her eyes, traced up his arm to his chest, across his broad shoulders, up his sturdy neck, along his strong jaw line, then paused at his full mouth. When his lips parted in a smile, she caught her breath as she studied his white teeth and followed the contours of his high cheekbones to those long dark lashes and sultry brown eyes.

She wasn't sure how long she had stood there like that staring into those eyes then back down to his mouth when he interrupted her thoughts.

"You're killing me," he said.

"What?" She asked innocently and batted her eye lashes at him.

"Your indecision…it's killing me," he said. He dropped his hand, ran it over his hair as he walked to the door.

"Just wait here. I'll be right back."

He was grateful for the cold air outside as he popped open the trunk and dug around for his evidence bag. It had been awhile since he had done the hands-on evidence collecting. This woman had him so flustered he doubted he would get any of it collected per procedure. He was already kicking himself for agreeing to do this.

Cat watched from the window as he gathered his things from his patrol car. She felt a rush of excitement when she saw him sit on the bumper of his car and run his fingers through his hair several times. She laughed out loud as she noticed he was talking to himself. She hoped he was feeling what she was feeling. What was she feeling? She asked herself. It was so strong, this tug at her heart.

When Sullivan came back up with his bag, he saw Cat in the kitchen putting coffee grinds in a paper filter.

Betsy Randolph

"Are you sure you want coffee this late. Won't you have trouble sleeping?" Sullivan asked her as he sat a large black nylon bag on the kitchen table. He unzipped it and pulled out some latex gloves and blew into them before he stuck his fingers in. He snapped the gloves in place as she turned to look at him.

"I always have trouble sleeping. Coffee relaxes me. I guess I'm weird. The caffeine doesn't seem to keep me awake, bad dreams do."

He nodded and looked serious when he said, "Oh, yes, I remember. Have you always had them, or has it just been recently?"

He took his camera out and removed the lens cover. He snapped a couple of pictures of Cat leaning against the counter with her hands behind her on the counter like she was about to push herself up to perch there. God, she's beautiful, he thought, as he looked through the camera at her. He ached to touch her. He decided he better get to work before he made a fool out of himself.

"I'll start with the letter. Don't let me keep you from doing anything, okay?"

"Well, I usually strip down as soon as I walk in the door, but I guess I'll wait to do that," she said with a laugh. She turned around, poured the carafe filled with water into the coffee machine and turned it on. Sullivan, whose mind was still stuck on "strip down," just stood there. He was trying to decide how to respond, when he bit his tongue, turned and briskly walked out of the room.

Worried that she had offended him, Cat walked into the living room behind him. Sullivan had knelt down next to the note and was snapping pictures.

"Sorry. I was just teasing," she began. "I hope I didn't make you uncomfortable by saying that." Slowly Sullivan stopped snapping pictures and stood up. They were dangerously close together. He looked down into her upturned face and looked from one hazel eye to the next measuring his words carefully.

"Everything about you makes me uncomfortable, lady, but in the very best way possible." He heard her quick intake of air, and without waiting for her response, he turned and walked to the bathroom.

He repeated the procedure of steaming the window with his hot breath and quickly snapped a few pictures.

"Come help me a minute, will you?" Sullivan called out.

When Cat peeked her head around the corner into the bathroom, he pointed to the mirror. "Will you hold this ruler against the mirror so I can get a measurement in the photo? Then blow your breath on there while I take some pictures? We could get the bathroom steamy and then take some pictures, but my camera lenses will just fog over."

She understood exactly what he meant about being uncomfortable. He was doing it to her as well. The bathroom was not big enough for the two of them to be in there together without touching. But without another word, she leaned over the sink and blew her hot breath out onto the mirror and then leaned back so he could get a good shot of it. As he leaned down and forward for the shot they bumped into each other, but neither moved away. She was so close to him, she felt like she would pass out. Her eyes studied Sullivan's profile approvingly until he finally dropped the camera and looked at her, then gestured towards the mirror with his chin.

"He must have had gloves on. I'm not seeing any prints here."

He looked so close at the mirror his eyes nearly crossed. "I can get the fingerprint dust out and make sure, but there doesn't appear to be any fingerprints on the mirror."

He told her that there could be prints on the envelope or note. He would have them processed tomorrow. He followed her out of the bathroom and watched her black slacks disappear around the corner. He gathered up his demeanor, camera and ruler and returned to the living room where he bagged the letter. Back in the kitchen he placed everything into his evidence bag and zipped it up. He laughed as Hannah proceeded to dance around the kitchen. Her little toenails, painted a rusty red, clicked on the ceramic tiles. Sullivan reached down and petted her fat little belly and glanced over at the coffee pot which had stopped percolating.

"Hey, I think the coffee's ready. Do you want me to pour you a cup?" Sullivan yelled. "I'm assuming you wanted to use these dainty little cups you placed on the counter?" he asked as he picked up a tiny cup with a thumb and index finger.

"Are they too frilly for you, Detective?" Cat asked. She appeared in the doorway with a warm smile on her face.

"You can get a regular mug if you like. They're above the sink." She pointed to the cabinet behind him.

"These cups will be fine. I was just giving you a hard time." Sullivan said as he lifted the coffee pot and poured the dark, hot liquid into two tiny china cups with red roses painted on the sides. He placed her cup on a matching saucer and handed it to her.

"Need any cream or sugar?" Cat asked as she opened the refrigerator and pulled out some Peppermint Mocha coffee creamer and splashed some into her coffee.

"No, thanks. I'll get my man card taken away just for drinking out of this cup. I wouldn't be caught dead with that stuff in it, too."

She laughed as they walked with their coffee to the living room where they sat on a southwestern print sofa. Sullivan sipped his coffee and looked at Cat over the rim of his flowered cup. It looked to Cat like Sullivan's eyes were smiling.

"What?" she asked at last. "Are you making fun of me?"

Sullivan shook his head, "No, Ma'am. Not at all." He placed his cup on the saucer and then set them both on the coffee table. "I need to ask you some serious questions, but I don't want to upset you again, especially now that you're being so hospitable." He smiled a sweet smile at her then.

"It's okay. Go ahead and ask."

He steadied his gaze on her face then started, "First of all, why do you park your car so far away from the building when you know you are going to have to walk out there by yourself after midnight?"

127

That was an easy one she thought. She sipped her coffee and replied, "Because when I arrive at work, it's the middle of the day, and there's no place else to park."

She appeared so relaxed and calm. He ventured to broach the Rick issue.

"Will you tell me what happened tonight at the station? I want to know what happened and what Rick said and did."

Cat looked into his brown eyes and felt herself wanting to trust him. She began where Sullivan and Bronson had left the radio station earlier in the day. She mentioned how Susan had been there and how Rick had acted towards her. She was trying to decide what if any part she had played in Rick acting the way he did. There had been a couple of times during her show where she had looked through the glass at him and he had appeared to be staring at her. She had smiled at him, and he had actually smiled back. Once, she might have even winked at him when a caller had commented on her voice. The caller had said it was sexy. She didn't even think about how Rick could have taken that wink, but now she had to admit that maybe he thought she was flirting with him.

She told Sullivan about what had happened and what Rick had done and how she felt about it all. Then she waited to see what Sullivan's response would be.

"First of all, I want you to quit trying to blame yourself for this guy's actions. Secondly, I want you to consider filing a complaint against him with the station manager."

He paused and looked into her hazel eyes. He saw himself there, with her, and happy. Forcing his eyes away and his mind to focus, he continued, "Thirdly, I wish you would write out a statement for me and allow me to pursue charges against him for assault and battery. I can probably even get the DA's office to go for sexual assault."

He noted the pain in her eyes as he finished, and he wanted so badly to comfort her, to hold her. Sighing out loud, Cat sat her cup down on the table and rubbed her hands on her thighs like she was cold.

"Wow! Well, I don't know." She shook her head slowly and shrugged her shoulders. "I need to think about that."

Sullivan placed his elbows on his knees and brought his face a little closer to hers. "Can I ask you something else?" She shrugged her shoulders again, but didn't move away from him.

"What did Rick mean when he said you didn't mind it before? Or whatever it was he said. He implied..."

Holding her hand up with her palm toward his face, she leaned away from him. Her color had turned bold red and her eyes flashing.

"Stop right there. Rick was lying. I don't care what he was implying." She started to get up when Sullivan placed a warm hand on her arm.

"Okay, take it easy. I believe you. Please think about what I said though. After seeing that note and the mirror tonight, I'm not so sure it wasn't Rick that did those things, are you?"

Cat didn't speak, but she laid her hand on top of Sullivan's that still rested on her forearm. They sat there like that for a minute or two before Sullivan told her he had to go. She tried to talk him into staying longer, but Sullivan knew he couldn't. He had to separate these feelings that were growing for her from the homicide case or risk losing it and his mind along the way.

He carried their cups and saucers back to the kitchen with her following him. He placed the dishes in the sink and took a deep breath before turning around to meet her eyes. He could see her fear had returned. He cursed his own resolve and grabbed his evidence bag.

With a final wistful look at Cat, he said goodnight and then was gone.

Chapter 15

Cat watched from the window as Sullivan drove away. She slowly made her way back to the kitchen where she stood for a long time thinking of him. He was so strong and confident. Those smiling brown eyes that crinkled at the corners made her lips turn up in a smile of her own. She reached above the coffee pot and opened the cabinet door and brought out a half empty bottle of rum. She measured a shot glass full and poured it into a glass tumbler and poured it over Coke and ice cubes.

Sipping the mixture she walked to her room and sat her drink on her bedside table. She was still thinking of Sullivan as she crawled into bed, grabbed her phone and called Susan.

"I have been dying to call you," Susan said when she heard Cat's voice. "Tell me what's going on, did Detective Tom show up?"

Cat pulled the covers over her body and took a drink. It was a bit too strong, but she swallowed it just the same. Leaning her head back against the headboard, she felt the warmth of her drink tingle in her belly and course through her veins.

Cat told Susan everything: she rehashed the Rick incident and how Sullivan had saved her and how they eventually made it to her apartment where just his scent and closeness drove her crazy. It felt like high school all over again as she told Susan about how his eyes lit up when she flirted with him. She described his eyes as caramel or golden chocolate. She felt ridiculously giddy as she remembered how his large hand felt on her arm. How remarkably soft his skin felt against hers. She threw the covers back and went to the kitchen. She made herself another strong drink and hurried back to bed, all the while Susan continued firing questions.

"I promise that's it. That is all there is to tell," Cat insisted while they laughed.

Cat and Hannah were curled up together on the bed and had the covers piled on several layers thick. Cat was getting really sleepy and closed her eyes while she talked. Susan asked about the missing bracelet before they disconnected.

"I'll check again tomorrow around the station. Maybe I'll put a little flier up about it or something."

"Well, if you don't get it back, I'll get you another one when I go to Colorado again or when I can talk you into going with me. I bought it in this great little jewelry store in Denver. You'll love it."

Cat laughed at her friend she affectionately had named "The Shopping Queen." "I'm sure I will. Okay, okay, enough for tonight. I'll call you later. I really have to get some sleep."

Cat hung up and pulled another draw of rum and coke into her mouth. Something about it suddenly felt wrong. So she sat the nearly-full glass down on the dresser table and pushed it away from her with a frown. Some unseen thing had begun to change in her.

Between the exhaustion and the rum, Cat never heard the creaking of the floors outside her apartment door. Hannah had stirred, but never barked. She simply slipped out of bed and made her way into the living room to see who was opening the front door. As the door swung open, a man in dark clothing stepped inside. Hannah began a tirade of barking and growling. She was rewarded immediately by the stranger with the hardest kick to the face she had ever felt. Within minutes the steel-toed boots had kicked, stomped and nearly killed the smallest member of the Carlyle family.

Somehow, Cat had slept through the whole horrendous thing. Now, the sinister figure stood in the doorway to Cat's room, watching her sleep and breathe heavily. He was so aroused just being in the same room with her. It was almost more than he could stand. He wondered what she was wearing, if anything at all. He watched the covers moving to the cadence of her sleeping breath. If he hadn't been so self-disciplined, he would have taken her then and there. But he had devised a plan and he had to stick to it.

It wasn't until ten o'clock the next morning that Cat found someone had been in the apartment overnight. She got up to go to the bathroom. When she called for Hannah to come back to bed, she didn't come. Groggily, she made her way through the apartment, calling Hannah's name.

"Come on, Hannah, I'm still sleepy. Let's go back to bed for awhile."

Cat wandered into the kitchen to find Hannah sleeping beside her water bowl. Cat knelt down and patted Hannah's head and saw what looked like blood on the floor.

"What's wrong, baby, are you hurt?" She asked as she played with the cropped little ears of her beloved pet. Suddenly, she realized Hannah was hurt badly and nearly dead. If she didn't do something quickly she would be.

Screaming for help, Cat jumped to her feet as she raced to the phone. Glancing down at her hands, she continued to scream. She dialed 9-1-1 and looked around the room in a panic. Someone had been there in the night. Someone had broken in and tried to kill Hannah. Before she realized she was sick, she turned to run to the bathroom, but didn't make it. Violently, she vomited on the kitchen floor. She heaved and heaved until there wasn't anything left to vomit. Gagging on her bile, she placed another call, this one to her parents.

Cat could hardly get the words out. Within the hour, the dog was in emergency surgery. The vet had described her wounds as life threatening. Phillip, Linda and Cat sat huddled in Cat's living room waiting for Detective Sullivan to arrive.

The Guthrie Police Department had been called. A detective and young police officer were in the next room gathering evidence. Cat was recalling the events from the night before and trying to make sense of what was happening.

"After Sullivan left, I went to bed. I didn't put Hannah in her crate, she slept with me," Cat explained. Her face was ghostly pale and her eyes were glassy with shock as she spoke.

"Why was Sullivan here?" Linda asked. "What did he want?"

Without waiting for Cat to answer, Phillip asked his own questions. "Did Detective Sullivan have new information or was he questioning you again? Are you a still a suspect in that man's murder?"

Cat didn't answer their questions directly. Instead, she confessed to her parents about the note and the message on the mirror. She told them about Warren, the incident with Rick from the night before and about everything that had happened recently. She cried as she told them she was hoping to save them from finding out about Warren Garrison and how he had treated her. She told them the whole ugly truth. It hurt, but at the same time, it felt good. She promised that she really hadn't meant to lie to them. She just didn't want them to worry.

"How many times have we told you - the truth will make you free?" Phillip chided. "Be honest, no matter what the cost. When you are honest you can look people straight in the eyes and know that you have spoken your truth." He shook his head as he stood. He threw up his hands then rested them on his hips. When Cat started crying again he sat back down and pulled Cat into his arms.

A few minutes later Sullivan knocked on the door and met with the detective and police officer from Guthrie P. D. They could hear him ask if they would send him a copy of their report as he handed the detective a business card.

135

Betsy Randolph

Sullivan glanced across the room, saw Cat, and made his way over to her. He silently exchanged glances with Phillip and Linda before squatting down in front of Cat and taking both of her tiny cold hands in his. She looked like she was in shock.

"Cat," He didn't know what to say. He searched her face for recognition. He wanted to tell her everything was going to be okay. He wanted to reassure her that he would find out who did this and make them pay. He couldn't believe someone had been bold enough to enter her apartment and try to kill her dog. He struggled with the idea that the killer hadn't harmed Cat. That meant something, but what?

He rubbed her hands with his thumbs and squeezed her fingers. She just sat there motionless. Her eyes were dazed and confused, her hair pointed in a thousand different directions off her head. It wasn't the dark circles under her eyes that made her look lifeless. It was the absence of light in her eyes that pierced Sullivan's soul. How could this have happened?

"I promise we will find out who did this. I give you my word."

Cat's eyes finally met Sullivan's. She didn't have the words to tell him how badly she was hurting, but she thought by his expression and the look in his kind eyes, that he must know. He pulled her closer to him and wrapped his arms around her. One of his hands stole around her back and cradled the back of her head. He gently guided her head onto his shoulder and just held her.

Phillip and Linda stared at them and then looked at each other. What it all meant, they didn't know. They all sat in silence waiting for the next move, not knowing exactly what it would be.

"I want you to go stay with your parents," Sullivan finally said. He pulled Cat away from him so that he could look deeply into her eyes. "It isn't safe for you here. Until we catch whoever is doing this, you have to go stay with your parents."

Cat shoved away from him and crossed her arms over her chest. "No. That isn't going to happen. I refuse to be run out of my house. I can't run anymore. I won't."

Everyone just stared at her as she stood defiantly. Linda and Phillip tried talking to her. They begged, pleaded, bargained with her. But she would not go. It might have been the first time in her life, she told them, but she was not going to run away. She was not going to be terrorized. She would die in this apartment on her own terms before she crawled out like a coward. She stood and walked to the tall windows and looked down on the street. Everyone watched her as she stood there. Each person wondered what was going through her mind. Each one of them felt proud of her, but terrified.

Phillip broke the silence by suggesting they go to the pet hospital to check on Hannah's status. Cat knew her dad was trying to get her out of her apartment, and, once in his car, she would be forced into protective custody.

"The vet said he would call. I'm staying, but you guys can go," Cat said. She placed her hands on either side of the wooden window frame and leaned her head in until it rested on the cool glass. Tears streamed down her face, and she didn't try to wipe them off. She just stood there as they dotted her blue cotton t-shirt like hot little raindrops.

"You can't stay here, Honey," Phillip stated with a growl. "Listen to Detective Sullivan."

Without turning around she barked back at him, "I am listening to him, Dad, but I can't run away from this. I'm staying."

"Then we're staying," Linda declared. "Dad and I will go get some things and we can stay in your extra room. You won't even know we're here."

Shaking her head from side to side, Cat continued in the debate with a quieter voice that came out as nearly a whisper, "I appreciate what you are trying to do, both of you. But I don't need you here. Dad, you can let me borrow one of your guns if that will make you feel better."

"No!" Sullivan, Linda and Phillip shouted in unison.

Cat turned then, her red eyes searching their faces. Without another word she stared at them before walking out of the room. When she returned a few minutes later she had changed into black bicycle tights, a biking jersey with a blue jacket over it and was carrying her pedal cleats. From the extra room she brought out a brilliant blue racing bike with a white seat and white handle bar grips. Her helmet hung from the chin strap on the handlebars. She slid her fingers into fingerless gloves and opened the door.

"Lock up when you leave, please," she said over her shoulder.

Chapter 16

She pushed her bike down the hallway to the back entrance of the building and carried her nearly weightless carbon-framed bike down the narrow steps. Once on the ground, she slipped on her cleats and threw a leg over the bike. She stepped into the first pedal, clipped in, and pedaled down the alley, clipping the other foot in before anyone could stop her.

It felt good to push herself further, faster than she'd gone or done before. She let her anger drive her on. Telling herself that she was in charge of herself, that she could bring her body into submission, she pedaled faster and stood to pump as she climbed a steep hill. She felt the sweat pouring off her head, running in little rivers down her temple to her ears. The cool fall day was perfect for cycling, and she felt the rhythm of the bike and her breathing sync.

Her thighs were burning as she topped another hill and sat to pedal. She pulled the cold water into her mouth from the water bottle. She slid it back into its aluminum holder and wiped her nose with her jacket sleeve. She didn't realize she was crying until her blurry vision finally made her stop. Her nose continued to run and her eyes burned from the mixture of sunscreen and tears. She cried and rode, prayed and rode and rode some more. Two hours and thirty miles later, she returned to find Sullivan and her mother gone and her Dad on the couch, watching TV.

"Your mother has gone to get some things. We aren't giving you a choice. We are staying."

She sighed as she leaned her bike against the wall in the living room, dropped her helmet and cleats by it and walked to the bathroom. Phillip could hear the water turn on in the shower and heard her jerk the shower curtain closed. He sighed and flipped through the channels on the TV, thinking about an afternoon nap.

When Cat emerged from the bathroom an hour later, she was dressed. Her hair had been washed and dried, but was pulled back into a ponytail. She had let little wisps of hair escape and they curled in ringlets near the nape of her neck. She had carefully applied mascara and eye shadow and used a dark raisin-red color on her lips.

She looked stunning, Linda thought, as she stirred sugar into a pitcher of tea. Linda had made lunch and set the table. She called Cat to join them, and the three of them sat around the dark oak table. Phillip held his hands out for his girls who took them and bowed their heads. As Phillip prayed for God's blessings on their food, family and lives, he thanked God for the life of the precious little dog that had brought such joy to their lives for so many years. He asked for healing for Hannah, protection for Cat and their family and asked that the person responsible be caught quickly.

They ate their lunch in silence until the phone on the wall rang. Cat got up and crossed to it. She picked up the receiver and said hello. She didn't say anything else for several seconds and then said hello again several times and finally hung up the phone. She had just gotten seated again and had picked up her sandwich when the phone rang again. She got up, made her way to it, picked it up and repeated the process of saying hello, getting no answer and then finally hanging up. She shrugged her shoulders and walked back to her seat.

"That's aggravating," she complained as she sat back down.

She placed her napkin across her lap and had lifted her tea glass to her lips when the phone rang for the third time.

"I wonder who that is?"

She sounded nervous, even to herself, as she walked quickly to the phone. "Hello?" When she got no answer, she slammed down the phone and stood there with her back to her parents. She felt how fast her heart was beating. She tried to breathe deeply to calm herself. He was terrorizing her. Whoever had broken in to her apartment and tried to kill her dog was now screwing with her head. She wondered who it could be. Rick? Warren? Or maybe someone from her past that she couldn't recall. How could anyone try to kill Hannah? Before last night and the incident with Rick, Warren would be the only person she would suspect. He was so mean sometimes. But she hadn't seen him or talked to him. Why would he start attacking her now? What had changed with Rick? He wasn't acting like himself either. He had always acted like he hated her, but now he was more venomous. His steely glare last night and those clammy hands he pawed at her with had made her feel nauseous. Who would do this, she wondered, and why?

141

Betsy Randolph

"What did the caller ID show, Cat?" Phillip asked.

He stopped eating and dropped his napkin in his seat as he walked over to where Cat still stood with her back to them. "Honey, who was it? Do you know?"

Cat didn't answer, just shook her head no. Phillip put a hand on her shoulder and she turned into him. She wouldn't cry. She had to be strong. She couldn't cry now, not with all this war paint on her face. A single tear escaped her defenses and slid down her cheek. She silently cussed it as it trekked southward across her face. She swiped at it angrily with her napkin and stepped away from her dad.

"The number says it's unavailable."

She and her dad walked back to the table and sat down when the phone rang again. This time Phillip beat her to the phone. He didn't say anything until someone on the other end spoke.

"Hello?" A male voice said. "Cat, is that you?"

Phillip relaxed a little as he spoke, "Just a moment, I'll get her for you. May I ask who's calling?"

Hearing a young man clear his voice on the other end of the line before he spoke again, Phillip waved for Cat to come to the phone.

"Yes, Sir, this is Pat Gilbraithe from the Sooner Broadcasting Network." Phillip covered the receiver with his large palm, "It's Pat from the radio station."

Cat reached for the phone. She listened as Pat described what was going on at the station. It wasn't a surprise that Rick had lied about what had happened the night before. But it was a surprise that the station manager hadn't even cared about her side of the story. Based solely on Rick's version, he had pulled Rick off of her show and placed Pat in his place.

"Won't it be great?" Pat was saying. He clearly was thrilled to get the opportunity to produce the live show. He didn't realize like Cat did, that there were larger implications to the move. Cat tried to think positively, though, and agreed with Pat that the show was going to be smoother with Rick out of the way.

"When do you start?" Cat asked.

She looked at her parents and tried a small smile. It felt unnatural, so she stopped.

"Today, can you believe it?" Pat replied.

He told her he would see her at the station in a little while and hung up.

"Well, that was interesting. Looks like Mr. Davidson replaced Rick with Pat for my show," Cat said as she plopped back into her chair.

"That sounds like good news. But since you don't seem happy, I am perplexed," Linda said with a frown. "You don't want to be around Rick anymore, right?" Linda asked as she looked into Cat's troubled eyes.

After a short pause, Cat continued. "No, I don't. But Mr. Davidson wouldn't have moved Rick off the show unless he said something to him. Mr. Davidson is likely to believe anything Rick said to him without giving me a chance to explain. It doesn't feel like a good thing, but I guess I'll have to wait until I get there to know for sure."

She picked up her sandwich and tried to eat it, but her appetite was gone. After clearing the table and enjoying a cup of coffee, they discussed alternate living arraignments.

"How about if I go stay with Susan when I get off work tonight?" Cat suggested. "I called Susan a little while ago to tell her what was going on. She asked me to stay with her. She reminded me that she only lives a few blocks from the station, and she said she would come meet me after work so I wouldn't have to leave alone."

Her parents looked uncertain as they exchanged glances. It wasn't fair to ask them to spend the entire evening there when she wasn't even going to be home. Since Hannah was gone…Hannah was gone! It hit Cat like a punch in the stomach. Hannah might never be coming back. Hannah might never sleep with her again or nuzzle her little nose in Cat's hair or wiggle her little body uncontrollably when Cat entered a room.

"I have to get out of here," Cat choked as she grabbed her bag and headed for the door. "Please go home. I'm going to stay with Susan tonight. I'll call you when I get to her house."

Chapter 17

Sullivan and Bronson worked all the leads they had regarding the Diaz murder, but they admitted they were no closer to arresting a suspect than they had been since the night of the murder.

"Let's have a couple of uniforms pick up Chaz Rodriguez again. I think we can rattle his chain a little more and squeeze some info out of him," Sullivan suggested.

He told Bronson what he had learned from Mrs. Diaz about the history between Chaz and her dead ex-husband. When Mrs. Diaz told Sullivan about the gifts that Juan had showered on their daughter for her birthday, it made sense that Diaz had gotten back into the business that had sent him to prison. There had to be a connection between his death and his recent increase in funds, Sullivan surmised.

"What did you learn from Warren Garrison?" Sullivan asked Bronson.

Bronson didn't answer. He sat at his desk and continued searching the internet. He had seen an advertisement on television the night before about a new cell phone, and he'd been talking about it non-stop since he had walked into the office.

"Will you please quit screwing off for a minute and give me an update on Garrison."

"There's not much to tell, Sully. The guy claims he hasn't seen or cared to see your girl in nearly a month. He had a pretty solid alibi for the night of the murder, and he didn't strike me as a killer."

"Did you actually check his alibi, Bronson?"

"Yes, of course I did!" Bronson looked at Sullivan with a frown that furrowed his brows. "Garrison claims to have been in the company of a young woman he met while drinking coffee at a McDonalds at I-35 and 122nd Street in Oklahoma City. Her name is Jill Warlick. She's a prostitute. Turns out she works close to that location at a truck stop. His story is a couple of weeks before the murder the two met and subsequently fell in love. Don't say it, I know."

Both men exchanged knowing glances and smirks. "Anyway, on the night of the murder they both claim she skipped work, met at her place and spent the night together."

"Have you scheduled a polygraph for her?" Nodding his head, Bronson responded, "Yes, Sir, she is supposed to come in the day after tomorrow." "And what about Garrison?" Sullivan asked. "No, I wanted to wait to see how hers turns out."

"Why wait?" Sullivan demanded.

Bronson admitted that he wanted to get him on a polygraph machine, but said he had a plan. He outlined what he had found in Garrison's past. Garrison had been accused of rape in high school, but the charges had never been filed because the accuser wouldn't testify and moved out of state after the incident happened. Then there was a similar incident in college, but Garrison had hired a high dollar lawyer who got the charges dropped down to a misdemeanor because Garrison had agreed to plead guilty to a lesser charge. Bronson pulled up Garrison's rap sheet and showed Sullivan that Garrison's previous convictions included two misdemeanor DUI's, assault and battery, assault, destruction of property and numerous traffic violations.

"Let's get him in here for a taped interview. We can hold off on the polygraph, but I want to get a feel for him myself." Agitated, Sullivan got up from his desk and made his way to the coffee pot. He knew he had consumed nearly a pot already, but he craved the black stuff.

As he poured the java in his cup and replaced the pot on the burner, he sloshed his cup causing coffee to splash on his pant leg. "Great!" He moaned, but inside he was screaming. He couldn't explain why he felt cross with the world today. While he was patting his pants with a paper towel he noticed that some coffee had splattered on the toe of his shoe. That's when it hit him.

"That's it!" Sullivan shouted.

He looked over at Bronson who was holding a finger up to indicate he needed a minute before Sullivan continued. Sullivan poured the coffee down the sink, dropped the Styrofoam cup in the trash and quickly made his way to Bronson's desk where he promptly unplugged Bronson's phone from the wall jack.

"What is wrong with you? I was on a call."

"Yeah, making personal calls on Department time. It's against policy. Come on, I just remembered something important." Sullivan pulled out his growing file on the Diaz murder and dropped it on the desk, while Bronson cussed him and fumbled with the phone jack to reinsert it.

Sullivan flipped through several pages in the file until he found the sheet he wanted. "Look." He pointed to the paragraph in Cat's witness statement where she had written about the killer's shoes. "See that? Remind you of anything?" Sullivan asked excitedly.

Bronson stared blankly at the statement, nothing was coming to him. He shook his head no and raised his hands palms up indicating such.

"Remember yesterday when we were in Rick's office? Remember those 'I love me' photos on his wall? Didn't you see the photograph where he was with the rock band, Poison? He was wearing similar shoes. I knew something was bugging me after we left. That was it!"

Sullivan walked around to his own desk that faced Bronson's and quickly called Judge Mason's office. He explained what he had and what he needed. When he got the verbal approval for a tentative warrant request he plopped down in his chair and began typing it up. Finally they had caught a break! He would have to call Cat and let her know what was going on. He glanced at his watch and realized she would probably be making the half-hour commute to Oklahoma City from Guthrie. He wondered how she was holding up.

Bronson interrupted his thoughts. "So you think Rick is the killer? That's not even possible, is it? Wasn't he working with Cat the night of the murder? How could he have gotten out to the parking lot before her and kill Diaz? Didn't she say she left the building first?" Bronson had forgotten about the cell phone now, he was engrossed in Sullivan's reasoning, or lack thereof.

"No one said the killer and Diaz were there first," Sullivan corrected. "In fact, Cat claims she was on the ground when the killer and Diaz came upon her, remember?"

"Oh, that's right, it's cutting it pretty close, but you are correct," Bronson admitted. "He could have done it. So you think the shoes she saw were Rick's? He actually has a photo on the wall where he is wearing the same shoes? Why wouldn't she remember those shoes as his?"

"It may be a stretch," Sullivan conceded, "but I'm willing to risk it, considering the killer is getting bolder. If we don't catch him soon, whoever he is, he is going to kill again. I can't let that happen." Sullivan finished the warrant request and printed it out.

Together they ran through the station and climbed in Sullivan's car. As they pulled away from headquarters, Bronson was still complaining about the deal he was sure he had missed on the new phone. Sullivan ignored his complaints and laid out the plan. The warrants would be delivered to the judge for his signature. With signed copies of those warrants, Bronson and Sullivan could begin the searches immediately. One team would arrive simultaneously at Rick's house and begin a search there while one team converged on the radio station. They needed the killer's shoes, and they needed the murder weapon. Both were crucial to the case. If Rick were stupid enough to keep either, he deserved to rot in jail.

149

When Sullivan and Bronson arrived at the radio station, they circled the lot a few times and noted the vehicles and tag numbers. Neither detective spotted Cat's car or Rick's truck. Something wasn't right, Sullivan thought. He suppressed the desire to start making phone calls. He pulled into the lot and parked close to where Cat usually parked. He reassured himself that he was early for Cat's shift. He gathered his thoughts while Bronson called back to headquarters to check on the other search team.

"We are good to go. I have four additional officers who will assist in the search and two of our forensic team members will document the evidence we find. They are en route and should be here any second." Bronson slid his phone shut and opened it again several times. "I'm surprised I can even get this piece of junk to work. It would serve you right for it to crap out right in the middle of this search."

Sullivan again ignored his complaining and zeroed in on a white car that pulled into the lot. He watched as the driver slowly entered the lot and parked near them. When Cat exited her vehicle, Sullivan's heart nearly stopped. Cat had chosen a black turtleneck with plaid slacks and low heels. She wore a black wool pea coat and looked like the picture of elegance. He got out of his car and stood watching her walk towards him. He felt his mouth go dry and silently cursed his hands that began to tremble.

With her hair pulled back, she looked taller than five-seven and a lot lighter than her license had said she was. He smiled, remembering the traffic stop. He had yet to mention that to Bronson. Her sleek, slender frame approached him with a confidence he had yet to see from her.

"Hello, Detective Sullivan. How are you?" She stopped a few feet from him. She was thinking he looked a little tired, but considering all the hours she was sure he had put in lately, he looked pretty good. Very good actually, she admitted to herself.

"I'm fine, Cat. How are you?" His husky voice drew her eyes to his lips. "You know, I could be better, but under the circumstances, I am alright. How are you, Mr. Branson?"

"It's Bronson," Bronson corrected her with a huff. "Clint Bronson. As in Charles Bronson, the movie star or like the TV show, *Then Came Bronson*."

Cat nodded her head, "Oh, okay," she murmured, never taking her eyes off Sullivan. Bronson could hardly believe this gal couldn't remember his name. He hadn't had a woman forget his name or mispronounce his name since he was in the third grade. The only logical reason for the conundrum was Thomas Sullivan. The idea of it had him smiling. He excused himself and pretended to make a phone call, walking away and leaving the two of them alone.

"If you don't mind my saying so, you look amazing," Sullivan declared. He slid his hands in the pocket of his slacks so he wouldn't be tempted to touch her. The compliment made her blush, warming her cheeks.

"Thank you. You look very nice yourself. Would you care to tell me what you and..." She pointed her eyes towards the retreating Bronson. "Charles Bronson are up to?"

Sullivan laughed and leaned back against his patrol car. He shrugged his shoulders and tried to act casual.

"You guys aren't here to escort me to work today are you? I don't think Rick is going to try anything else." She said. She told him about the phone call from Pat. She promised Sullivan that she was filing a formal complaint with the station manager and based on the outcome of that would let him know if a criminal complaint was necessary.

Sullivan didn't admit why they were there. He didn't want Cat to know, and he didn't want her to inadvertently spill the beans before the other warrant team was in place. Instead, he told her about what he had found out about Garrison. He asked if she knew of his background and prodded for more information about their relationship.

"I had no idea he had been in any kind of trouble before. He sort of had the bad-boy image, but I thought it was more of a show than anything else," Cat said with a shrug.

Sullivan grew serious and looked her right in the eyes. "Maybe it's just my law enforcement experience, but I can't imagine dating someone before knowing if they have a criminal past." He looked away then because the shocked look on her face had him wishing he hadn't been so blunt. It would have been gentler if he had just slapped her.

"Are you suggesting that I am so naive or stupid, that I would date a violent criminal? As if I could spend time with a rapist and not have realized it?" She didn't wait for a response. She launched into Sullivan. She was angry. She could admit that. The truth was she was mad at herself. She should have known Warren Garrison was dangerous and evil. She did know it, but she discovered it too late. Still, she verbally attacked Sullivan as if he were the enemy. She left him standing in the parking lot bleeding from his invisible wounds.

"What just happened?" Bronson inquired as he came jogging back to where Sullivan stood like a statue nearly weeping.

"I'm not entirely sure. I tried to talk to her about Warren Garrison, and I guess I hit a sore spot. She all but clobbered me."

Sullivan stood there rubbing his chin analyzing where he had gone wrong. They both watched Cat stomp off towards the radio station.

Chapter 18

C at sat in the station manager's office, explaining her side of the confrontation with Rick from the night before. It appeared to Cat that nothing she said was convincing Mr. Davidson of her innocence and Rick's guilt. His eyes never stayed on hers for long as she tried to explain. He was a weasel.

"It isn't that I believe either story over the other, Cat. I just think it would be in the best interest of the station if you and Rick didn't work so closely together from now on. We will find a suitable replacement for the producer and in the mean time Pat can handle the calls. When he isn't here, you will just have to run a regular music shift with news and weather without the live call-ins."

Cat bit her tongue and pressed her lips together firmly to keep from spewing all over him. "I agree with your decision about removing Rick. Pat only works two days a week, though. I have sold advertising spots for that live show, Mr. Davidson. The station will lose money, and I will lose my commission from those sales. Doesn't that count for anything?" She could feel the heat beneath the collar of her sweater.

Davidson held his fat hands up in defense, "For now, that's the best I can do. If there isn't anything else, I have other things to attend to."

Cat was fuming at being dismissed in such a manner. She quickly left his office and made her way to the break room where she searched for something to punch. Her tears were near the surface – she was struggling to keep them contained, making her throat burn. She stood clinching her jaw and fists, staring out the grimy window in the break room when she heard a commotion up front.

When the warrant team arrived, Bronson and Sullivan converged on the radio station with zest. They entered the building practically at a run producing a copy of the warrant to the receptionist who took off down the hall towards the station manager's office. Without waiting for her to return, they strode to Rick's office and knocked loudly on the door. The receptionist and station manager met them outside Rick's office and produced a key that allowed them access.

Once inside, they began a systematic search and seizure, tagging and bagging evidence as they went along. They were informed by Mr. Davidson that Rick had called in sick. Immediately, that information was relayed to the warrant team at Rick's residence.

After nearly three hours at the radio station, Sullivan, Bronson and their teams, left. In their wake was a mess that would take several people, several hours to clean up. Before departing the radio station for a rendezvous with the other warrant team, Sullivan motioned for Cat to come out of the sound booth. They stood in the hall and briefly discussed getting together after she got off work.

"I don't know Detective; it doesn't sound like a good idea to me." She reminded him of what he had said the night before and what he had implied in the parking lot.

"Cat, please call me Tom. I know what I said last night, and I have apologized for what I said earlier. I didn't mean it the way it sounded."

She stopped him with a flat, dead stare.

"Oh yes, you did. You basically said I was an idiot for going out with a guy who I should have realized was a rapist."

Before she could continue, he interrupted by saying, "I only meant to…"

Cat was shaking her head no and through narrowed angry eyes sliced him in two by saying, "You only meant to make me feel like a fool. I shouldn't have even told you about Warren to begin with."

Sullivan insisted he didn't mean to make her feel foolish. He tried to explain, to apologize again and then giving up, he grabbed Cat's hand and just held it gently.

"I'm sorry. Okay?"

The pleading look on his face and in his eyes had Cat easing back. "Okay," she finally said as she dropped her eyes to their joined hands. Pat poked his head out of the control room then.

"You're back on in thirty." Then he disappeared back in the room.

"He means thirty seconds," Cat clarified.

She asked if Sullivan would meet her at the radio station at midnight again, and he said he would.

"I don't want to find you wrestling with anyone else when I get here, though," he joked as let go of her thin fingers and waved goodbye. She laughed and went back to work.

"That police detective really likes you, Cat," Pat commented through her headset.

She smiled at him and gave him a thumbs up as she brought her mic volume up and began the top of the hour state and local news. About an hour into the show, a caller told Pat he wanted to request a song for his girlfriend and gave Lewis as his name. When he was live on the air with Cat, however, his story changed dramatically. "Hey, Kitty Cat," he purred into the phone.

"How's your little dog doing? Did I kill that mutt or what?" Cat froze.

Not only could she not speak, but the world was spinning violently around her. Her head jerked up to see Pat tapping furiously at the window. He didn't know what to do. Before the long silent pause ended, the caller managed to ask one more frightening question.

"I have your bracelet. Want me to bring it back?"

Pat finally realized he needed to disconnect. He went straight to a commercial that would run for sixty seconds and rushed in to the sound booth where Cat was violently throwing up in the trash can.

"I am so sorry, Cat. I didn't know what to do. How can I help you? I am so sorry."

157

He kept saying how sorry he was over and over as he held her hair back away from her face. He reached for a roll of paper towels that sat next to the ancient record player. The phone lights were all lit up with callers, and the commercial was coming to an end. She pointed to the sound board as she dropped to her knees and leaned closer to the trash can.

"Go start some music," she choked, "any music. I have a CD ready in player number two." Gasping for air, she rushed with the instructions, "just push play and roll the sound up on the number two controller," she gagged again.

Dry heaves wracked her body as she crawled towards her purse that hung on the back of her chair. After getting the music started, Pat rushed back to Cat's side.

"What are you looking for?" he asked excitedly. He helped her get her purse off the chair and unzipped it for her.

"My phone! Get my phone!" she gagged.

"You need some water. Stay right there."

Pat rushed from the room to the bottled water holder and pulled a paper cup out of the dispenser. He filled it with cold water and rushed back, forcing Cat to drink it. Then he ran to get wet paper towels for her face. She wiped her face with one and folded the other, putting it on her forehead.

"Thanks, Pat," she murmured weakly.

The phone lines were still lit up and the music ended before Cat could compose herself. Pat scrambled around to find another music CD, put it in player number three, pushed play and lifted the volume control. There was a full twenty seconds of dead air before the first notes began to play.

Pat sank on the floor next to Cat as she called Sullivan. She told him what had happened. Sullivan said he was back en route. Since she always recorded her show, he was going to get a copy of the call.

Pat and Cat were sitting on the floor wondering what to do next when the door flung open. "What in the hell is going on in here?" Mr. Davidson demanded.

He stood with his hands out waiting for an answer. "Well?" he shouted loudly. Pat tried to explain, but was rudely cut off by Mr. Davidson.

"Get up off the floor!" he shouted at Cat. But she just sat there looking at him blankly until he screamed, "You know what? You're fired!"

He stalked to the control room, picked up the phone and started making phone calls.

Cat looked at Pat, but no tears came. She felt nothing so nothing came out of her mouth. Pat helped her up and sat her back in her chair, but she made no move to take over the controls. So Pat pulled the extra chair to the desk and worked the sound board from there. He played music, gave the weather and news at the top and bottom of the hour. When Sullivan showed up, he tried getting Cat to talk, but she could hardly speak. The dry heaves she had suffered earlier returned each time she tried to tell him what had happened.

Sullivan called Susan and asked her to come to the station. When she arrived, Sullivan left Cat in her care. Mr. Davidson had retreated to his office, so Sullivan stalked in unannounced and asked for a copy of the show. After being denied, Sullivan walked to the door as if he were leaving then stopped and shut the door, turning the lock before he turned back to Davidson.

Fire lit his eyes an eerie golden color as he walked briskly back over to Davidson's desk and around the side. He spun Davidson in his chair with his foot, pushing the large leather chair and Davidson's fat body against the wall violently. Resting his foot on the chair between Davidson's legs, dangerously close to the family jewels, Sullivan asked politely again for a copy of Cat's show. He explained the situation in a manner that Davidson and his tax-evading ways would understand.

"Fine. I'll have Pat make you a copy," Davidson consented as he continued cupping his crotch with his hands for protection. He wiped his upper lip with the sleeve of his shirt and sighed as Sullivan retreated to find Pat.

Meanwhile, Susan had gotten Cat out of the building and into her car and was preparing to take Cat back to her place, when Sullivan stopped them. He lowered his tall frame to a squatting position next to the open passenger door where Cat sat catatonically. He looked into her eyes and saw no hope in them.

"Listen to me, Cat. We are going to find this guy. I have my team working on a warrant for the phone records as we speak. I want you to go on home with Susan and stay there until I come. Okay?"

He got no response even when he lifted her hand to his lips and kissed the back of her knuckles. He buckled her seatbelt and resisted the urge to kiss her lips before shutting the door.

"Take good care of her. Call me the minute you get there and don't let anyone in except her folks, okay?"

Susan nodded, "She'll be fine. We'll call you in a few minutes," Susan reassured him. She hopped in, buckled up and put the car in gear. They had barely gotten out of sight when Sullivan's phone rang. It was his partner.

"I just got the message. Where are we meeting?" Bronson asked enthusiastically.

"Headquarters, for starters." Sullivan briefed him on what had transpired. They agreed that they would bring in Chaz Rodriquez, Warren Garrison and Rick Hurley for formal interviews. Sullivan made the calls to get the men rounded up and brought to police headquarters.

After hearing the tape of the radio show and getting his copy, Sullivan made some calls to the phone company and the on-call judge. He began the tedious process of getting a warrant for the phone records.

Chapter 19

Inside Cat's apartment, the killer decided to wait to begin his chore until he was certain the antique shop below had closed for the night. He intended to make a little noise and did not want to be caught in the act. After waiting as long as he thought was necessary, he stood and stretched. Slowly he exchanged his leather gloves for purple latex ones that he had stored in the front pocket of his jeans. As he snapped them in place, he smiled at the destruction he could already picture in his mind.

He pulled the knife from its sheath in his boot and began slicing the pastel-colored pillows that lay neatly on the couch in the living room. The southwestern printed pillows shredded easily, and he spilled their billowy contents out onto the floor. He kicked the rustic pine coffee table over on its side, breaking the Indian pottery that set on it.

He laughed as he threw the heavy wooden sugar mold that served as a candle holder into a rustic hutch that held delicate looking blue and white dishes. After overturning, slicing, and smashing everything that caught his eye, he made his way to Cat's bedroom. He opened her dresser drawers slowly and began touching all of her clothes. It was thrilling to be this close to her. He picked up a pair of light blue panties and held them to his nose. He sniffed deeply while he buried his nose in them. This in itself had been worth breaking in for, he thought. How arousing it was to have Cat's personal items against his skin.

He had never been a thief before, but he couldn't resist the urge to take part of Cat home with him. He stuffed several pairs of panties and stockings into his jacket pocket before moving to her closet. After ransacking the closet and the entire room, he paused to study his handiwork. "My darling Cat, you are going to love what I've done to the place!" He made his way to the front door, dodging piles of broken knick knacks that Cat had collected over the years. Just before he opened the door to make his departure, the phone rang. It startled him.

Cussing at the phone, he waited while it rang and rang. Finally, on the fifth ring the answering machine picked up. The caller identified herself as "Miriam, next door." He swore again, and as he heard the voice of what sounded like a little old lady saying she was concerned. She had heard all the banging and what sounded like things breaking. Her squeaky, old voice sounded scared. She pleaded into Cat's machine for her to please call back right away. He sighed as he erased the message from the machine. Tightly he gripped the handle of his trusty knife and headed towards the door. He'd have to reassure Miriam that everything was "just fine."

****

While Bronson and Sullivan interviewed the three suspects, Susan, Cat and Cat's parents sat in Susan's living room discussing travel plans. They had decided that it would be best if Cat left town for awhile. Susan and Cat would fly to Colorado the next day and spend a relaxing week at a moderately priced spa that Susan had visited numerous times.

"Consider it an early Christmas present," Phillip said. "Your mother and I were thinking of doing it for you anyway."

"Practice what you preach, Dad," Cat reprimanded. "Honesty, remember?" she added sarcastically.

Susan flashed a smile at Cat's parents. When they had finally convinced Cat that she should go, they quickly made the plane reservations and discussed the various spa packages. They decided upon a five-night deal with everything included. The girls were going to lie around in steamy rooms and mud baths. They would get manicures, pedicures, and facials, do some yoga, eat some tofu and get their Zen on. Cat had never done any of that. It actually sounded more like torture, but she was willing to try it at least once. Since it was a gift, how could she refuse? Besides, it wasn't like she had a job anymore. What difference did it make? Cat remembered that she didn't have Hannah waiting at home for her either. Her heart ached at the thought. Just that morning, the doctor had told them that Hannah might not survive. She would have to stay at the vets for the better part of a week, maybe more.

For now, Cat's other best friend, Susan, was taking her on an adventure. Susan was a freelance journalist, so her time was her own. She loved the jet-setter lifestyle and frequently picked up and flew to some destination and wrote about wherever she was. Cat often envied her best friend. She began thinking what it would be like to travel all the time, to have exciting adventures to write about. Cat could feel her energy returning as she made a list of things to pack. They would sleep a few hours then drop by her apartment on the way to the airport to grab a few things. She thought about splurging and buying everything she needed when she got where she was going, but she was too frugal to be so spontaneous. Besides, now that she was unemployed, she'd have to tighten her belt a bit.

Sullivan called just as they made the reservations with the spa. When he heard of their plan, he agreed that Cat needed some time away.

"I think it will be good for you to get out of here for awhile," he told her. He wanted to say that he would miss her and that he didn't want her to go, but she needed this, he decided. "Are you planning on going home before you fly out?" He didn't want her returning to her apartment alone. He wished they were already out of town.

After laying eyes on Chaz Rodriquez and Warren Garrison, he was afraid for her. Not to mention the slime ball, Rick Hurley. He realized it could be any of them terrorizing her. They all had the opportunity and ability. He hadn't decided if Chaz had motive, but the other two clearly did.

"Yes, our flight leaves at 1:05 p.m., so we'll just run up there, grab some things and head back to the airport. I think we'll have plenty of time."

"Well, I would really appreciate it if you didn't go alone. I didn't have anything to hold my suspects on, and I don't want anything to happen to you."

Nothing had turned up on the search warrants executed on Rick's house or the radio station, except for the discovery of Rick's adult porn, some misdemeanor marijuana and a lot of alcohol. From the look of Rick's house and the stashed bottle at the station, Rick might have been an alcoholic, but Sullivan wasn't too sure about him being a stalker and killer. Rick had suddenly disappeared though, and that was troubling Sullivan.

Chaz was an ex-con. He had spent time in prison for drugs, possession of stolen property and intent to distribute a controlled dangerous substance. He didn't have an alibi for the night of the murder or the night when the dog was nearly killed. Chaz said he was attending an AA meeting when the harassing phone call at the station had taken place. He was one to keep close tabs on, Sullivan decided.

Warren was a different animal altogether. He could be their guy. He had an alibi for every event. He also tried too hard to please during the interview. He was polite and respectful until Bronson pushed him about the alleged rapes in his past. There was a moment that both detectives discussed afterward that sent chills up their spines. It was when Warren answered the rape questions and his smile remained plastered on his face. His eyes were dead and emotionless. They discussed the possibility that he was a sociopath and possibly psychotic.

"Sometimes, you just have to go with your gut on these things," Sullivan had told Bronson. "My gut says this guy is a rapist. Let's get with our sex crimes unit and find out about any unsolved rape cases. We may have opened a new can of worms here." Bronson agreed and contacted the sex crimes unit himself. He sent them Warren's information. The detectives decided to go home, rest and meet back at Headquarters at 9 a.m.

Cat reassured Sullivan that she wouldn't go alone to her apartment. Susan would go with her to pick up her things. She promised him that if she needed anything she would call the local police department. They disconnected the call after a few minutes of stalling on each end. Several hours later, after a fitful night of haunting dreams, Cat roused herself off of Susan's couch and splashed warm water on her face. She pulled her hair back and secured her hair in a ponytail. She took a quick shower and brushed her teeth. She dabbed on a little eye makeup and studied her reflection in the mirror.

Criticizing her frizzy hair, a blemish that had appeared overnight on her chin and her overall shabby appearance, "What does he see in you?" she asked herself out loud. "He is way out of your league."

When Cat walked into Susan's kitchen she found Susan making muffins and brewing some strong, black java. "Ummmmm, smells good," Cat purred.

"Don't you look cute," Susan greeted her with a chipper smile. "Breakfast will be ready in a minute. Are you getting excited about our trip?" she asked with a smile.

"Yes and no," Cat confessed. "I slept terrible. I don't really want to leave town with my dog in the hospital. Besides, I feel like I'm running away from my problems. I still can't believe I got fired from my job last night." Her shoulders slumped forward; she would have started to bawl if Susan hadn't lovingly grabbed her shoulders.

"Listen, kid, everything changes, that's life. Instead of focusing on all the bad, focus on the positives."

"What positives?" Cat asked pathetically.

"Well, for starters," Susan said while pointing at Cat with a spatula, "your parents are paying for your vacation, you get to find a better job and a gorgeous man is crazy about you. What do you have to complain about?"

Cat blushed and looked somewhat innocent with big questioning eyes. "You really think he's crazy about me?"

Susan just laughed. "Don't be silly, Girl, that boy has it bad for you."

After eating their blueberry muffins, Cat and Susan drank their coffee and finished getting ready for their big day.

Chapter 20

When Cat opened the door to her apartment nearly an hour later, she nearly fainted. Everything was destroyed. She stood there with the door opened but didn't enter. Susan pushed past her and screamed. She raised her arms to shield Cat and backed out of the apartment, taking Cat with her. Pulling her cell phone out of the back pocket of her blue jeans, Susan called 9-1-1 with steady fingers and reported what they saw. They were instructed not to enter the residence or touch anything.

Guthrie police officers arrived within a couple of minutes, searched the premises, and took statements from the two women. Susan had called Sullivan and Cat's parents. The cavalry was en route from Oklahoma City.

Sullivan arrived first. He urged Cat and Susan to leave for their trip without taking anything from the apartment. Phillip and Linda agreed and gave Cat extra spending money to cover the added expenses.

"Have you told anyone other than us where you are going?" Sullivan asked Cat.

"No, you and my parents are all that know."

Sullivan turned his gaze on Susan. "What about you, have you told anyone?"

Susan shook her head no, but then added, "I told my boyfriend. He lives in Denver. I was planning on seeing him while we were there. He wouldn't tell anyone though."

Sullivan whispered for them to keep it between them as he made a circular motion with his hand indicating the five of them that stood in the circle in the hallway outside of Cat's door.

"We have to get back to the city before we miss our flight," Susan urged as she looped her arm through Cat's. "We will call you guys when we land in Denver. Don't worry, I'll take care of our girl," she said as she smiled at Sullivan. She added a wink that had him turning a nice shade of cranberry.

After hugging everyone goodbye, including Sullivan, Cat walked quickly with Susan to Susan's waiting car, and they made their way to the airport in Oklahoma City. Cat was silent most of the trip. When she did speak it was about everything that she had lost or that had been damaged in her apartment. They had done a walk through with the police officers. Cat was crushed by the things that were ruined. She knew when she got back, her parents would have paid for someone to come and clean everything up. She had confessed that she didn't think she could do it without suffering a major nervous breakdown.

"I don't think I can live there anymore. I feel so violated. I'll never be able to sleep there again," Cat confessed to Susan as they parked in the covered airport parking. They quickly got Susan's luggage and were walking towards the shuttle buses when Cat remembered her promise to call Miriam for their date for the Bluegrass Festival.

"I have to call Miriam real quick. I just realized I had promised to take her somewhere tomorrow," Cat said. She stopped on the sidewalk beside the shuttle bus to place her call on her mobile phone. After several rings she finally hung up. "That's odd. She didn't answer, and her voice mail never picked up. I guess I'll try her again later."

They loaded the shuttle and headed to the terminal. Once they were checked in, Cat called her again and still got no answer. She worried a little about her neighbor and tried to think back when she had seen or talked to her last. She couldn't remember. She asked Susan to remind her to check on Miriam again when they landed in Denver.

Back in Guthrie, the police secured Cat's apartment and began asking the other residents of the building about any noises or strange people coming and going. They got no response from the resident across the hall from Cat.

****

The next day Cat called Sullivan and asked him to check on Miriam. "I may just be being paranoid, but I can't get a hold of my elderly neighbor. She and I had plans today, and I've been trying to get in touch with her to tell her I had to cancel. But she doesn't answer her phone. Will you please have someone go by her place and then have her call me back?"

Susan was smiling at Cat as she disconnected from Sullivan and laid her phone down on her lap. They were sitting across from each other in large leather recliners getting the best foot massage and pedicure money could buy at the Three Star Spa in Boulder.

"I had to call him," Cat said unapologetically. "Who else could I have called?"

Susan rolled her eyes, "Oh, I don't know, Guthrie P.D. maybe. You do realize he works for a different police department, and in a different town, right?"

"Well, I just figured he could call and ask them to check on her. I didn't mean he personally had to go."

"Riiiiiiight!" Susan laughed. "I don't suppose you were missing his voice and just wanted to talk to him."

"No, that wasn't it. I really am worried about Miriam."

"Uh-huh. It had nothing to do with Tom."

"You mean Sullivan?"

Susan shook her head no and smiled. "No, I mean Tom," Susan said with a wicked laugh. "You suck at lying, Sister. You always have."

They both laughed and swapped comments about Sullivan's looks, clothes, and body configuration. Cat was having a wonderful time. This was exactly what she needed, she decided. She was still thinking about Sullivan and his tall lean body when she and Susan made their way through the candlelit lobby of the spa to their next appointment with a masseuse. The brochure described it as a deep-tissue massage with a chocolate body-scrub. She was anxious to see herself in chocolate and couldn't wait to phone her parents and thank them again. This was the best vacation she had ever had. She smiled as she removed her thick, terry cloth robe and wrapped a large, warm towel around her body.

"Please, no phone." The petite Asian masseuse objected as Cat slipped her phone out of her robe and carried it with her to the table. Cat relented and laid it back on the chair that held her robe.

"You turn off phone?" the masseuse asked politely.

"No, I am waiting for a phone call." She couldn't explain why she thought she should leave it on.

"You must. No interruptions, please. Turn off." She palmed her hands together and bowed slightly.

Cat couldn't refuse her polite gesture. So she walked back and turned the phone off completely. An hour later after being kneaded like dough, scrubbed with a delicious chocolaty substance, rinsed and soaking in a hot tub, Cat turned her phone back on. She had missed five phone calls. Three were from Sullivan and two were from her parent's home.

Every measure that had been taken to relieve her stress level was instantly reversed. She knew something was wrong. While still in the tub, she called Sullivan back first. She sat up when he answered after the first ring. Her heart was pounding in her chest as she listened to what he had found. He told her that he had gone personally to check on Miriam after calling and learning that the small police force in Guthrie had their hands full with all the extra traffic in town for the Bluegrass Festival. When he got to her apartment, he could not get her to answer the door or the phone. He finally had gotten the owner of the building to use his key to open the door. Inside they found Miriam unconscious. Someone had stabbed and beaten the senior citizen and left her for dead on her kitchen floor. She had been taken by a medical helicopter to a trauma center in Oklahoma City. The prognosis wasn't good. She had lost a great deal of blood and had slipped into a coma.

"She is in very good hands. They are doing everything they can for her now. She is a tough old bird," Sullivan told her.

He reassured Cat that everything was going to be okay. He suspected that Miriam had heard or seen what was going on inside Cat's apartment and that the suspect tried to eliminate Miriam as a witness. His hope was that she would pull through and be able to identify her attacker.

"We have her on twenty-four-hour police guard. There is an officer with her right now and will be until she either wakes up or..." he hesitated. He instantly wished he hadn't. He could hear Cat's quick intake of breath and was certain by the silence that she had understood what he hadn't meant to say.

"I'm sorry Cat. Let's just hope and pray for the best."

He confessed about some other disturbing news, too. What he said made her furious and frightened at the same time. She hugged her naked body with one arm and sank back into the water as he told her about the phone records they had subpoenaed. The caller that harassed her during her radio program had been calling from Cat's home phone.

"What am I going to do? He's going to kill me isn't he?" Cat's voice quivered as fear began squeezing her chest tightly. Sullivan's face grew stern as he fisted his hand as he spoke,

"No! That isn't going to happen. I won't let it," Sullivan said, with conviction. "Nothing is going to happen to you, I promise."

Sullivan convinced Cat to stay in Colorado. With the urging of Susan, Phillip and Linda, she decided to try to enjoy the rest of her stay. It wasn't any use though; all she could think about was Miriam. She wracked her brain wondering how anyone could be so cruel and twisted as to attempt to kill a little dog and an old woman. Whoever this person was, he was exceptionally evil. What could he possibly want, or did he just want to cause her pain and suffering? Cat nervously ran her hand along the silver chain around her neck. She had added a silver dove pendant she purchased at the mall. She centered it on the necklace with shaky fingers.

The pink and burgundy colors used in decoration of the dining room where she and Susan sat had a very calming effect on its patrons. Susan had chosen to wear an elegant black dress that flattered her thin shape. Cat had chosen a turquoise cable knit sweater and slacks. Both women chose heels to adorn their feet, and both admitted feeling elegant and refined after their day of pampering. They had ordered identical meals of steamed chicken breast in white wine sauce with a vegetable medley on brown rice. Sipping a dry red wine, they appeared lost in their own thoughts as they watched the candle dance on the table between them. Susan broke the silence first.

"Did you enjoy that chocolate scrub today?"

Cat fiddled with her linen napkin in her lap and met Susan's eyes with a shrug of her shoulders, "Uh huh, I love how I felt afterwards, but you know I am not crazy about being touched so much."

Susan smiled knowingly and raised her wine glass as if in a half salute. "Some people say they can get a sensory overload if they aren't used to having a massage." Maybe that was what she was feeling, Cat mused. It felt like all her senses were on overdrive or high alert. Of course, it could be the nagging fear of going home and seeing Miriam. In spite of the massage, her neck felt tense and stiff. It could have been the wine, she wasn't certain, but something was making her head ache right above her right ear. She put a couple of fingers on a bulging vein that was throbbing and pushed the wine glass away. She picked up her ice water and drained the glass of its contents.

"Does your head hurt?" Susan asked, growing concerned for Cat. She replaced her own wine glass and stared across the table at her best friend.

"Yeah, right here," Cat pointed to the vein on her skull.

Susan didn't know what to think. She stared at her friend and wondered what was going on inside her brain.

"Are you okay?" Susan asked her after a few minutes, "Do you need to go lie down?"

Cat nodded. She looked away so Susan wouldn't see the tears in her eyes, "After dinner I'll lie down, but I still won't feel better until I know Miriam is going to pull through."

Susan worried about her friend across from her and reached a hand out to comfort her. "Miriam is going to make it," Susan said with more confidence than she felt.

Cat looked at her, and her eyes screamed the pain she was trying to hide. "If Miriam dies...it will be because of me. It will be my fault," Cat said with a sob. She brought her napkin up to cover her mouth. She couldn't stop the tears. There was no point in trying. Susan came around the table and leaned over Cat like a mother hen, putting her arms around her best and oldest friend and just held her.

"What happened to her is not your fault," Susan chided with a rough hug. "Besides, if you hadn't called to have her checked on, she would have died for sure. You just remember that when you are beating yourself up. You saved her!"

Cat hadn't thought of that. It comforted her a little. She wiped at her tears and looked at Susan with red, bleary eyes. The look that passed between them was one of acceptance and gratitude. "Thanks," Cat whispered. "I hope so."

After dinner the two returned to their room and lay on their beds fully clothed. They had kicked off their shoes and were discussing the plans for the next day. Cat seemed to be feeling better, Susan thought. She discussed the idea of Susan's boyfriend picking them up and taking them shopping all day. They both agreed it would be fun.

With their plans made, they decided to take a short stroll through the spa's gardens before they called it a day. They had been told by a young man at the front desk that the beautiful rose gardens had put on a magnificent fall bloom. He described the scent as overpowering.

"Since the wind has died down today the blooms in the rose garden have filled the air. If you miss it today, you will be sorry," the young man had urged.

He displayed several large roses in a cobalt vase on the granite countertop. He claimed the head gardener had cut them just that morning. Cat and Susan had stuck their noses into the peach, red, white and yellow blooms and breathed in deeply. They didn't want to miss the rose show or the heavenly scent that had been described to them, so they slipped their heels back on and headed out to the garden.

While gently holding a rosebud the size of her fist, Cat closed her eyes and inhaled the deep, red-rose fragrance. The antique rose smell reminded her of her grandmother, Millie, and it made her smile.

"My Granny had a rose bush just like this one, right outside her front door." Cat said as her nose lingered near the petals.

She smiled at the thought of her Granny and her roses. Millie was a Master Gardener and had the greenest thumb Cat had ever seen. There wasn't anything she couldn't grow, Cat thought.

Just then, her phone buzzed in the pocket of her slacks. It didn't strike her as odd that the caller ID said, "Withheld." Sometimes, that happens even with numbers that are stored in your phone, she assured herself as she answered it.

"You better go home, little girl."

A male voice slithered menacingly into the earpiece. Cat froze in place, releasing her grip on the rose as terror crept into her ear and seeped throughout her body. She was white as a sheet when Susan grabbed her arm and pulled the phone to her ear so she could listen in as well.

"We wouldn't want anything to happen to you so far from home," the voice continued.

"Who is this?" Susan demanded. She pulled the phone away from Cat and yelled, "What do you want? Where are you?" Then she yelled expletives into the phone and challenged the manhood of the caller before he disconnected with a hideous laugh.

"Do you think someone followed us here?" Cat asked. Her voice trembled as she looked around nervously. Susan guided her quickly back to their room. They closed the door and locked the dead bolt, then slid the safety chain in place.

"Let's call your folks and Tom and see what they think we should do?" Susan suggested.

Her voice had raised a full octave. Cat dialed her parent's home number first. When she got no answer, she called both of their mobile phones. She was in a full panic when she couldn't reach them. She fumbled with the phone as she dialed Sullivan's number. Her worst thoughts and fears were surfacing as the phone rang and rang. Sullivan picked up on the fourth ring and sounded out of breath. When she asked what took him so long to answer, he hesitated then nervously laughed into the mouthpiece. It embarrassed him to admit that he had been in the shower and was now standing dripping on the rug outside of the shower, answering the phone.

Cat stammered with her own embarrassment and asked him to call her back once he had dried off and dressed.

Cat smiled a crooked smile at Susan with a devilish gleam in her eye. Susan just slapped at her arm and threw her head back laughing at the sight of her friend's discomfort. Cat hung up the phone and fell on the bed. She closed her eyes, trying futilely not to picture Sullivan naked and dripping wet talking to her on the phone.

"Okay, back to the issue at hand," Cat finally said, propping herself up on her elbows.

She had a sick feeling in her stomach thinking that the killer had followed them there. And what about her parents, had something happened to them? Her phone rang just then and the caller ID said it was Linda Carlyle.

"Hi, Honey. Sorry I missed your call. Is everything alright?" Linda asked.

"Yes," Cat lied, "is everything okay there?" she asked, as Susan tried to take the phone away from her. Cat slapped at her hands and turned away to try to keep her from getting the phone.

"Everything is good here. Your dad and I just got out of the hospital. We went to check on Miriam. She hasn't changed, but she is holding her own."

Cat thanked her mom for checking on her friend and asked about Hannah. She was told that Hannah was recovering and would be released from the vet in a couple of days. Relieved, Cat started to end the conversation without telling her mom why she had called. The look on Susan's face stopped her, though.

Susan stood there silently judging Cat, with her hands on her hips and shaking her head. Cat conceded to the truth and earned an approving nod from Susan as she told her mom about the phone call. She mentioned that she was waiting for Sullivan to call her back and omitted the details of why he had to. Linda and Phillip suggested that the girls should come home right away. They would wait to hear what advice Sullivan would give and made Cat swear she would call them back after talking to him.

Chapter 21

W hen Sullivan returned the call, the girls were already in bed. They had changed their clothes after turning on the gas fireplace in their room and had snuggled in for the night. They each sat in their beds with books purchased from the spa's gift shop. Susan's book was a sleazy romance paperback, but Cat had splurged on a hardcover book about garden design. The cover was an explosion of color with deep blues, vivid reds and bright oranges. She wasn't reading the pages, she simply flipped through the book and studied the pictures of gardens from all over the world and marveled at the various choices of designs. She promised herself that one day she would have a glorious garden where she could linger amongst the sky-blue delphiniums and run her fingers through the soft, blue fescue grasses. Yes, she would have lots of blues in her garden, one day.

The phone interrupted her blue, flowery thoughts. "Sorry it took so long to call you back," Sullivan said. "My partner called me with an update on the case."

Cat sat up and pushed the phone closer to her ear, "Anything you can tell me about?" Cat asked. She noted something in Sullivan's voice that made her concerned.

"Well," he hesitated, and then decided it wouldn't jeopardize anything to tell her. "The stabbing victim Juan Diaz was running buddies with Chaz Rodriguez and Chaz is associated with your pal, Warren Garrison."

"Warren is not my pal," Cat protested. "We were co-workers and dated a short time, that's all."

Sullivan let his head drop and ran his fingers through his thick wavy hair. "I didn't mean anything by that. Take it easy." Sullivan said and then hurried through the last part so that he could get to the real reason he called. "We believe that Chaz and Warren got acquainted while performing court-ordered community service in Oklahoma City. We also got word from our Sex Crimes Unit that Warren was a prime suspect in a rape case they worked last year. He was never prosecuted because the witness disappeared."

"Disappeared?" Cat nearly shouted. She cast a worried look at Susan.

"That's what they are telling us," Sullivan added. "The victim left work one night and no one ever saw her again. A missing persons report was filed by her roommate, but no one has seen or heard from her since," said Sullivan.

Cat closed her eyes as she put her brain in gear. Had she heard something about that, it didn't seem like it was that long ago. "I think I remember hearing about that case. Was Warren a suspect in her disappearance?" she asked, almost afraid of the answer. She cast a fearful glance at Susan. Susan, sensing a dark cloud forming, got out of bed and climbed into bed with Cat.

They shared the phone between their heads and listened as Sullivan explained that Warren was indeed a suspect, but his alibi for the time of her disappearance had come from an unusual source. With the air-tight alibi in place, the police had to look elsewhere and the case had gone cold.

"You are telling me that Rick Hurley was Warren's alibi?" Cat shouted.

She sat upright on the bed, inadvertently pulling the phone away from Susan's ear. Susan sat up and stretched her head and neck closer to Cat's to remain included in the conversation. It wasn't until Sullivan confessed that he missed Cat that she moved the phone to the other ear and shoved Susan away with a playful nudge of the elbow.

After a brief whispered exchange between them, Cat finally told him why she had originally called. Remembering the recent phone call made a shiver run through her body. "What do you think we should do? My parents suggest we cut our trip short and come back."

"No, don't do that," Sullivan instructed. "There is no reason to believe that someone followed you. It is more likely that whoever called realizes you are gone and wants you to come back. Stay put unless you hear from me otherwise. Okay?" Sullivan suggested.

After disconnecting, Cat called her mom back with the update. Cat was about to hang up when a thought popped into her head. She quickly asked her mom about getting her old job back at her dad's radio station.

"Let me your dad on so you can ask him yourself." Linda said.

Phillip reassured Cat that he would always have a place for Cat at the radio station. They agreed to discuss all the details when she got back to town. After disconnecting the call, Cat sighed.

"That's a relief. I hadn't realized how stressed I was about finding another job."

They leaned against the headboard and talked for nearly an hour before Cat finally yawned and Susan copied her. "What is it about yawning that makes people close to you do it too?" It was a rhetorical question that Susan didn't answer. She simply got out of bed, extinguished the gas to the fireplace and flopped down in her own bed. Cat watched as she fought with the covers to get them just the way she wanted them.

"Why are you such a freak about the covers?" Cat asked while she laughed.

"I guess we all have our little quirks, huh?" Susan said as she pointed to Cat's black high-heeled shoes which had been carefully laid by the wall not touching each other with the buckles refastened.

"You're right. We all have our little quirks," Cat agreed with a chuckle. She sunk under the covers and then immediately sat upright with a look of eureka on her face.

"Quirks! Of course! Why hadn't I seen it before?" Cat asked. Without waiting for a response, she continued, "Warren had this quirk about that silver necklace he gave me. Remember?"

Susan shook her head no, but without replying urged Cat on by motioning with her hands for Cat to continue. "He wanted me to wear it constantly. Remember how angry I told you he was when he saw that I put the little dove pendant on it? He was furious and wanted me to remove the dove. I called you and told you what a freak he was, and you just said something about him being sentimental, remember?"

"That's right," Susan recalled. "Didn't he ask for the necklace back when you guys broke up?"

"Yes, but I told him no. I despise people that want gifts returned. I didn't ask him for stuff back that I had given him," Cat added angrily.

"I know, but didn't he return your gifts to you?" Susan chirped.

"Very funny," Cat said. "You know very well he ripped that book to shreds. I paid forty dollars for that thing."

Cat began to make a mental drawing about the timelines and events surrounding Warren's employment and their courtship. "Here is what I don't get," Cat admitted. "If Warren was a suspect in a rape and then the disappearance of the victim, how did we not know about it?" Cat asked. She raised her hands as if the answer would somehow fall from the sky into her hands.

Susan drew her knees up in bed and wrapped her arms around them. "Let me see if I understand this right. Warren was suspected in two crimes, he used Rick as an alibi and Rick covered for him by lying?"

Susan turned her head to look at Cat, who hadn't answered her. Cat stared off into space as if she were replaying some event in her mind. "What is it?" Susan asked. "Are you remembering something important?"

Susan waved her arms back and forth across Cat's field of vision. Breaking her stare, Cat replied, "I don't know. I keep thinking about how Warren and Rick interacted at work. They appeared to have nothing in common and, although they worked together, I wouldn't have called them friends."

Cat's mind reviewed the past six months, and she forced herself to concentrate. Nothing more was coming to her. "I'll check my journal when we get home, but I don't remember anything unusual about their relationship and can't understand why Rick would lie for Warren, if he did."

Deciding to let it go for the night, they settled in and each drifted off to sleep. Somewhere in the night, deep in the subconscious of Cat's brain a video played over and over. In the dream, a man was choking her with the silver necklace. The dream ended the same way each time: she died. She saw the knife and saw the pools of blood that lay at her feet. She was certain it was her own.

At 4 a.m. she awoke with her heart racing. She was covered in sweat. She quietly got out of bed, her mind wild with fear. Creeping to the bathroom, Cat turned on the hot water for the shower. Numbness began to seep into her harrowed brain. Without peeling off her sweaty night clothes, she stepped into the tub as if in a trance. As the bathroom filled with steam she flashed back to the steamy bathroom in her apartment and slowly opened the shower door, frantically searching the mirror for any cryptic messages. When she failed to find any, she shut the door and fell exhausted to the bottom of the tub and let the hot water fall on her.

That's how Susan found her nearly an hour later, fully clothed, soaking wet and disoriented. She couldn't remember how she had gotten in the shower. Susan's gut began to churn. She got Cat some warm, dry clothes, helped her change and get back into bed.

She would have to call the Carlyle's.

Susan sent her boyfriend a message and told him what was happening. He endeared himself to her by suggesting they cancel their shopping plans for the day. Maybe they could still have dinner out somewhere if Cat were feeling better that evening.

With the plans made, Susan laid a hand on Cat's back. Whoever was behind this was messed up in the head she decided and they were determined to drive Cat insane. Susan sat by her best friend and tried to read her book, but her mind kept returning to the silver necklace. While Cat slept, Susan quietly pulled the bedside table drawer open where the girls had put their jewelry in the night before. She removed the necklace and held it in her hands. It wasn't anything special. It wasn't even that pretty. She ran it through her fingers while studying it. She wondered why Cat had been so adamant about not giving it back to Warren.

Chapter 22

He paced the floor in his living room, kicking trash and dirty clothes that covered the floor. His thoughts were uncontrolled mumblings. They were shouts and whispers colliding. Voices that were his, but others, talked all at once about nothing and everything. It was maddening! He wondered if he was losing his mind or if it was the meth. He picked up a can of warm beer that sat on a red milk crate he used as a coffee table. Tilting his head back he swallowed the stale beer and gagged. In a rage, he threw the can across the room and kicked the milk crate, sending it bouncing into the television set that no longer worked. *Who cared?* He thought. He didn't care about anything anymore. He knew he had to stop smoking the stuff. It had only taken one time to be addicted. Now it was all he thought about. All he wanted. All he needed. He hadn't slept in days, but yet he wasn't tired. There wasn't any point in eating – he wasn't hungry and couldn't taste the food anyway.

He needed another fix. He couldn't let this high wear off. He panicked when he realized he didn't have any more meth. He would have to steal his next hit. He slid the knife into the leather sheath, attaching it inside his boot next to his skinny leg and pulled his jeans down over it. He would have enough meth to last him a week before he came back to this over-priced dump, he didn't care what it took to get it either.

He scratched nervously at his neck and then each arm as he walked down the street glancing from side to side. People were watching him. He could feel their eyes on him. Scratching at millions of tiny bugs on his arms, that only he could see, he cautiously left the street and entered a narrow alley. His head swiveled and bobbed. Evil people were following him, he just knew it. They were after him. They would try to hurt him or even kill him. Feeling the knife tap against his ankle he grinned. They better not get too close to him or he'd cut them. He'd laugh as he watched them bleed. He was scratching his arms and talking to himself when Bronson and Sullivan spotted him stumbling towards them.

They were sitting in Bronson's parked Charger in the narrow alleyway behind a large liquor store. Trash spewed over the large metal can they parked beside, it littered the ground in every direction. Sullivan's informant had sworn this is where they could find who they sought, so they sat and waited. The man's appearance had dramatically changed since they saw him last.

"He is tweaking pretty bad today," Sullivan commented. He noted the sores that covered the man's face, neck and arms. "Don't spook him. I want to surprise him and get him subdued before he has time to react," Sullivan instructed.

He placed a restraining hand on Bronson's arm when Bronson grabbed the gear shift and started to throw it into drive. "Chill out, let him come closer," Sullivan warned.

He waited a couple of minutes more before saying, "Now, go now!"

Bronson dropped the gear shift into drive and spun the Charger's wheels. They converged on him like vultures. They were out of the car and on top of the meth head before he knew what had happened. With their weapons drawn, they ordered him to the ground and handcuffed him. Sullivan removed the knife and the sheath from inside his boot and held up a tiny clear plastic bag, its interior was coated with a chalky white film. "What do we have here?" asked Sullivan.

"Get your hands off me. I haven't done anything, pigs!" He shouted, "That isn't mine," he claimed, as his eyes tried unsuccessfully to focus on the baggy Sullivan held.

He cussed and struggled all the way to the car, where Bronson shoved him in the back seat, buckled him in and slammed the door. Sullivan bagged the knife and sheath as evidence and placed it and the baggy containing the residue, in the trunk. They drove straight to police headquarters while their prisoner yelled, swore and occasionally spat at the metal cage that separated them from him. When they got to headquarters, they had to drag him out of the car, up the stairs, down the hall and into an interview room. They shoved him down hard in a heavy metal chair and chained his feet to the floor in a leg restraint.

"Stay," Bronson ordered, as he pointed a single finger at Chaz face.

Chaz' pock-marked face was nearly purple with anger as he yelled and screamed. He cursed in Spanish and in English for several minutes before running out of steam and finally laying his greasy head on the table in front of him.

Sullivan and Bronson met in the observation room after retrieving a cup of coffee. They congratulated themselves on their catch, noted that no one had gotten harmed in the process and hatched the plan for the interrogation. Bronson would be the bad cop and Sullivan, the good cop. A paramedic from the fire department would come check the vitals of their witness. He was blitzed out of his mind, and they wanted to ensure he didn't' stroke out when they interviewed him.

The paramedic informed them that their witness had admitted to using meth and that he would probably be cooperative after he settled down. They knew from past experience that Chaz would be truthful, but only after shaking him up a bit. They let him rest awhile before they started. They enjoyed another round of very strong coffee, which tasted a bit burned, and walked into the interview room with their roles firmly in place. After listening to Chaz ramble for about twenty minutes, Bronson slammed his hand on the table and screamed for Chaz to give them something useful. Bronson threatened jail time for the baggy with residue and suggested that Chaz was reaching for his knife when they arrested him. That would be an additional charge.

"Come on, man. I don't know nothing else," Chaz started. His head hurt and his fingers were tingling. He agreed to tell them more if they took his handcuffs off. He said he couldn't feel his fingers any longer. So Bronson removed his handcuffs and allowed him to rub his wrists before handcuffing him with his hands in front of his body.

"There, now spill it!" Bronson demanded.

"This guy told me he'd give me a thousand bucks if I could get a necklace back from some chick. So I got my buddy Juan to lift it. I was gonna split the profits with him," Chaz admitted.

He told them how slippery Juan Diaz had been and how he himself was still on probation from a previous drug charge. He said if there was any way to steal the necklace, Diaz would have gotten it. No doubt about it. He didn't know what had happened to Diaz, he still couldn't believe he was dead. Chaz swore that he hadn't killed Diaz.

"It's not that we don't believe you, Chaz," Bronson said, flashing his best smile at Chaz then over to Sullivan, who only rolled his eyes. "It's just that we don't believe you. You understand, right?" Bronson paused, but when Chaz just stared at him with watery, bloodshot eyes, Bronson continued, "I mean, come on, Chaz, who would pay a thousand dollars for a silver necklace? You didn't think that sounded a bit odd?" Bronson asked.

Chaz just stared back at him; sweat seeped out of his pours filling the tiny room with a combination stench of chemicals and alcohol. Meanwhile, Sullivan pretended to be taking notes. Instead, he drew a picture of a hangman's noose on the yellow legal pad he held. Being the good cop during an interrogation was boring work. The senior detective continued to doodle on his note pad, periodically glancing from Bronson to Chaz.

Chaz' bloodshot eyes burned as he thought about the last question he was asked. He felt sweat forming on his bald head. He used his handcuffed hands to wipe at the sweat. "I dunno. What did you ask me again?"

Bronson repeated the question, and Chaz finally admitted that the unknown guy had given him 500 bucks and said he'd give him the other $500 after Chaz had brought him the necklace. No one was supposed to get hurt, and Diaz needed the money.

"But Diaz never saw any money, did he?" Bronson asked with a smirk. "All he saw was the business end of a blade."

Chaz hung his head and began to cry. "I know, man. I know," he sobbed. "I've been thinking about that a lot."

Sullivan piped up then, "Chaz? How was the guy who paid you supposed to get in touch with you. Did he call you? Do you have his phone number? Were you going to meet somewhere?" Sullivan asked rapidly. Chaz just looked bleary-eyed and confused.

Bronson took over again by asking, "Why would Diaz meet with the guy that hired you if you were the one he gave money to, Chaz? None of your story is adding up."

Bronson got up from his chair as he spoke. He circled the tiny dingy room as he rolled his head and neck relieving the stiffness. Chaz didn't respond, he just looked down at the table, his tears beginning to fade. Bronson circled behind Chaz' chair and leaned down to whisper in his ear.

"You are a liar. You killed Diaz!" He hissed. "We intend to prove it. You are going back to the big house."

Chaz was alive then, screaming, "No." Straining against his restraints he yelled, "I didn't kill him." His ugly face was twisted with anger. "I've never killed anybody. I ain't going back to prison."

The Spanish cursing began again and neither detective attempted to stop it. They just looked at Chaz and waited for his ranting to subside. When it did, Chaz was breathing heavy. The odor coming from his breath and person was filling the small room. It nauseated Bronson. He began fanning the stench away.

"So when was the last time you talked to this unknown guy who just handed you a fist full of money?" Sullivan asked.

"Like I told you, dude, I don't know when I talked to him last – a week ago, maybe."

Chaz appeared to be coming down off his high. The detectives watched as his hands began to shake a little. His eyes, although still bloodshot, tracked a little more together, giving the appearance that Chaz was a little more in control of his faculties.

"Is it possible you talked to him the night of the murder?" Bronson asked, as he glanced at Sullivan who was sketching something with his pen. Bronson walked slowly around the table behind Sullivan while waiting for Chaz to respond.

"Maybe he called me that night, or the next day. I can't remember exactly."

Bronson scratched his chin, acting like he was thinking, "Did he mention anything to you about killing Diaz?" Chaz worked hard to focus his eyes on the detectives face, "No, he was still asking me about that stupid necklace. I didn't even know that Diaz was dead yet."

"Do you think he killed Diaz?" Bronson asked. There was a long pause as Chaz thought about the question. He stared at his handcuffed hands before he answered.

"Yes, I think he killed him," Chaz admitted. "He killed him, but it's my fault that little girl don't have no daddy now."

Chaz's high was gone. In its place was the despair and emptiness he always felt when he was sober. It bore into his haunted conscience with ease and celebrated his miserable life with constant whispers of self destruction. His own selfish greed had cost someone their life. He glanced helplessly at the shackles that held him in place. These chains might be the only thing that could one day set him free from his addictions.

Chapter 23

Cat slept all morning. When Susan's boyfriend, Jackson, showed up fifteen minutes past noon, she was still sound asleep. Jackson handed Susan a gift wrapped box for Cat and sandwiches from a nearby deli. She placed it all on the table next to the sleeping Cat and hugged him tightly. It hadn't even been a week since she had last seen Jackson, but so much had happened since then. She started a fire in the fireplace and pulled the comforter off her bed. She placed the pillows on the comforter for seats in front of the fireplace and motioned for him to sit down.

After lunch, they talked in hushed tones about what they were going to do. Susan agreed that she probably would have to take Cat back to Oklahoma sooner than expected and voiced her concern about her mental well-being.

"It was scary finding her that way this morning."

She hoped Cat could snap out of it, but she had to admit that the amount of stress Cat had endured was overwhelming. They thought she was waking up when they saw her moving around on the bed. She rolled over a couple of times before they heard the first moans. When the crying started they both got up and hurried over to her side. Cat was saying, "No!" loudly, over and over and thrashing around. Susan sat on the edge of the bed and rubbed Cat's shoulder as she hushed her sleeping friend. Cat quieted down and stopped moving.

"I don't think she's going anywhere tonight. You can hang around if you want, I'd love for you to, but I think I'd better just stay here." Susan said.

Jackson agreed, "I could always pick up Chinese food complete with chopsticks, fortune cookies and sake later tonight?" He suggested. Susan wrapped her arms around his neck and clung to him several minutes before leading him by the hand back to their picnic by the fireplace.

"What are you two kids doing down there?" Cat asked after waking up and spotting them on the floor an hour or so later. She threw the covers off and walked towards the bathroom "Excuse me a moment."

When she returned, Susan introduced Cat and Jackson. They shook hands politely before she spotted the beautifully wrapped box that sat on the little table next to her bed.

"What's this?" Cat asked as she pointed to the box.

"Open it and see for yourself," Susan suggested. She and Jackson began picking up after their picnic. Cat tore into the little box with reckless abandon. She had the paper off, the box open and the silver bracelet on her arm in seconds.

"It's perfect. Thank you, Susan. This means a lot to me. I hated it that I lost the other one."

She hopped in the bed and pulled the covers back over her flannel pajama pants. "What are you guys gonna do this morning?" Cat asked. "I think I'll just lie around and read if you two don't mind."

Jackson and Susan looked at each other. Susan made her way to Cat's bed and sat down. She peered into Cat's hazel eyes and lifted her hand to look at the bracelet. She was relieved to see the familiar engraving on its silver edge. She patted Cat's hand and told her what time it was and what all had happened. Cat couldn't believe it.

"Wow! Well, let me jump in the shower, and we'll get out of here. Have you guys been cooped up here all day?" she asked.

"I didn't want to leave you," Susan said. "You needed your rest. Besides, we've have had a nice time just being together."

"You must have really been tired to have slept that long, kid," Jackson added. "I had Susan check a couple of times to make sure you were still breathing."

Cat could see why Susan liked Jackson. He seemed to have a great sense of humor and the most amazing gray green eyes Cat had ever seen. His thick blond hair was cut short and parted on the side. He was very handsome.

"Thanks for having her check on me, Jackson. Sounds like I was a zombie. I'm sorry I ruined you guy's plans. Why don't you go out for a date tonight? I'll be fine."

Susan patted Cat's arm gently. "There isn't any way we would leave you here alone. If you don't feel like going anywhere, we can order some Chinese food and just watch a movie or something."

Suddenly Cat was crying, or laughing. No, she was definitely crying, Susan decided. She hugged her best friend and rocked her gently back and forth. "There now, it's gonna be okay. Don't cry. Please don't cry," Susan comforted her.

"Bring me that little orange bag on the counter, honey." Susan told Jackson. She searched the bag and found a brown pill bottle and twisted off the white lid. "Here, take this," Susan said. "It's a muscle relaxer."

"No, I don't think that's a good idea." Cat said. "Look, I'm fine now. It was just shocking to hear that I had slept all day and that you two looked after me. I feel stupid and help-less." Susan tried to reassure Cat that it was okay. "That's what this trip was about," she said. "Getting away and relax-ing."

"I still don't want your muscle relaxer," Cat said as she ran shaky fingers through her matted blonde hair. "It's two in the afternoon, and I am still in pajamas. If I got any more relaxed, I'd be dead."

The all laughed and Jackson suggested that he and Susan get some ice from the ice machine and grab some sodas.

After they left, Cat took a few minutes to call her parents and check in. She felt better just hearing their voices. Since Susan and Jackson hadn't returned, she decided to get a shower. She jumped in and quickly lathered up. Her stomach, making growling noises and aching a bit, reminded her she hadn't eaten all day.

When she emerged from the shower with fresh clothes, wet hair and a little make up on, she felt like a new woman. The three of them watched movies, ate, talked, laughed and enjoyed their evening. When Jackson left around ten, Susan walked him to the doorway to tell him good-bye. She said they were probably going to go home the next day, and she'd let him know what their travel plans were. After relocking the door, the girls changed back into their pajamas and slid into bed, but Susan could tell by the look in Cat's eyes that she was frightened.

"What's wrong?" Susan asked.

Cat explained that they had gone all day without a single incident, but the nighttime terrified her.

"I have an idea. Why don't I sleep with you in your bed tonight?" Susan suggested. "It will be just like when we were kids." Without waiting for a reply, Susan jumped on Cat's bed and bounced around. She flapped her arms and acted crazy. After destroying the covers with her bouncing, Susan did the Nestea plunge and nearly knocked heads with Cat, who was laughing so hard she snorted like a pig. The two of them laughed and laughed. They were just drifting off to sleep when Susan's phone vibrated as it sat on the table between the two beds. Cat grabbed it without looking at the caller ID and handed it to Susan.

"I think you ladies should come home," Sullivan said. Susan didn't recognize his voice, but before she could question him he went on. "Miriam isn't doing well and isn't expected to live." They spoke only for a few moments about Miriam's condition before Sullivan asked to speak to Cat.

"What's happened?" Cat asked him quickly. "Tell me everything." She sat up in bed and leaned against the headboard.

Sullivan told her about Miriam's deteriorating condition, about the interview with Chaz Rodriguez, about not being

201

Betsy Randolph

able to locate Warren Garrison and finally about the bizarre behavior of Rick Hurley. They spoke for nearly twenty minutes before Sullivan said he really thought Cat should come home. With the killer still on the loose, he said he would feel better if she were closer.

"I want to see you," Sullivan told her before they hung up. "Be careful," he added.

She hit the end button on Susan's phone and pressed the phone to her chest. If Susan were right this gorgeous man really was interested in her.

She handed the phone back to Susan, scooted back down under the covers and told her what Sullivan had said. They would go home tomorrow. Susan made the call to the airlines and had the confirmation emailed to her phone. Then called the hotel salon and made an 8:00 a.m. appointment for them to get their hair done before flying home.

Cat was admiring her friend's self-confidence. She was so sure of herself. Cat was thinking it was probably Susan's red hair that made her that way, she smiled thinking to herself that redheads were outgoing, fiery and ostentatious.

"Maybe I could use a red tint to my hair too," Cat said as she combed her hair with her fingers.

"You know, I've never told you this," Susan said as she twirled Cat's hair with her fingers, "I was always envious of your auburn hair. I wish you would go back to your natural color." Cat only laughed.

"Fine, I'll consider it," Cat said before asking about their return flight home. Susan said the earliest flight they could get was one o'clock. So they would have plenty of time.

When the hotel phone rang at 6:00 a.m. for their wake up call, Cat was certain she hadn't slept at all.

"Rise and shine, sister. We've got to get moving," Susan said as she threw the covers off and sprang out of bed.

She made her way to the sink where a coffee pot sat. She set the coffee to brew and quickly put on her workout clothes.

"Come on, sleepy head, we have an 8 o'clock hair appointment and I want to hit the gym before we go." When Cat only grunted and didn't stir, Susan ripped the covers off the bed before Cat could react.

After a brief tirade of threats and swears, Cat finally swung her legs off the side of the bed. Her frizzy blond hair with brown roots was plastered down against her head on one side and waving to an unseen crowd on the other. Susan laughed at her hair and threw her some sweats.

"Let's go! Move it, move it, move it!"

Once they had downed a cup of coffee apiece, they headed to the gym for some cardiovascular exercise then grabbed some breakfast from the continental breakfast bar. After a quick shower they headed to the salon. Cat and Susan flipped through hair style magazines and examined several styles, but didn't seriously consider any of them. Finally Cat saw what she wanted. A lady sitting next to Susan had a *People* magazine with Reba McIntire on the cover.

"That's what I want, right there," She said, as she pointed to the lady's mag.

The beautician was a beautiful black woman who appeared to be in her late thirties. Her caramel-colored skin was flawless and her own hair was cut short and spiked with flaming red tips. After borrowing the magazine, Cat pointed at the picture and asked if she could make her hair look like Reba's.

"If that's what you want, I can do it." She replied confidently. Her cocoa-colored eyes were encased with long fake lashes that had gold flecks embedded in them. Cat liked her immediately.

"I'm Celeste. I have been making ladies beautiful for nearly ten years," She said as she shook Cat's hand. Cat noted her long graceful fingers and the red polish that coated her nails. "I got a late start because I kept changing my degree. It took awhile, but I finally figured out what I loved and what I was good at."

While Cat's hair was getting washed, conditioned, cut, colored and styled, Susan and Cat chatted with Celeste like they were old friends. Nothing was off limits and every topic was covered. By the time they left, the girls had made a new friend and had exchanged email addresses.

"I don't even look like the same person." Cat exulted, smiling at herself in the mirror. "I love the new look. You did a fantastic job, Celeste." She hugged her new friend tightly and slipped her a healthy tip. They said good-bye and went across the lobby to the boutique where Cat splurged on a gorgeous blue dress. Then they hurried back to their room to pack and change for their flight home.

Susan sent Sullivan a text while they sat in the terminal in Denver. She told him what time they were arriving in

Oklahoma City. She suggested he meet them at the airport and claimed it was for Cat's safety.

"What are you smiling about?" Cat asked her with a grin.

"Oh, nothing," Susan laughed. "I'm just happy to be going home, that's all.

Chapter 24

During the flight, Susan drifted off to sleep, but Cat was wide-eyed and awake. As the airplane descended through the billowing cumulous clouds, Cat stuck her face close to the window and looked down on the state that she loved. It looked so different from the sky. She admired the green rolling hills, acres of wheat fields, the lush foliage of trees, and the beautiful red clay earth. This was her home, it stirred her heart to know where she belonged after years of searching.

When they touched down, Sullivan was waiting for them. He watched them exit the concourse through security. He didn't even recognize Cat, but he knew it was her. His heart told him so. He stood there with his eyes fixed on her and his mouth nearly hanging open.

She had worn her black heels with the tiny buckles at the ankles and her new blue dress that fit her hourglass shape perfectly and plunged discreetly at the neckline. The silver necklace hung from her neck, and the descending silver dove rested between her breasts.

She noticed him standing there the minute they walked through the inner glass doors. Her heartbeat increased in rapid tempo at the sight of his tall, rugged form with his perfectly masculine face and those sweet brown eyes she wished to lose herself in. She felt shy and slightly embarrassed as her heels clicked on the white marble floors. The closer she got to him the faster her heart raced and the more she wanted to run toward him.

"Marry me!"

That's all he said when they got close enough to hear him. Susan and Cat both died laughing and thanked him as he took their bags from them.

"You look marvelous, Cat," he exclaimed, looking her over from head to toe.

"Did you even notice me?" Susan pouted, jokingly.

"Of course," he smiled. "You look great, too."

They made their way to the entrance of the airport before it dawned on Cat that Sullivan had met them on arrival.

"How did you know when we were getting in?" She asked him, with a serious look on her face. She had stopped in her tracks refusing to take another step until he answered.

"I can't reveal my sources, but suffice it to say, I'm glad I was informed correctly." He held out a hand for Cat to take. She slid her fingers into his large, warm hand and waited for her heart to slow before she spoke.

"Thank you," was all she could think to say. Susan just smiled.

Sullivan's patrol car was parked just outside the front doors of the airport lobby. He drove to Susan's car which was parked in the long-term parking garage. Sullivan asked if Cat would ride with him to the hospital to see Miriam. She agreed and Susan said she'd follow them there. On the way to the hospital, Sullivan brought her up to date on the investigation. He nearly rear-ended someone twice while stealing sideways glances at Cat. He couldn't keep his eyes off her.

Sullivan told Cat that Bronson had found another associate of Diaz' that corroborated Chaz' story about some man hiring him to steal the necklace. She looked down at the necklace, then back to Sullivan.

"Why would he care so much about this necklace?" She asked. "It's pretty, but I am certain it isn't that expensive."

Sullivan asked her why she chose to wear it all the time then. He had to keep his eyes from wandering down the chain, to the dove and beyond as it rested against her creamy white skin. He cut his eyes back to the road ahead of them.

"Why didn't you just give it back to him when he asked for it?"

"Because it's rude and immature to give someone a gift, then ask for it back." She touched the necklace with her fingertips.

"Well, I have to admit," Sullivan said with a grin, "it does look good on you."

Chapter 25

When they arrived at the hospital, Cat went straight to Miriam's room in the intensive care unit. The glass walls, rubber tubes, beeping machines and weird smells made Cat cringe. She hated hospitals, and she hated seeing people she cared about in them. She leaned close to Miriam's ear as she whispered to her dear friend that she was finally there. She brushed silver curls off Miriam's bruised forehead and adjusted her gown which had slipped off a bony shoulder. Cat pulled the covers higher and tucked them around her sleeping friend.

The visible bruises and cuts on Miriam infuriated Cat. She clenched her fists and gritted her teeth. Someone would pay for doing this, she silently swore. A tear slid down her cheek and dropped on Miriam's pillow as she bent over and planted a gentle kiss on the grandmotherly figure's cheek. She wanted to wrap her arms around Miriam, but afraid of hurting her, she just stood there seething. Gently she touched Miriam's arm on the single piece of fragile skin that wasn't purple, blue or black. Sullivan put his hand on Cat's shoulder when she stood back up. He gave it a squeeze and Cat turned towards him. Uncontrollable tears gushed out of her eyes as she fell against him. She sobbed as he held her. He promised they would catch whoever had done this to Miriam.

Cat had quit crying, but was still dabbing at her eyes with a tissue when Susan got there. One look at Miriam and Susan was crying, too. A nurse came in to check on Miriam and asked them to step outside while they gave her a breathing treatment. The three walked down the wide, sanitized hallway and entered the ICU waiting room. Just then, Sullivan's phone rang. He held a finger up to the girls and walked away to talk into the phone. When he came back he said he needed to go, but wanted to stay informed of their movements. Cat said she was going back to Susan's to get her things and then would probably be staying at her parent's house until she made other arrangements. Susan would be traveling again the next day, flying to the east coast travel article she was writing.

Cat watched as Sullivan's tall, lean figure disappeared down the hallway in his starched Wrangler jeans and cowboy boots. He was beautiful. When she hugged him she had felt his duty weapon under his left armpit and had seen the shoulder holster when he was at her apartment. It was a combination of leather, elastic and Velcro and it crisscrossed over his muscled back and shoulders. Under one arm the holstered black pistol hung and under the other were two additional magazines that held extra bullets. She wondered what made a person want to carry a gun for a living.

She had always thought it odd that someone would be willing to risk his or her life for the safety and protection of others. She figured the job of a law enforcement officer was often unappreciated by the people they served. Maybe that was it, she thought. Maybe the draw for Sullivan had been the service part of it. She admired him for his commitment.

Cat called her parents and told them that she would be coming to their place after picking up her things from Susan's. But once she was behind the wheel of her trusty car, she made her way north to Guthrie instead. She couldn't explain why, but she needed to see her apartment. She wanted to see the carnage, the waste. She wanted to keep this feeling alive inside her that wanted revenge. It made her feel strong and confident somehow. The familiar rumbling of the car tires across the red brick cobbled roads told her she was getting close to home. When she pulled into one of the two narrow parking spaces available in the alley behind her building, she looked around cautiously before getting out. She climbed the metal stairs as quickly as she could with heels on and inserted the key into the outside door.

Entering the long hallway, she listened for any sounds as she tiptoed down the wooden floor to her apartment. There were no signs indicating the police had been to her apartment or to the one across the hall. Her hands shook as she unlocked her front door and stepped quickly inside, shutting and locking the door behind her. Cat looked around and couldn't believe her eyes. The place was spotless. Aside from the obvious missing items, it looked pretty good.

She walked silently from room to room investigating. She wondered why her bicycle had been spared in the melee, but considered it a blessing. Quickly she changed her clothes, gathered her biking gear and packed it and more clothes into a big suitcase with wheels, and pulled it out to her car. She went back up one last time for her bike.

Before locking the apartment, she took another look around. This place would never be home again if Hannah and Miriam didn't survive. A deep sadness filled her. The hollowness she felt as she looked around the room seeped into her soul. Tears blurred her vision as she locked up the apartment. Once outside, she wiped the tears off her face and secured the bike on the carrier attached to the roof of her car and took off.

Phillip and Linda could not believe their eyes. The girl who had left home seventy-two hours before had been transformed into a beautiful graceful woman.

"Wow! Look at you, sweetheart!" Phillip exclaimed as he embraced Cat.

He pulled her inside after she rung the doorbell. "Why are you ringing the bell? Why didn't you just come in?" he asked as he studied her in the entryway.

"Who is it?" Linda asked as she rounded the corner.

She was drying off her hands with a dish towel and nearly threw it in the air when she laid eyes on Cat. She could hardly believe her eyes. "Catherine!" She rushed over to where the two of them stood and threw her arms around Cat, kissing her on the neck.

"Honey, you look so beautiful. I love your hair. Come in, come in! Tell us all about your trip."

They settled on wrought iron bar stools that sat beneath the center island in the kitchen. Cat rested her elbows on the granite countertop and caressed the surface with her hands.

"I love this." She said pointing at the turquoise, cream, pink and rust colors that ran like rivers through the granite surface.

"What did you tell me this was called?" she asked as she studied it like art.

"It's Italian marble. It's called 'Blue Louise.' Isn't it beautiful?" Linda asked.

She hugged Cat again and asked if she had eaten lunch. Cat said yes, that they had eaten in Denver before boarding the plane. She admitted that she was still a little hungry and accepted her mom's offer to heat up some chicken enchilada casserole. It was one of her favorite dishes, and no one, including Cat, could make it like her mom could.

While Cat ate, she told her parents about everything that had happened on her trip. Between bites she answered questions and frequently accepted their compliments with grace. Both parents had mentioned over the past few years how they would like to see her hair return to its natural color. Every time they had mentioned it, she had run right out and bleached it or put a color streak through it, just to irritate them. She couldn't explain why, she just did. It made her sad all of a sudden to recall her juvenile antics.

"I'm sorry for being so hard to get along with in the past. I don't deserve you two. Thank you for my vacation. It was wonderful."

Who is this person? Phillip asked himself. Who was this gorgeous young woman sitting in his house, admitting her mistakes? He was blown away by her candor and willingness to accept responsibility for her actions.

"We love you, or else we would have killed you long ago," Phillip laughed he hugged her tightly and planted a loud kiss against her auburn head. "Besides, we knew we had raised you right and that you were just trying to find your own way."

He laid an arm around her shoulder and squeezed her again. "I've already told your mom that you are going to work for me at the radio station. When do you think you want to start?"

"As soon as possible, is tomorrow okay?"

Phillip nodded his head in agreement. After cleaning up her lunch plate and glass, she brought her stuff in from the car.

As she was walking her bike up the sidewalk, a black pickup drove slowly down the street. Cat turned and stared at its tinted windows as it crept slowly by. She didn't recognize the truck and couldn't see the driver, but she figured she should tell Sullivan about it.

Early the next morning, she showered, dressed and met her parents in the kitchen. She sipped on some coffee but refused breakfast. "No, thank you. I'm not really hungry. I guess I am just excited about getting to the station," she told them. She was rewarded with smiles from them both.

"I'll give you two an hour before you are choking each other," Linda said with a laugh. She was thinking it would be a miracle if they could actually make it an hour before trying to kill each other. "I'll check and see who is still living at noon. One of you is taking me to lunch" she stated as a matter of fact.

The hours flew by as Cat recorded promos, greetings, station identifiers and made a few telephone sales. She called Sullivan to let him know what her new work number was and invited him by the station for a visit. She told him about the ominous looking truck and promised she would be extra vigilant of her surroundings. When Cat and her parents went to lunch around 12:30, she was feeling great.

"Well, since it appears that you are both alive, I guess I'll buy lunch in celebration," Linda joked.

They ate salads and enjoyed fresh fruit from a local deli around the corner. They were about to head back to the radio station when Phillip spotted a truck he thought looked like the one Cat described to them the day before.

"Is that the truck?" He pointed out the window to a black Chevy truck parked across the street. The windows were darkly tinted, preventing anyone from seeing if it was occupied. "I don't know. Why don't we go check it out? We could get the tag number and call it in to Sullivan!" Cat suggested.

With her parents in tow, Cat emerged from the deli first and walked in a straight line across the street towards the truck. Without warning, the driver accelerated quickly and lunged the truck towards Cat. She dove out of the way, just in time, as the truck sped past her and down the street. Her parents raced to where she lay on the pavement and helped her up.

"Cat Honey, are you okay?" her mom yelled. "Where are you hurt, did he hit you?" She asked as Phillip screamed at the retreating driver to stop and come back.

215

"I guess that was a stupid idea," Cat said as she dusted off her slacks. She had managed to scuff one knee and ruin a good blouse judging from the looks of one of the elbows.

"Call Sullivan," Phillip demanded as he turned and ran. "Tell him what happened. I'm going to get my car and see if I can find that guy."

He was off and running before either woman could stop him. Cat quickly dialed Sullivan's number, gave him the information and begged him to hurry. She was afraid of what would happen if her dad did find the truck and the driver.

Several people had come out of the deli and from a service station across the street. They said they had witnessed the incident. One witness thought he had gotten a good look at the tag. He repeated it to Cat who repeated it to Sullivan who called it in. The dispatcher gave him the bad news a minute later, just as he was pulling up at the scene.

"That tag comes back not-on-file," she informed him. He scratched his head and listened to the witness tell his version of the story again, remaining quiet so as not to disturb the witness's recollection of the events. The witness repeated the same tag number and said that he was pretty sure that's what he saw. A uniformed officer had arrived and was busy getting witness statements, so Sullivan took Cat and Linda back to the radio station. Linda called Phillip. He hadn't been able to spot the truck, so he was reluctantly returning to the radio station. When he got there he asked Sullivan to step outside with him.

"Thank you for coming so quickly. I need to ask you a legal question," Phillip said. He looked around nervously to ensure no one would overhear him. "I'm going to start carrying a gun. I want to make sure that I am legal to do so."

Sullivan gave him a quick version of the Concealed Carry Law. As Phillip understood it, he was going to have to fill out a bunch of paperwork, pass a background check, attend some classes, qualify on the weapon and pay a fee, before he could carry a gun to protect his family. He could feel his blood pressure rising at a dangerously fast rate. His head was pounding. The men walked back into the station where Linda met him at the door and ushered him into his office after seeing how red his face was. She asked Cat to bring him some water and she loosened his tie. She took off his suit jacket and hung it on a hanger on the coat rack behind the door.

"Now you just sit here and calm down. Drink this," she instructed, holding the cup of cool water to his lips. Sullivan told them what they had talked about and apologized for Phillip getting so upset.

"He will be fine in a few minutes," Cat reassured him. "Come on."

She held out her hand and led Sullivan out of the office and closed the door.

"It's not your fault. He has high blood pressure. He'll probably just break the law and carry his gun anyway. I don't even know why he bothered to ask you."

Continuing to hold his hand, she took him on a tour of her father's station. Sullivan's heart beat wildly with her delicate hand in his. He tried to focus his attention on what she was saying. He decided he liked the homey feel of the small station. The crisp white walls were in stark contrast to the dingy, worn-down office building where Cat had worked the week before. It made him feel better knowing she was here where the carpet wasn't frayed and dirty. He noticed the control booth didn't look like she could catch a dangerous disease just from being inside it.

This is really nice. It's a whole lot cleaner than the last station."

She smiled her thanks. "I agree, I can actually wear nice clothes and not worry about them getting destroyed at work. Well, that is until today."

She held her elbow up for him to inspect. She had gotten a nice patch of road rash on her elbow and knee. Her clothes had taken the worst of it, she assured him.

"No more bravado, got it?" he instructed. He tapped her nose as if she were a dog that had peed on the carpet.

"Yeah, whatever! It didn't seem like bravado to me. I mean, it was broad daylight, in public and I had my parents with me."

His eyes were deadly serious when he looked at her and said, "Just be careful, okay? That's all I ask."

She agreed with a nod and a handshake. Her hand lingered in his for a moment longer. He said he had to get back to work and would check on her later. Leaning down, he pecked her cheek with a friendly kiss and then was gone.

The next several days went by without any further sightings of the mysterious truck. Cat worked at the station, hung out with her parents, rode her bicycle and sat with Miriam at the hospital, reading to her occasionally. Miriam wasn't getting better. The doctors had prepared them for the worst. Only time would tell.

Susan had been in and out of town repeatedly in the last few weeks. She stopped by when she had time. Hannah had been released from the vet's, but was taking a long time to heal. It made them all sad to see the little dog once full of life, moving like an old worn out dog.

Chapter 26

C at was growing more and more relaxed. He could see it. She didn't look around nervously nearly as much anymore when she left the house or work. Sometimes she wouldn't even turn around when she was walking alone on the street. He smiled at himself in the rearview mirror of the stolen sedan.

He imagined himself forcing Cat in the car. He would take his time with her. It wouldn't be like the others. He watched as she came out of her parents' house in her skimpy biking outfit. She looked like a whore. Just like all the others. She wasn't any different. Except that he hadn't killed her yet. He licked his lips as he watched her sit on her bike seat and put her feet on the tiny plastic petals. He laughed out loud as her foot slipped off the pedal and nearly falling over. She looked around then, he noticed.

"You are more worried about looking like a fool on that stupid bike than you are about me," he chided her aloud. He imagined how she would look naked, tied up and gagged.

He wanted so badly to hurt her that it made him ache all over. He continued to watch her as she pedaled down the street. He didn't start the car until she was a block away. The windows weren't tinted in the sedan, so he would have to be careful.

He hung back while she was in residential neighbor-hoods. He wanted to take her when no one was around so no one would hear her when she screamed. Fifteen minutes later he was getting frustrated. She usually went out on the two-lane road north of town. The hills were challenging out there. He watched through binoculars on more than one occasion from a seldom used birdwatching tower in the park that paralleled her favorite route.

He wiped his sweaty hands on his jeans and took another swig of beer from one of the cans he had brought along in a mini-cooler. He was relieved when he saw her finally take a right turn out of the ever-expanding housing addition and stand up on the bike to pedal uphill. He tossed the empty can onto the floorboard next to the nylon rope. He'd brought it and a large kitchen knife, pliers, and a gag for her pretty mouth that had made from a pair of her own panties. He watched her buttocks and legs as she pumped the pedals over and over. He swallowed the saliva that had pooled in his mouth.

Cat was admonishing herself for riding on an empty stomach, she felt exhausted as she pushed and pulled the pedals with her legs. She felt the cool breeze rush through the air vents of her helmet as she dipped her head. She was cold when she first started riding and thought about just staying in the neighborhood. But the longer she rode, the better she felt. So she got out on the newly resurfaced road and challenged herself.

Her thighs and lungs burned as she reached the top of a little hill. She coasted and took a swallow of water from the water bottle that was attached to her bike frame and repositioned her sun glasses. As she started up the next hill she caught a glimpse of a tan sedan in the little side mirror attached to her helmet. She saw how fast it was driving, so she got as close to the right-hand side of the road as she could. She couldn't see the driver clearly, but she could tell it was a man. She waved her arm, signaling for him to go around, but he didn't. She watched as the car got danger-ously close to her rear tire and then slowed, backing off.

Several times the car got close to her and then retreated. Cat's heart was crashing against her ribs. She prayed it wasn't the killer, but her gut was screaming that it was. She stood and pumped as hard as she could, her mind racing to think of a plan. The next cross street was nearly a half-mile away. If this was the killer, she was alone on a two-lane stretch of highway outside of town and no way to escape.

Her eyes darted to the side mirror on her helmet. Where had the car gone? She thought it had disappeared when she heard the roar of its engine. She dared a glance over her left shoulder just as the tan sedan smashed into her back tire. The force knocked her violently off the bike and slammed her in a rolling heap onto the blacktop road.

She rolled and tumbled for what seemed like an eternity. When she finally came to a stop she lifted her head and looked at her bloody knees. She didn't feel the pain at first – it just stung a little. Then she glanced at her elbows, hip and shoulder. All of a sudden, they were burning like fire. She lay still, but then lifted her arms off the ground. The pain was intense as she attempted to move.

"You are going to be okay," he was saying. "Just be still. Do you hear me?"

It felt like he was dragging her. She couldn't be certain, but it felt like he was checking her for injuries. His hands were all over her body. She slid in and out of consciousness moaning and groaning from her wounds. She was thinking she knew him when she caught a whiff of his cologne. He smelled familiar. He managed to lift her up and lay her in what she thought was the back seat of his car.

She couldn't understand what he was doing with the rope. Her injuries must have been severe, because he was tying her down so she wouldn't roll around. The searing pain had her trying to rise off the seat, but the rope held her arms down firmly. Why was he tying her up? She tried focusing on his face as he bent over her and took her helmet off. He had a hat pulled down on his head and the dark glasses prevented her from seeing his eyes. She thought she was dreaming and closed her eyes until he stuffed something into her mouth with a hard shove. Then he cussed her as he lifted her head and tied the gag tightly behind her left ear with a jerk.

He whispered some horrible things in her ear then. He promised to hurt her. He said she would bleed. He swore it would hurt horribly bad and she would scream, but no one would rescue her. He slammed the door as she rocked with fear and disbelief. She watched with crazy, pain-filled eyes as he slid behind the wheel and jammed on the accelerator.

Her racing bike lay mangled in the street. It was in two separate pieces when a lady in a red sports car started to go around it a few minutes later. When she realized what it was, she slammed on her brakes and reached for her phone. She dialed 9-1-1 as she exited her car and hurried around the mangled bike, frantically searching for the bike's rider.

Several miles away, while sitting at one of only a half-dozen stop lights in Guthrie, his mind was running through the next several hours, maybe days. He would have so much enjoyment with Cat. In less than five minutes, he would have her safely tucked away in a large wooden shed behind his house. She would be naked, scrubbed clean and chained up within the hour. And she would be all his, to do with as he pleased.

He turned up the radio to drown out her whimpering and gagged cries from the back seat. He didn't know a semi driver directly behind him at the traffic light could see into the back seat of the sedan. The frantic semi-truck driver had called the police and they were working their way through traffic behind them.

One minute he was congratulating himself on his catch and plotting Cat's demise. The next, he spotted a black and white car weaving through traffic behind him, approaching quickly. The blue and red lights came on as the black and white patrol car went around the semi and behind the stolen sedan. He screamed a list of expletives, slamming his hand on the horn. Without so much as a good-bye, he jumped from the car, with it still in gear and ran like a rabbit from a wolf.

He sprinted through an intersection, narrowly missed a guy on a motorcycle, jumped over the hood of a parked car and plowed into an old woman carrying groceries on the sidewalk. He was up and running again when he heard the squeal of tires followed by the crinkling of metal and breaking of glass.

Scaling a wood fence, he fell to the hard ground on the other side. It knocked the wind out of him, so he lay there cussing, sucking air in and pushing it out with exaggeration. Before running again, he crouched behind the fence and looked through the slats for trouble. When he saw none, he ran around the side of the house, straight into the path of the biggest pit bull he had ever seen.

Chapter 27

All they could do was wait. They had heard more than one uniformed person tell them that today: First, the police, and now, the nurses and doctors. Phillip and Linda paced the living room, then the kitchen, then the dining room and finally the waiting room at the hospital. They checked the home phone a dozen or more times to make sure it was still working. Then they checked their cell phones and waited. They prayed, they cried and they waited some more.

When they received the call that her bike had been found, they were hysterical. They rushed to the scene and helped search for their only child. They looked everywhere for Cat. Without knowing what to say, they made the calls to Susan and Sullivan and waited while the Oklahoma Highway Patrol was called in to investigate the collision.

When the trooper showed up in his brown uniform and round, Smokey the bear hat, he didn't appear concerned about the missing rider. He said someone probably stopped and rendered aid to her and had probably given her a ride to the hospital. His nonchalant attitude rubbed Phillip and Linda the wrong way. They tried to get the young trooper to understand what Cat had been through recently. He seemed oblivious to what they said as he got his large roll-a-tape out of the trunk of his patrol car and started taking measurements. He finally got into his car and started typing on his computer that was mounted on a black metal stand in the center console of his black and white Dodge Charger.

When Sullivan arrived he took Phillip and Linda aside. He put an arm around each of their shoulders. "Let me talk to the trooper and see what I can find out. My dispatch is already making calls to all the local hospitals. If she was taken to a hospital, we will know about it soon. Why don't you guys head back to your house and I will be right behind you."

Phillip thanked him profusely, but Linda just stared at him as if he spoke another language. Phillip guided her back to their car. When they got to their house there was already a police car in the driveway.

"Please, God, no!" Linda shrieked.

She clutched her chest as she got out of the car and stumbled towards the police officer. He was standing on the porch talking on his hand-held radio. He saw them park next to his patrol car, so he replaced the radio on his gun belt and readjusted his hat. He walked down the sidewalk to meet Phillip and Linda. He saw the fear in their eyes.

"Good afternoon, my name is Officer Weatherly. I've been sent here by Detective Sullivan. He said he will be here shortly, but he wants me to wait with you until he arrives."

"Has something else happened? Did they find her out there after we left?" Phillip asked. He put both hands on his head, waiting for the bad news.

"No, Sir, nothing like that. You probably know more about what's going on than I do. I'm just suppose to wait here with you."

He motioned for them to continue up the path to the front door. They walked together to the front door and were surprised to find it unlocked. Had they really run out of there earlier and forgotten to lock the door?

"I thought you locked this, Babe," Phillip looked accusingly at Linda.

"You were the last one out. Remember?" she replied defensively. "I was already in the car when you came out."

Phillip looked at the police officer and held a finger up across his lips to motion for them both to be quiet. He had started through the door when the officer grabbed his arm and pulled him back outside.

"Wait a minute. You stay out here with your wife. I'll call for backup, and we'll search the premises. If someone is in there, you don't want to confront them unarmed.

"Who said I was unarmed?" Phillip said as he slid his fingers around the stainless .380 he had tucked into his waistband.

"You got a permit for that thing?" the young cop asked. He smiled when Phillip didn't reply. "Come on, keep your head down," the officer said.

The police officer radioed in to his dispatch that they would be searching the house and then turned his radio off. Phillip looked at Linda and said, "You stay here. We will check the house." Phillip pointed at the porch swing with his non-gun hand and bent his elbow, raising the pistol skyward.

He motioned for the officer to follow him, and they crouched down as they silently swung the door open and crept inside.

Linda walked to the end of the porch and sat in the swing. After searching the house and finding it as they had left it, Phillip returned to the porch and pulled Linda to her feet. He took her inside, laid her on the couch, covered her with a blanket and sat beside her. He rubbed her shoulders gently as he leaned over and whispered in her ear. "She's going to be all right. Rest now, rest."

He got up, walked slowly to the kitchen and poured himself a cup of cold water and offered some to the police officer who paced the floor while looking out the kitchen window periodically.

When Sullivan arrived, the young officer walked out to meet him. Phillip watched as the two men talked briefly by Sullivan's car. Then Sullivan turned and made his way up the walk and to the door. Phillip opened the door as Sullivan's hand was in a mid-air knock.

"Come on in Detective and tell us what you know."

Sullivan motioned toward Linda, "Get Mrs. Carlyle. We are heading to Baptist Hospital. Cat's in the emergency room there. She is pretty banged up, but she's alive."

Phillip rushed to Linda's side while Sullivan was still talking and shook her shoulder. Cat had been found.

Cat was conscious and screaming when they rushed into the emergency department. They could hear her all the way down the hallway. She settled down a little when her mom and dad pushed past the half-drawn curtain and up to her bed.

The only place on her body not scraped up was her head. Even her chin had suffered some abrasions. She was a pitiful sight. The large male nurse with an evil looking rubber scrubber had been cleaning her up. Between the iodine bath, the blood, the torn biking clothes and the obvious struggle Cat was putting up, the place looked like a war zone.

Linda held her hand over her mouth and tried unsuccessfully to stop crying. Several times, she tried to speak but only a sob would emerge from her thin, tight lips.

"Try to relax, I know it hurts. Here hold my hand," Sullivan said, trying to soothe Cat. He held a burly hand out for her tiny one. "Go ahead and squeeze when it hurts."

"It hurts constantly," she said, almost screaming.

"Tell this barbarian to stop," Cat yelled, but the nurse continued to scrub her wounds. It appeared to Phillip and Linda that Cat's skin looked more like hamburger meat. It was more than either of them could stand.

When Phillip's legs quit holding him up, he leaned sideways and hit the wall before Sullivan grabbed the back of his jacket and eased him gently to the floor. Another nurse came running in and rolled him over. She checked his vitals, determined he had fainted and asked for Linda to help her get him up and out into the waiting room. Linda gave Cat a pitiful glance and did as she was asked.

Sullivan continued to hold Cat's hand and tried to get her to look into his eyes so that she wouldn't watch what was being done to her. Cat didn't seem to notice that Sullivan saw her wearing only her panties and bra. She tried to recall everything that had happened and all that she had seen and felt. She gave a description of the man who had hit her. The police had recovered the sedan with her in it after it crashed into a bus at the red light. She was taken by ambulance to the burn center because her injuries essentially were burns. After discovering that her left leg, right arm, two ribs and collarbone were broken, they began the process of splinting, casting and scouring the wounds.

"I'm going to kill him with my bare hands when we find him," Cat swore through clinched teeth.

She squeezed Sullivan's hand hard and looked directly into his eyes. His words were like balm to her soul and she allowed herself to get lost in his eyes as he clasped his other hand on top of hers.

There would come a day when she would be safe again, Sullivan vowed to himself. He would do everything possible to ensure it. He would capture or kill whoever had done this or he would die trying.

Chapter 28

He carried the alcohol, bandages and a bottle of Ibuprofen to the counter and pushed them all towards the old woman behind the register. Without looking up, she began ringing up the items.

"Did you find everything okay?" She looked up and stared at the badly injured man.

"Oh, my goodness, you need to go to the hospital. What happened to you?"

He gritted his teeth together and pushed out a few words, "Nothing. I'm fine."

He used his shirt to apply pressure to the deep gouge wounds on his forearm. He was bleeding badly. He knew he needed stitches, but he couldn't risk going to the emergency room.

"Please hurry," he begged.

She totaled everything, took his money, and gave him his change. While she bagged everything up for him, she leaned over the counter and saw that he had bled all over the floor.

"Please let me call an ambulance for you. You have lost a lot of blood."

Without a word he turned and made his way quickly out the door carrying his medical supplies with him. The store clerk picked up the phone and called 9-1-1. The dispatcher on the other end of the line had the clerk look out the front door to see what sort of vehicle the man had left in, but the store clerk didn't see any vehicle.

"He must have left on foot. There aren't any cars in the lot."

When a police cruiser showed up seven minutes later, the clerk was cleaning up the mess. She pointed to the blood on the floor and showed the officer where the man had dripped all over the floor as he had shopped, but the blood trail ended in the alley behind the store.

After leaving the store, the injured man kicked the dirt over the drops of blood in the dirt, then hid behind the building, sitting against the cinderblock wall that surrounded the large metal dumpsters. He opened the bottle of Ibuprofen while cursing the excessive packaging. His bloody fingers tore through the safety seal and pulled the cotton ball out. He could probably use that, he thought. He poured the Ibuprofen in his mouth without counting the pills and leaned his head back against the wall.

Over the next several minutes he poured the alcohol over his wounds, packed as many clean bandages as he could on the large gashes the dog's teeth had made and cussed his bad luck. He swore that someone would pay for the pain he felt. He knew exactly who it would be, too – Cat. She had been the source of his internal pain for some time. Now she was the source of his external pain as well. He would make her suffer. She would suffer more than he had ever made anyone suffer before.

Betsy Randolph

He was cussing her out loud when he heard the back door of the business open and shut. He quickly and quietly squeezed himself between the wall and the dumpster and silently winced at the pain in his legs where the dog had ripped them to ribbons. He still didn't know how he had gotten away alive. That dog was every bit of a killer as he was. He lay down as quietly as he could on the cold concrete when he heard the front doors of the dumpster open and heard something being placed inside. Then the metal doors slammed shut. He closed his eyes while he waited for whoever was on the other side of the dumpster to leave. He could smell the burning cigarette and knew whoever was there would be there for awhile. So he relaxed a little, thinking of how close he had been to Cat. He could still smell her on his arms where he had carried her. He sniffed the air as if she were there.

When he woke up several hours later, it was dark. He moved as slowly as possible to avoid tearing open his wounds that appeared to have stopped bleeding. There was just enough light from a light pole in the parking lot for him to see. Once he was out from behind the dumpster, he looked himself over, inspecting his wounds. The bleeding hadn't stopped; it had just slowed due to the cold. He limped to the corner of the building and looked both directions before he entered the alley. He could make it home from here. He began walking and planning his next move.

Chapter 29

After everyone had left her to sleep, Cat lay in the hospital bed wishing she could make the madness stop. Her mind replayed the events of the last two weeks. She wondered why her life had spiraled out of control. Tears streamed down her cheeks as she accepted her part for allowing Warren and Rick to treat her as they had. She had been weak. There was no denying that. Just acknowledging that she hadn't ever stood up for herself was a new development. She would look back later with pride when she finally realized that she was worthy of love. Catherine Carlyle, victimized time and again, was worthy of love. She could accept love as well. She deserved to be treated nicely. She wondered why it had taken all of this for her to accept herself and for her to be able to admit openly what had happened to her in the past. She had never been willing to be honest with herself, let alone anyone else.

Suddenly she realized that she could respect herself. Silently she thanked God for helping her escape from what she reasoned was certain death. She thanked Him for her wonderful parents – not perfect ones, but ones that loved her beyond belief, parents that always stood by her when her choices took her places she didn't really want to go.

Mentally, she took an inventory of her life and the relationships in it. Cat thought about her parents again, her best friend Susan, and her neighbor Miriam. She was truly blessed. Her tears continued as her mind recalled warm memories with each of them and Hannah, also. She lay there for a long time thinking of her loved ones and wondering how they would have felt if things had turned out differently that day.

Time for some honesty, she thought. She wiped her tears off her face with her un-casted arm. She was thinking it was time to evaluate the other relationships in her life, too. Sadly, she admitted she had accepted whatever treatment people handed out to her. For the first time in her life she realized that she must have been showing with her actions how she truly felt about herself. She didn't like herself very much, and it showed. By allowing them to treat her with disrespect and violence, she was saying it was okay because she didn't value herself either. When she was finally able to admit this, her feelings about everything changed almost immediately. She had to stop feeling sorry for herself. She must stop accepting what was happening and act.

She rang the buzzer for the nurse and waited. She cringed when the large male nurse that had tortured her earlier, appeared in the doorway. For a second she thought about telling him she had pushed the button by mistake. She had already pulled the covers around her chin before she realized she was regressing to the old Cat. So she stopped, looked the horrible scrubs-wearing man in the eyes and asked for paper and a pen. He stood there a moment deciding what to say and then without a word, turned and walked to the small dresser against the wall. He pulled a drawer open and pulled out a note pad and pen with the hospital's name on them. He brought them to Cat and held them out to her.

She looked into his eyes as she thanked him. He turned to go, but just before he walked out the door, she stopped him.

"Sir?"

He turned slowly with a questioning look on his face.

"Thank you for cleaning me up earlier. I hope you hated doing it."

He smiled then, and she noticed that his whole face lit up when he did. He had very kind eyes, she thought. He told her then that it was the worst part of his job, but one that had to be done. When he left, she sat there for a moment feeling more alive and stronger than she could ever remember feeling before.

She would stop the killer. All she needed was a plan. Using her casted right arm, she slowly scribbled some notes on the paper.

The next morning, Sullivan relieved the police officer who had guarded Cat during the night. He entered her room expecting to find her timid, broken body cowering beneath the sheets. He couldn't blame her. He would probably have lost it by now if the truth were told. She had been through an extreme amount of stress, mental anguish and physical pain. He wasn't prepared to find her sitting up in bed with a cup of coffee in her left hand and a notebook in her lap.

"Good morning, Detective. Would you care for some coffee?"

"Aren't you bright-eyed this morning?" he asked and smiled. "Looks like you got some much needed rest. How are you feeling?"

"I might have some broken bones, but I feel pretty darn good. Let me show you something."

She motioned for him to come to her bedside. She showed him the notebook and what she had been writing. He raised his eyebrows and mulled over what she proposed.

"There isn't any way I can allow you to use yourself as bait like you're suggesting. Besides, you aren't in any condition to do any crime fighting. If you haven't noticed, you are in the hospital."

He stood with his hands on his hips and looked down on her bruised, injured face and body. It hurt him to see her like that. He wanted to get the guy so badly he would be willing to do anything to catch him, but he would never put her in harm's way to do it. He was thinking how different she seemed when she reached a casted arm out to him. Her cold fingertips rested against the skin on the back of his hand. He looked down at her hand and then back to her face. Their eyes locked for a brief moment and the look that passed between them had both of their hearts pounding.

"You are an amazingly, resilient woman, Catherine Carlyle."

She smiled and batted her naked eyelashes at him. "And you are an amazingly astute man, Tom Sullivan."

He caught his breath as he beamed at her. "I believe that's the first time you have ever said my name."

The huge grin on his face said it all. He moved closer to her bed and leaned his face down to hers. Gently, he brushed his lips on her cheek and then stood back to examine her reaction. She had closed her eyes when he moved closer. She expected to feel his lips on hers. When she felt them on her cheek instead, she was embarrassed.

Seeing her cheeks redden made him almost laugh. He loved to tease her. He placed a rough hand under her chin and lifted it gently towards him. She didn't lift her eyes to his until his face was inches from hers.

"You are beautiful, do you know that?" he asked with a husky voice.

Her whole face was ablaze now. Her hazel eyes widened as he put both of his hands on either side of her slender face and pressed his lips to hers. Her mouth was so sweet, he realized. He parted his lips and breathed in through his mouth. Then he took her lips again, his warm, gentle mouth welded to hers in a kiss that Cat thought could put her into cardiac arrest. She could kiss this man for the rest of her life. He broke the kiss by pulling away. Then he moved the bedside table that she had in front of her. It held her coffee cup, notebook and pen. He pushed the button on the remote to lower her bed. Then he took her casted arm and laid it gently by her side. Pulling the covers over her body, he tucked the blanket around her shoulders and down her arms so that he tucked the blanket completely around her.

"I'm going to have the nurse come and give you some pain medicine. Then I want you to go back to sleep. After you have had some rest, we'll discuss this plan of yours some more."

Before he moved away she stopped him with a warning. "Sullivan, don't you ever kiss me like that again unless you really mean it."

She waited for a response, but he didn't say anything. He just leaned over and kissed her again, this time with more passion than she had ever felt. No one had ever kissed her like that, no one. She snuck her good arm out of the blankets and shot it around his neck, pulling him closer. Her heart monitor was beeping wildly when the nurse walked in.

"What is going on in here?" She demanded. "Excuse me, Sir, you need to leave. You are disturbing the patient." Sullivan took a step away, his fingers immediately going up to cover his mouth as if he could hold her kiss there forever.

"I'd say he is disturbing the patient," Cat murmured as a sly smile crept onto her face.

She turned smiling eyes to Sullivan who backed away slowly from her bed as the nurse began checking her vitals and clearing the alarm on the monitor above Cat's bed.

"Go on, get out," the nurse demanded of Sullivan.

He waived a goodbye to Cat, blew her a kiss and slipped out the door.

Cat spent the next three days in and out of sleep. While she recuperated, Linda and Phillip took turns staying with her. Sullivan, Bronson and their homicide team searched for Warren and Rick, both of whom had virtually disappeared without a trace. It was unclear if they were partners, but one thing was solid in Sullivan's mind: one or both of them was a rapist and a murderer. Sullivan was going to catch them, dead or alive.

Linda was reading a book when Cat woke up. She put her bookmark between the pages and laid the book down. Standing up, she touched Cat's shoulder.

"Hi, Honey, how are you feeling?"

Cat looked around the room groggily, "I'm really thirsty."

Linda handed her a cup with a straw and held it to her dry lips. Cat drank and drank and finally withdrew her lips and let her head fall back against the pillow.

"What time is it?" Cat asked. She looked around the room as if she would see a clock somewhere she had never seen one before. "How long have I been out?"

Linda rested her hand on Cat's forearm and leaned over her trying to get a good look at Cat's eyes. They appeared distant and wobbly.

"Are you hurting anywhere?" Linda asked as she looked Cat over.

Cat's bruises, which had been bright blue, were beginning to fade to purple. The damaged skin continued to heal, but with the daily iodine scrubbings, she couldn't imagine how the skin was ever going to heal properly. Linda looked at Cat's wounds and winced. It hurt deep inside her womb to see her own flesh and blood in so much pain. She held her hand over her own abdomen and rested the other across Cat's brow. She felt hot, Linda thought.

"Please ask Sullivan to come back in now," Cat pleaded. She tried to shift her weight in the bed to sit up, but the pain sucked the air out of her, causing her to freeze in place. "Is he still here?" Cat's red eyes were watery and swollen as she scanned the room.

"No, Honey, he hasn't been here today. You have been pretty much out of it for the last three days. I told him I would call him when you woke up."

Sullivan smiled at her as he entered the room. He brushed her cheek with the back of his hand and said something about how good she looked considering all she had been through. He told Linda he would sit with her for awhile if she needed to go home and get some rest. Linda refused, but did excuse herself from the room so the two of them could talk. When the door closed behind her, Sullivan looked down at Cat. His eyes filled with concern as he saw tears form in her eyes and threaten to pour out over her lashes.

"What is it? Why are you crying?" he asked quickly, he leaned down to hear her response.

"Please don't let him get me. He's here! He's going to kill me."

Fury raged in his heart, he laid a strong hand on hers and spoke gently.

"No, he isn't going to get you. I promise."

Her eyes still looked terrified. The pain or the pain medicine was to blame he guessed. The pupils of her eyes were so large that the irises of her eyes were barely visible. He watched as her eyes darted around the room in fear. He placed a hand on her forehead and realized she was burning up. He pushed the call button for the nurse and waited for her to arrive.

"You again, why am I not surprised?"

As fate would have it, the same nurse was on duty that had sent him packing on his last visit. Without acknowledging what she said he told her that Cat had a fever and maybe was having hallucinations. To be certain and to see how high it was, the nurse retrieved a digital thermometer and ran it across Cat's forehead, down her temple to her ear.

She adjusted her IV drip and gave her some pain medication in her catheter. She told Sullivan to stay with Cat until the doctor came. When Linda returned a few minutes later carrying cups of coffee, she was alarmed to see the nurse, the doctor and Sullivan circling Cat's bed.

"What's wrong. What's happened?" Linda said hurriedly.

Sullivan explained that the doctor had ordered a CT scan fearing Cat's brain may be swelling.

As the nurse and an orderly wheeled Cat from the room, Linda and Sullivan were left to hope and pray for the best.

Chapter 30

It had been the longest three weeks of his life, Sullivan told Bronson. He had spent many hours at the hospital and had gotten to know Linda and Phillip better as the three of them, and occasionally Susan, took turns staying with Cat. Besides the constant police protection, Cat had never been left alone a single minute. Bronson looked at his friend and partner with concern and voiced what the two of them had avoided mentioning the last few days.

"They aren't going to come out of hiding until she is where they can access her. You know that, right?"

"Don't go there," Sullivan said, holding a hand up like a stop sign.

"If we can't find them, they can't be found. Maybe they killed each other. That would save us a lot of trouble." Sullivan said as he nervously tapped his fingers on his desk.

"You know that would be too easy," Bronson replied. He exhaled and plopped down hard into his office chair. He spun it around and lifted his feet so that he twirled in a tight circle like a sitting ballerina. His eyes were still spinning as Sullivan stopped the chair mid-spin with a large boot.

"Knock it off. You're making me dizzy."

Bronson laughed and stood up. He staggered to the fridge where he opened the door and stuck his head all the way

inside. He pulled out two cold cans of soda and tossed
Sullivan a can without warning. He was rewarded with a few
colorful words about Bronson's mother to which Bronson
just laughed, opened his drink and guzzled most of it in one
long noisy swallow. Sullivan set his unopened can on his
desk and frowned at his partner.

"Relax a little, Sully," Bronson said. He placed a hip on
Sullivan's desk and loosened his neck tie. "Okay, here is my
theory. Tell me what you think."

Bronson outlined how he believed it was a coincidence
that Rick and Warren came to work together. How they both
had a weakness for alcohol and or drugs or both and how one
or both of them enjoyed hurting women. He couldn't decide
which was the killer, but thought that both could easily have
done it. He paused, giving Sullivan time to absorb what he
had said and to reply.

Sullivan thought about it. He agreed with Bronson's
theory and reminded him about what Cat had said about the
reports of rapes and how she had taken the self-defense
classes. Then he reminded Bronson of what she had said
about the necklace that Warren had given her and how he
wanted it back. He mentioned how Cat had lost her favorite
bracelet the night of the murder, how he thought the
murderer returned to the scene, slashed Cat's tires and had
possibly found the bracelet that their team somehow had
missed. He recalled the radio caller that mentioned the
bracelet to Cat and how the call was traced back to Cat's
residence. Maybe what the killer was searching for at her

apartment was the necklace. Maybe it was something else, something she didn't even know she had.

"I'm going to check with Miriam again today and see how her memory is coming along. The doctor said she might wake up one day and remember everything that happened and who attacked her," said Sullivan.

It had been a few days since he had last spoken to her. Maybe she could recall something now. Anything would help. All they needed was a small break. He was thinking they just needed one tiny thing to go their way for a change when the phone rang. Answering the phone he said, "Homicide," then paused. It was a lieutenant from the sex crimes unit. He told Sullivan he needed Sullivan's team to respond to a report of a nude female body that had been found in a shallow grave near the Oklahoma River.

The next several hours were spent at the crime scene, followed by a couple of hours at the morgue, where they waited for the preliminary report. The medical examiner looked over his glasses at Sullivan and Bronson. His bushy white eyebrows shadowed his light blue watery eyes; he rubbed them as he spoke.

"Your victim was sexually assaulted and then strangled to death with a thin rope or chain," he said. "As usual, it will be awhile before we get the toxicology results back on the blood."

"Thanks, Doc'," Sullivan said, patting him on the shoulder. "We'll be in touch."

Bronson followed Sullivan as they exited the building and walked outside into the bright sunshine. Sullivan told himself there wasn't any way to prevent what had happened to the latest victim, Jillian Warlick. Anger had him balling his fists, he wished for something to punch. He squinted as he slid his sunglasses on his face. Sullivan waited until they were back inside the patrol car before he reminded Bronson about the young prostitute who claimed to be Warren Garrison's girlfriend and alibi for the night of the Diaz murder.

She had given her name as Jill, when they questioned her. She hadn't showed up for her polygraph as promised and when they went looking for her they were told that she had moved out of her apartment and hadn't left a forwarding address. Warren claimed Jill was upset with him because he had broken up with her, he suggested she had returned to Colorado where she had family.

Sullivan and Bronson had hoped for a different outcome, but they knew this would be her fate if she had been lying for Warren Garrison. They were fairly certain he was their guy. They had to find him and soon.

****

Over a cold beer in a downtown pub, the two voiced their opinions, doubts and discussed what their next steps should be.

"I'm meeting with Miriam tomorrow," Sullivan said. "Do you want to come along?" He asked Bronson.

"Sure, my youngest has a doctor's appointment at two o'clock, but we can go earlier," said Bronson. "I'd like to be there when she points the finger at our man. Care to make a friendly wager on who her attacker was?"

"Nope," Sullivan said, as he finished off his ale and threw a crisp bill on the bar. "I don't want to take your money. Besides, you'll need all the cash you can get if you keep making them babies."

They laughed as Bronson elbowed Sullivan, nearly knocking him off his barstool.

"You're just jealous, Sully."

Sullivan laughed, but secretly admitted he was jealous. He wanted what Bronson had and he wanted it with Cat.

The next day as he and Bronson stood beside Miriam's bedside, she struggled with their names, asking them several times who they were and why they were there.

Sullivan was growing frustrated and was about to suggest that they leave when Bronson held his cell phone up where Miriam could see the tiny screen. "Look at this, Miss Miriam. Do you recognize this young lady?" He asked.

He showed her a photo of Cat. She looked beautiful in the photograph and as soon as Miriam saw it, she clapped her hands together in front of her mouth.

"That's Cat! Something terrible happened to her, didn't it? I knew something bad was happening in her apartment. I knew I should have just called the police," she said.

Miriam struggled with her breathing, she was beginning to hyperventilate. Sullivan put his hand on her shoulder and motioned for Bronson to get the nurse. Sullivan tried to calm Miriam, reminding her to breathe. Miriam looked into his eyes. Through her tears he saw her fear and pain, it knotted up his stomach.

"I called Cat that day," Miriam said. "I wanted to see if she would answer the phone. Afterward, when someone knocked on my door, I just knew it was her. I didn't even look out the security hole. I just yanked the door open, and there he stood. The look on his ugly face told me all I needed to know." Miriam said as she put her hands on either side of her head, covering her ears.

"Who was it Miriam? Who came to your door? Do you remember his name? Sullivan asked excitedly.

He could feel his knees shaking. Their mystery was over. Rocking back and forth, still covering her ears, Miriam began to hum. Sullivan prodded her to continue, but she didn't. She just rocked back and forth, back and forth. Finally she looked up at him with innocent, wondering eyes and asked, "I'm sorry, but who are you again?" Sullivan didn't respond. He knew it was futile.

Bronson reentered the room with the nurse as Miriam sighed, exhausted from the conversation.

"Tell us his name, and we'll let you rest," Sullivan pleaded, he hated to admit defeat.

"His name?" Miriam asked, confused. She tilted her head back and her mind wandered off again.

"Do you know his name, Miriam?" Sullivan asked wearily. He leaned closer to her trying to get her to stay focused.

"Of course, I remember his name, it was Robert Archie Martin. He and I were married for sixty-two years. Sixty-two years." She said again then she began to cry softly.

It was over. Both Sullivan and Bronson knew it. They said goodbye and walked silently through the halls of the rehabilitation hospital. She was doing so much better, but she still had been unable to help them determine who had ransacked Cat's apartment and then beat, stabbed and nearly killed her and left her for dead. It was depressing, Sullivan thought. He slid his hands in his pants pockets and hunched his shoulders as if a huge weight were resting on his back. He felt so weary.

"One of these days she'll wake up completely," Bronson said. "She'll remember everything. You'll see," Bronson encouraged him. But Sullivan didn't speak. He had nothing left in him today.

Bronson pushed the down button for the elevator and didn't say anything else for several minutes. They rode down in silence and were nearly all the way to Sullivan's patrol car when a light bulb inside Sullivan's head flipped on.

"When Cat is able to come and visit Miriam, she'll tell Cat who it was," Sullivan said. "We already know it was either Rick or Warren. Hey, by the way, why didn't you have a picture of those two on your phone to show the old lady?" Sullivan asked, turning toward Bronson. His five o'clock shadow accentuated the cleft in his chin as he frowned. He stopped to stare at Bronson who only fidgeted with his tie and looked uncomfortable.

Bronson didn't want to admit that he had taken Cat's picture at the radio station when they interviewed her for the first time. He had hopes of torturing Sullivan at some point with her photo, but now it just seemed creepy and hard to explain, so he quickly changed the subject.

"Showing Miriam pictures of Warren and Rick is a great idea. I don't know why I didn't think of it. I guess that's why you're in charge, huh?" Bronson asked. He slapped Sullivan on the back as they walked through the parking lot toward the patrol car.

Whatever Bronson's excuse was for the photo of Cat, it didn't matter, Sullivan thought. *It was probably just to needle me anyway.*

Chapter 31

Cat slowly walked up the sidewalk to her parents' house with the assistance of a fancy wooden cane. Her mother had purchased it few days before Cat was release from the hospital. She glanced down at it now, marveling at the intricate carvings and clear glossy finish. Her physical therapist had said Cat would have to perfect walking with the cane before the doctor would release her to go home.

Besides the brain swelling scare, there had been a couple of set-backs with her therapy, but Cat had worked hard to get better. Her will and determination made her a pleasant patient and her physical therapist coached her as she mastered walking with the use of the cane. When she walked out of the hospital, she told her mom and dad that she felt like she was getting released from prison.

Cat's friends and family had worked together and moved Cat out of her apartment while she was recovering. They put most of her stuff in storage. The rest of her belongings were moved back to her old bedroom at her parents' house. It was decided that she would live with them until she was able to take care of herself again. Even though she admitted to Susan she was dreading living with her parents again, Cat knew she didn't have any other choice for the time being. She needed them.

The next few weeks were spent in daily physical therapy sessions, doctor's visits and resting. She was getting stronger everyday and feeling more like herself.

"I'm going to take a walk by myself," she said as she emerged from her bedroom one morning. Her parents, still clad in pajamas were sitting around the kitchen table, drinking coffee and reading the morning newspaper.

"A walk? Really?" Linda asked surprised, looking over at Phillip. "Are you sure you are feeling up to it?" Linda asked.

"Just wait a few minutes and I'll go with you. Or Mom will," Phillip said as he sipped his coffee. "Why don't you sit down and have a cup of coffee first."

Shaking her head no, she raised her hands to indicate they should remain seated.

"Nope. You two sit right there. I am going alone, and I am not even taking this nasty old thing." She took her trusty cane and hung it on the door knob to the pantry.

Phillip and Linda looked at each other then back to their daughter. They started arguing with her about what she should and shouldn't do, but were met with a wave and a smile. Cat had made up her mind and she would not be stopped. She shut the front door behind her and stood on the porch. She slid her sunglasses up the bridge of her nose and, without moving her head, used her eyes to scan the street. The plan she had decided upon could not wait any longer. She knew the only way to catch the killer was to make herself available to him. She was what he wanted. He had told her so himself.

Betsy Randolph

She walked slowly down the front path, limping every step of the way. A soft north wind played with her auburn hair that fell loose on her shoulders. She studied the flowers her mother lovingly tended and inhaled the earthy scent of the cool fall morning. The early December temperatures hadn't affected the blooms of the maroon pansies or cheery yellow chrysanthemums. Their happy faces welcomed her to the garden, encouraging her to feel better, stronger, more sure. When she reached the driveway she paused, slowly walked down the driveway to the edge of the street then stopped as if she were winded. She spotted the parked car at the corner. Her heart began to race. She knew it was him, so she bent at the waist and rested her hands on her knees. She pretended to breathe heavily before holding her ribs as if they hurt.

Slowly she stood while stretching her back. She glanced at her wrist watch to note the time then limped her way back up the driveway and up the front path. She was smiling as she stepped through the front door of her parent's house. She leaned heavily against the large wooden door, looked at her watch again and breathed normally for the first time in exactly seventeen minutes.

It was going to work. Her plan was going to work!

She wanted to scream, to tell someone it was going to work, but she knew she couldn't. Everyone said it was entirely too dangerous. So she walked to her room, pulled a brown notebook out from under her pillow and flipped through the pages to where a paper-thin, wooden bookmark held her place. She wrote down the date, the time and the vehicle description she believed the killer drove. Then she replaced the notebook and slipped her shoes off. She lifted her right shoe and examined the long metal blade that she had secretly placed under her orthotics inside her shoe.

"You will come in handy someday, friend," she promised the blade then slid the shoes under her bed.

The afternoon passed quickly as she helped her mom clean house and got caught up on some reading. It was nearly five o'clock in the afternoon when she closed the bathroom door behind her. She locked the door before undressing. She would never feel totally safe again, no matter where she was she thought as she unholstered her pistol. It was a .380 she had strapped to her ankle. It had been with her since Sullivan slipped it to her at the hospital. She was never without it.

She folded her clothes and laid them on top of the pistol on the edge of the bathtub. While the water ran in the tub, Cat lay face down on the floor and pressed her palms to the cool tile. She began pushing her rigid body up, extending her elbows and then slowly bending her elbows and lowering her body to the floor again. Only her hands and toes were touching the floor. Up and down, up and down. She performed forty pushups while the tub filled with hot water. She turned the water off and then lay on her back on the floor and did as many tummy crunches as she could.

"I'll be ready next time," she proclaimed as she stood and looked at her well toned body in the mirror. "He'll be sorry he didn't finish me off when he had the chance."

She combed through her hair. It had grown several inches since her last trim. She admired her natural hair color and wondered why she had ever bleached it blonde. Sullivan said he loved her hair either way. She smiled at herself in the mirror as she imagined him running his fingers through her thick hair. She had been daydreaming about Sullivan when she suddenly remembered that they had dinner plans together. She needed to get moving. She slipped into the tub and let herself sink beneath the steaming water. It caressed her skin and rejuvenated her mind.

After dressing, reattaching her hardware and applying some light makeup, Cat followed her nose to the kitchen where her mom was making chicken parmesan. Linda was stirring her prized homemade marinara sauce and sprinkling in more oregano. Cat peered into the oven window at the chicken beginning to bake. "Wow! That smells great! Maybe we should stay and eat with you guys."

Linda turned and looked at Cat with shining eyes. "You're welcome to stay. Your dad and I would enjoy visiting with Tom. I've made plenty," Linda said as she opened the canister with the dry pasta inside. She began measuring out enough pasta for four people.

Immediately Cat was sorry for having suggested it. She began back-pedaling when Phillip walked in. Linda told him she had invited Cat and Tom to eat with them. Phillip agreed, he'd wanted to visit with Detective Sullivan and check up on the investigation.

"Why don't you call Tom and ask him to cancel your dinner reservations? We'd love for you both to spend some time with us here tonight," Phillip suggested as he swung an arm around Cat's thin, but muscular shoulder. Looking at her dad's face, she could tell he was really sincere. They were still worried about her, she thought.

She was looking forward to having Sullivan all to herself, but it wouldn't hurt to ask him what he thought about her parent's idea. So she went into the living room to place the call. When Sullivan answered his cell phone, his happy voice tickled her ear. He seemed genuinely pleased by the invitation. He smiled at the idea of being invited to eat with Cat's family. He stopped on his way to buy both ladies a fresh spray of flowers.

He was singing with the radio as he pulled onto the Carlyle's street. But the song died on his lips along with his light-hearted mood when he spotted a maroon car parked against the curb a few houses down. The house was up for sale and had been empty for several months. He knew because he driven past the Carlyle's house numerous times in the past few months.

His cop instincts told him to be wary, almost as if he heard a little voice telling him what to do. He started to go on past Phillip and Linda's house and drive straight to the maroon car, but he was off duty and in his own personal car. He had to force himself to remember that he wasn't on duty. Besides, he assured himself, he was being paranoid. If the car was still there after dinner, he would investigate it then. For now, he wasn't Detective Sullivan, he was Tom, and he was hungry.

He forced himself to avoid looking at the maroon car as he parked, got out and carried two bouquets of fresh flowers to the front door. Cat opened the door. He thought she had never looked more beautiful than she did right then.

She had piled her hair high on her head allowing little pieces of it to fall freely around her face and neck. Her cheeks were pink, but it didn't look like makeup to him. She hardly had any on. He did notice that her lashes had been lightly touched with mascara, and little gold flecks of glitter lay on her eyelids. He wanted to kiss each little sparkle as she closed her eyes and stuck her perfect little button-shaped nose in the roses he presented to her. He couldn't think of anything to say but, "Wow!" It made her laugh.

"Thank you, their beautiful!" Cat exclaimed.

He gave her a little hug as she pulled him in the open door. She caught a whiff of his masculine cologne mixed with soap and flowers as her cheek met his chest. She felt light-headed just being close to him. When Sullivan presented Linda with her bouquet, she nearly cried.

"Phillip hasn't brought me flowers since he crashed my car, ten years ago," she told him.

Her glance at Phillip said he was overdue.

"Sorry," Sullivan mouthed to Phillip, who waved off the complaint and motioned for Sullivan to join him in the other room as the women finished the last of the dinner preparations.

"How's the investigation coming?" Phillip asked once they were alone.

He nervously looked over his shoulder. It was obvious to Sullivan that Phillip didn't want to discuss the investigation in front of the women.

"Unfortunately," Sullivan hesitated.

He hated to tell Phillip of Jill Warlick's fate, but it was only a matter of time before he found out. So he told him about the discovery of her body and what they supposed had happened to her and by whom. He told Phillip about Rick Hurley being fired from the radio station when he didn't show up for work for three straight days. Sullivan admitted that it was a bad sign. Either Rick was the killer or he had fallen victim to the killer.

Every law enforcement agency in the state was looking for Rick and Warren. They would eventually be caught. When Cat called the men to dinner, no further discussions of the case was mentioned and the evening passed as casually as if Sullivan were an old family friend. Sullivan seemed to enjoy himself and interacted with Linda and Phillip easily. Cat decided she could get used to having Sullivan around more, she thought with a smile. After dinner, the men washed the dishes, per the Carlyle custom, and the women sat at the kitchen table drinking coffee and whispering about the men.

"Is there anything sexier than a man washing dishes?" Cat asked her mother in hushed tones. She nearly died laughing at her mother's reply.

"The only thing sexier is watching a man change a baby's diaper."

Sullivan and Phillip were beginning to feel self-conscious about being whispered about.

"Okay, enough magpies. Out of the kitchen," Phillip demanded.

He shooed Cat and Linda out of the kitchen with a dish towel, which only made the ladies laugh harder. He and Sullivan were nearly done anyway, but he had one more question for Sullivan and this presented a good excuse to get the girls out of earshot.

"Let me ask you one more thing. Did you ever find out from Miriam who her attacker was?" Phillip asked.

Sullivan took a deep breath and exhaled. He shook his head no. He explained what happened when they went to see Miriam at the rehabilitation hospital. He told Phillip that when Bronson took the pictures of Warren and Rick back for Miriam to see, she became hysterical. Bronson couldn't get her to say which one of the men had tried to kill her before one of the nurses asked him to leave. It felt like a lost cause, Sullivan told him, but he encouraged Phillip to take Cat back to see Miriam sometime. Maybe Cat could jog her memory, he suggested. With a quick glance at his watch, Sullivan decided it was time to go. He thanked the Carlyle's for dinner and walked out to his car with Cat. She was desperate to touch him, but forced herself not to make the first move. She saw the car parked down the street so she limped a little as they walked and pulled her sweater tighter around her.

Sullivan pretended not to see the parked car. Instead, he focused all his attention on the hazel-eyed beauty that smelled like warm vanilla and roses. He felt intoxicated being near her.

"Thank you for dinner," Sullivan said, his voice low and sultry. "I can tell your leg is hurting, so I won't keep you." He casually leaned his back against his car door and took Cat's hand in his. He pressed his warm lips to her cold knuckles.

"Thank you for the beautiful flowers, Tom." she replied.

The urge to pull him to her was so great it made her heart ache. It took all the restraint she had not to attack his lips. Her eyes looked at his mouth before meeting his eyes. She could see a smile forming on them.

"I really like you," she finally ventured. "I'd like you to come for dinner again soon."

Smiling he nodded his head and said, "I'll be waiting for the invitation."

He opened his car door, took another look at Cat and smiled again. "I really like you, too," he said at last, then slid behind the wheel and started the engine.

He drove away with her scent all around him. He would dream about her sweet face tonight he thought as he circled the block to come up behind the maroon car that sat parked on her street. But the car was gone. He punched the steering wheel and swore. He wanted the tag number or a closer look at the car and its driver.

Cat watched from a darkened window in the library as Sullivan pulled away. Less than thirty seconds after he disappeared from view, the maroon car followed him. She thought about calling or texting him, to see if the car was an unmarked police cruiser, but changed her mind. She didn't want him to worry and she didn't trust her feelings enough to hear his voice again so soon. There was something about Thomas Sullivan that had her heart and imagination working overtime.

Chapter 32

Vivid, horrible dreams woke her in the night. After several attempts to go back to sleep, she finally gave up, picked up her current book from beside her bed and began reading.

She loved mystery novels. She wondered if she could pen a novel herself about all that she had recently been through. She laid the book on her chest and visualized her novel. The next thing she knew the sunlight was sneaking past the blinds and making vertical circles on the wall.

After her morning rituals, Cat headed out the door to visit Miriam. She was planning on going to the radio station for a few hours after seeing Miriam. The cold air greeted her as she stepped outside and trudged to her car. The bitter cold seeped under her coat seam and crawled up her back.

She had only driven her car a couple of times since the accident, but she looked forward to being in control of one aspect of her life again. She fired up the engine and backed slowly out of the drive. She saw a blue minivan at the end of the street and tried to quell the nagging fear that every unfamiliar car held the killer. She was so focused on the minivan that she didn't notice the guy dressed in black leathers riding the motorcycle. He followed her through the neighborhood and out onto the two-lane road.

Miriam was tickled to see Cat. She talked non-stop about all that she had been doing.

"That's wonderful," Cat exclaimed, as she watched Miriam lift five-pound weights.

Miriam curled her arms and pumped the little barbells up and down. Cat clapped, making a grand gesture of congratulating Miriam. Cat knew it was an accomplishment since she had been through weeks of rehabilitation herself.

"Can you remember anything about the attack?" Cat asked her abruptly when Miriam finally replaced the weights on the weight rack.

A deep frown perched on Miriam's lips, and she looked around the room as if her attacker might be close by. She shook her head no finally and sat down next to Cat on a short bench.

"I know it was that fella you introduced me to, but I can't remember his name," Miriam hesitated. "He is evil. I guess you know that, now."

Cat slipped her arm around Miriam's shoulders and squeezed her.

"I am so sorry he hurt you, Miriam. Was it Warren? Is he the one that hurt you?"

Cat looked into Miriam's clouded eyes. She looked confused. She finally shook her head no.

"It wasn't Warren. I'm sure of that. But I just can't remember his name right now."

Before Cat could ask any further questions, Miriam picked up the magazine that Cat had brought her and pointed to a photo on the cover.

"You see that quilt? I'm going to make you that quilt, Emily," Miriam said looking at Cat earnestly.

Cat hugged her while a tear slid down Cat's cheek. Emily was Miriam's daughter that had been killed at the age of four. Cat knew then that Miriam would never be the same.

"I looked forward to seeing your progress on the quilt," Cat whispered.

She left the hospital feeling downhearted and phoned Sullivan to tell him what she had learned from Miriam.

"Homicide." Bronson's voice barked into the phone.

He rested the receiver on his shoulder and leaned his ear against it to pin it in place. Cat told Bronson why she was calling after Bronson told her that Sullivan was in a meeting.

"I don't know if it was Warren or not. Miriam seemed so confused one minute and then really clear-minded the next," Cat admitted as she sat at a red light nervously drumming her fingers on the steering wheel. That's when she realized she had forgotten her silver bracelet. A frown crossed her mouth as she listened to Bronson talk. She hated to be so forgetful.

Bronson mentioned what had happened when he and Sullivan paid Miriam a visit. He said he would advise Sullivan that Cat had called. Two stop lights later the phone rang and she hurried to answer the call, hoping it was Sullivan.

"Hey, Baby," a sinister voice said into her ear. "I've been missing you."

His voice shredded her nerves, constricting her heart. She felt the first signs of perspiration begin to seep out of her pores. It took a second or longer for her voice to work. When it did, she wondered how she sounded so calm and sure.

"Really?" she asked. "Funny thing is, I've been missing you too," she lied. "When am I going to see you again so I can thank you properly for these nice scars I have?" she asked through her teeth.

She gripped the steering wheel hard as she thought about poking her fingers through his eye sockets.

"Tell you what, kitty cat. I'll surprise you sometime soon, so you can thank me in person." Then he disconnected the call.

She was so furious that she nearly ran the red traffic light in front of her. She steadied her nerves by calmly closing her cell phone and laying it in the center console. She patted her pistol, promising to empty it into him on their next meeting.

"He will be sorry he messed with me," she promised herself as she gunned the accelerator when the light turned green. She sped across town and pulled in front of her dad's radio station still angry from the phone call.

She was thinking of all the torturous things she would like to do to the caller when she walked into the station. She didn't realize how the adrenaline had caused her eyes to turn hazel-golden with fury. Even her eyebrows were arched as if in battle mode. When her dad saw her, he was alarmed.

"What's happened?" he asked as he got up from behind his large antique desk and approached her.

His face was filled with concern and his own eyes had grown large with dread. He couldn't remember ever seeing Cat look the way she did just then. With his hands still on

266

her arms, he pulled her towards him in a rough embrace. She felt stiff and cold in his arms. When she didn't answer he pushed her back enough to stare into her eyes. His face was ashen she realized. Grudgingly she told him about the phone call, but made him promise not to tell her mother. She rationalized that it would only make her mother more nervous and upset every time Cat tried to leave the house. She should have known that her father felt the very same way.

They tried going on about their business the rest of the day, but the dark cloud of fear hung over them both. Around four o'clock they gave up pretending that everything was fine and walked to a coffee shop about a block away.

"It's expensive, but that is a delicious cup of coffee. Thank you," Cat said as she tipped her cup to her lips again.

She continued sipping the dark, motivating liquid. She rolled her shoulders to the front, then to the back, and then bent her head to each shoulder as she stretched her tense muscles. She rubbed her neck as she looked at her dad. He looked as stressed as she felt.

"I remembered something about the murder last night," she began. "Would you care to hear it?" She asked.

"Sure, what was it?" he said and laid a large familiar hand on top of hers on the table.

"I remember screaming and someone coming to me. I thought it was a stranger, but I remembered last night that it was Warren. He picked me up off the ground after I saw that guy stabbed. I thought for a second that he had come to help me. Then he spun me towards him and slapped his hand over my mouth. He dug around my neck with his fingers like he was searching for something. I didn't realize what he was doing at the time," she said as she looked around her cautiously before she continued. "He was searching for this."

She held the silver necklace out for Phillip to see. "Warren gave this to me when we first started dating. It doesn't look expensive, but when I broke up with him he asked for it back. I refused."

Phillip inspected the necklace and shrugged his shoulders.

"Why did he want it back?" Phillip asked.

"I have no idea. Sentimental reasons, I suppose. It made him furious when I would not return it. He started threatening me shortly after."

Phillip suggested that she call Sullivan right away. Cat told him that she would and that she had planned on telling him about today's phone call anyway. They sat in silence for a few more moments, each lost in their own thoughts. When their cups were empty and their nerves a little more calm, they agreed it was time to head home.

As they walked back to the radio station Cat's phone rang. She stopped dead in her tracks when Miriam's charge nurse told her how sorry she was. Cat's eyes wandered to her father. He watched as nearly all the color drained from Cat's face. She squeezed her eyes shut and said no over and over as the nurse told her that no one had anticipated Miriam's sudden passing.

"That just can't be," Cat pleaded with the nurse. "I was just there. I was just with her. She was fine."

The nurse assured her that she had died peacefully, "She must have died in her sleep," the nurse said gently.

"You're not listening to what I'm saying. I was just there an hour or so ago and she was fine." Cat screamed.

She was shaking, Phillip realized, as he put a hand on her shoulder. He guided her back to the station. Cat handed him the phone and stumbled toward her car. She had to get out of there. She needed to see Miriam's body with her own eyes. Phillip got the information about where Miriam's body had been taken and stood debating with Cat about him driving her home for several minutes before he finally gave up. She would go see Miriam alone.

He watched Cat in his rear view mirror. He saw her slide behind the wheel of her Ford as he rounded the corner and headed for home. He immediately called Linda and began telling her what had happened. He asked if Sullivan could come to dinner. He would force Cat to tell Sullivan what had happened and what she had remembered about Warren. Linda agreed. She would call Sullivan herself and see if he were free for dinner.

Cat sat in her car for several minutes without moving. Rage, fear and disbelief took turns stomping on her heart. When she finally inserted the key into the ignition she had made up her mind. *Miriam hadn't just died in her sleep. He must have gotten to her. He must have killed her. But why?* Miriam couldn't remember anything. She didn't know who had attacked her or why.

Betsy Randolph

Cat punched the steering wheel until her hand hurt, then she turned her anger on the ceiling of her car, punching and screaming obscenities until her rage subsided.

Tears finally replaced the anger. She sat for a long time crying. Uncontrolled sobs shook her body until she was spent. She laid her head against the driver's side window, an occasional whimper escaping her lips. The tears were gone, but an immense sadness and hurt had taken its place.

She put her hand on the key in the ignition, but just before turning the engine over, she paused. Something wasn't right – she could feel it. It was him. He was close – she knew it. Every hair on her body felt electrified. Without a single thought for her safety, she got out of the car and ran back to the station. Quickly she unlocked the door and went in. Purposely leaving the front door of the business unlocked, she made her way by feel into the back office that was pitch black. She waited until her eyes adjusted to the dark before pulling the pistol out of the ankle holster. She steadied herself for the possibility of what lay ahead and she waited.

Chapter 33

The hairs on his arm stood rigidly at attention. He could smell her. The fear that emanated from her body was like a calling card. He had watched her from the alley across the street. He laughed while she cried. He nearly cried with pleasure watching her lose it because he had smothered the life out Miriam. He felt powerful. It was thrilling to know he had caused her such pain. There would be more pain before the night was over.

He watched her run back into the building. He wondered what she was up to. When she didn't lock the door and she didn't come back out, his hands began to sweat. A single idea danced in his brain. He could take her here! That would be exquisite.

Before he could talk himself out of it, he sprinted across the street to the radio station.

He pulled the glass door open and waited for the chime to announce his presence. When he walked into the front office, he knew she knew he was there, so he dispensed of any pretense to hide.

"Here, kitty, kitty," he began calling as he walked through the building. He made his voice high pitched as he scratched the walls with his finger nails.

His steps were light, his thoughts jumbled as his mind whirled with evil ways to make Cat suffer. His shoes squeaked as he walked through the offices with a large knife clutched in his hand. Every few seconds he called out to her. Each time she heard, "Here, kitty-kitty," sickening nausea, like fingers - stuck in her throat. Her original plan was to lure him inside, hide and call Sullivan. She thought she was prepared for this. She thought she could take him on her own. But fear slapped at her brain. Its fierceness grew exponentially with each sinister word that he spoke.

She cowered behind a nearby desk with a pistol in one hand and her cell phone in the other, suddenly forgetting how to use both.

Tonight would be the last night she mocked him, he thought, as he crept from room to room. His eyes worked hard to adjust to the darkness. He scanned methodically while he continued to torture her mind.

"Here, kitty-kitty. Come out, come out wherever you are."

He planned to carry her back to the wooden shed behind his house. Only special girls got to see it. She would be pleased to know that she'd be the first to use the small second-hand cot he had recently added for her comfort. It's not like he was a monster or anything, he thought, with a wicked smile. He could hardly wait to hear her scream, to watch her suffer and plead for her life – it was exhilarating just thinking of it.

Cat knew she had waited too long to use her cell phone. She saw a tiny gleam of light reflecting off the large blade he held in his hand. Before she realized it, her shaky hand raised the pistol and pointed it up at him.

He intended to spend some quality time with Cat; hours, if not days, teaching her to respect him. That's what every female needed to learn: respect. His plans were changed instantly when he felt a burning sensation in his right shoulder. The sound of the gunshot seemed to stun his senses for a moment. He was trying to figure out what had just happened when he heard another pop. The second shot spun him completely around. He dropped to the ground face first.

Cat held the pistol in both of her trembling hands. She got up slowly and walked closer to the crumpled form bleeding on the carpet. Head to toe, he was dressed in all black. She didn't recognize him until she nudged him with her foot and saw his face. That's when she saw his sharp profile. The thick brow, the stellar nose, the square jaw: it was Warren Garrison.

She circled his body, walking carefully around his head and stooped to pick up her cell phone which she had dropped during the shooting. She pushed the number 9, but that was as far as she got.

Warren lashed out like an injured tiger with the knife he still held in his hand. It sliced a nasty gash in Cat's calf. Her scream pierced the air as she grabbed for her injured leg and stumbled a few steps. Warren wrapped his arms around her ankles, pulling her to the floor with a thud. Losing her balance, she dropped the gun before she fell on top of him. Struggling to break free of his grasp, she thrashed and kicked. After several unsuccessful attempts, she managed to knock the knife from his hand, but he held tight to her legs with vice-like claws. They rolled together on the floor, tumbling into a wooden desk, the wall, and several chairs while each tried to yank fists full of hair from the other's head. She clawed at his eyes with her nails, gouging his cheek in the process.

With every scream, his grip grew tighter. With ever scratch or punch, he laughed. He wrestled her over onto her back and pinned her arms down to the ground, then straddled her. Blood dripped off his wounded chest and on to her moist cheek as he yelled for her to stop fighting. But she didn't. She couldn't. She fought like a wild beast, bucking and kicking. She scratched at his wrists as he held her to the floor. Promising to kill him, she spat in his face.

Clearly, he was winning. His strong legs had her pinned beneath him to the floor, and he wasn't letting her go. He smiled a sinful knowing smile at her. She drew in a deep breath and squeezed her eyes shut while visions of what he had done to her previously flashed torturously in her mind.

Just as she was getting her mad renewed, she envisioned her elderly neighbor, Miriam, sprawled on the floor, bloody, beaten and now dead because of him. Somewhere deep within, Cat could feel the hate brew inside her. Like a liquid heating to a boisterous boil, she exploded with a shrill howling scream. Her eyes flew open, and the hidden warrior inside her raged. With a fury she didn't know she possessed she used her powerful muscular legs to propel Warren off of her. She planted her feet on the floor and used her hips to buck him off and away. She sprung up like a spider and spun away from him before he could react. As fast as her legs could sprint, she darted through open doors, around corners and up a flight of stairs. She never looked back as she ran. She didn't dare stop to check if Warren was close behind her. She knew he was or soon would be.

When she got to the top of the stairs, she unlocked the rooftop door with a quick twist of her hand, flinging the door wide open. She was out on the flat rooftop in a heartbeat. She ran to the roof's edge and peered over the side of the building, mentally weighing her options.

"Trust me, you will die if you jump," Warren laughed. His voice was raspy and weak as he struggled to breathe.

She took one look at his bloody chest and scratched face and smiled at having caused him a little damage. She leaned her back against the low edge of the concrete wall and rested her hands on her hips.

"You've lost a lot of blood," Cat said with no empathy. "You look like you're not gonna make it. I've wanted to watch you die for quite some time now. Looks like I'll get my wish." She nearly laughed at the sound of own her voice which sounded unfamiliar to herself.

"Listen to you, Cat. You sound evil. Look how I have changed you," Warren alleged with a smile.

"You haven't changed anyone, Warren. You are so pathetic," Cat laughed.

Both of them stood there looking at each other, sizing up the other's wounds. Warren put his hands on his knees and bent over at the waist. He coughed up some blood and spit it on the ground by his feet. His eyes never left Cat's face. He

275

licked his lips and began telling her what he intended to do to her. Cat wasn't listening anymore though. She knew she only had one choice. She was alone and no one was coming to her aid. She would have to finish Warren herself. She silently prayed for God to help her.

Warren's whiney voice interrupted her prayers, "I brought you something, Kitty Cat."

He held up her silver bracelet where she could see it. Blood was smeared all over it. His nasty fingers twirled it around and around. He held out a single bloody finger and motioned for her to come to him.

"Why did you do it, Warren? Why did you kill all those women? Why did you kill Miriam?"

She didn't expect a reasonable answer. There wasn't an answer that would make sense or matter now anyway. She was just trying to buy some time. She needed to reassure herself that she had the courage, the strength, the will to see this through, no matter how it ended. Warren didn't answer her. He just smiled at the knowledge of how much pain he had caused her. His eyes took on an eerie gleam.

"How could you hurt a little old dog?" Cat screamed. "You nearly killed her. She won't ever be the same!" Cat screamed again.

Warren just laughed. He ran his bloody hands over his chest. "Honey, no woman is ever the same after being with me."

Cat smirked. She rolled her eyes and just shook her head. "Whatever, Warren. You disgust me." She pretended to gag a little before she forced a grin across her face.

Her disrespect hit Warren like a searing slap. Cat watched as he stood to his full height and wrapped his fingers around the silver bracelet. She felt his icy stare as a cold wind whipped at her body. She knew he was about to try something so she kept him talking, hoping to keep him distracted.

"I have something for you too, Warren."

She pulled the silver necklace from her shirt and showed him the silver dove pendant. She ran the pendant up and down the chain and watched as his face changed from anger to pure rage.

"Quit calling me Warren and take that stupid bird off my necklace," he screamed.

She watched as his eyes appeared to bulge as he yelled. She wondered if he had quit breathing, his face was so red and the veins in his neck were thick as ropes. Whatever his reasons were for wanting the necklace, she knew without a doubt that he wanted it desperately.

"What is the big deal with this piece of crap? Why do you want it back so badly?" she asked as she held the necklace out from her body.

"Shut your mouth, you whore!" Warren screamed. He shook with fury.

Cat watched as his foamy mouth spat as he yelled. She saw that his legs were shaking. Feeling panic begin to rise in her throat, she swallowed a few insults she wanted to yell back at him. She wasn't ready yet to send him reeling.

"Where did you get this necklace, Warren?" She softened her tone a little as she asked. "Who else did you give it to, besides me?"

He shook his head no and yelled, "Trailer trash like you wouldn't understand."

"Come one, Warren, tell me."

He relaxed a little by looking around before he spoke. Using the back of his hand, he wiped at the corners of his mouth.

"Well, since you won't live to see tomorrow. It won't matter if I tell you or not." He cackled. "That necklace was my mother's. I killed her with it. I killed every whore I ever knew with it, just like I'm going to kill you with it."

He threw his head back and laughed like a lunatic then. He laughed so hard and for so long that fear began to plague her mind. She could feel her old self-doubt crawl up her leg like a spider; it clawed at her back and settled like a monstrous weight around her neck. Suddenly, she had a thought! She unfastened the silver chain and held it up for Warren to see. She watched his eyes follow her every move as she slid the dove off the chain and placed it in her pocket. His eyes looked feverish and yellow as she held the naked chain up for him to inspect.

Cat yelled, "Give me the bracelet and the chain is yours!" She watched as he appeared to be thinking over her offer. She knew she sounded scared, she could hear her voice cracking. Her mind was racing with ideas to distract Warren when she thought of the man who she watched die.

"Why did you kill that guy by my car? What did he ever do to you?" Cat asked.

"That loser died because he was incompetent," he yelled. "You should have died too that night."

She shuddered at the thought.

"What is the deal with this worthless chain, Warren? Why not just get another one?"

Cat could tell Warren was getting tired of talking. He ignored her and examined his wounds. He was losing a lot of blood. She watched as he straightened his shirt collar and tucked his shirt back into his pants. She could almost see his anger renew his resolve to kill her. He appeared confident that he could. He believed he could snuff out her life like that of all his other victims. He smoothed his hair back with a hand covered in blood and narrowed his nearly black eyes at her. The sinister smile that crossed his face had bile filling Cat's mouth.

For a brief moment the thought crossed her mind that today would be her last day on the planet. She cursed her weakness and forced herself to stand tall and face him. She could hear a voice screaming inside her head as Warren walked slowly towards her like a jackal waiting to pounce on his prey. The closer he came, the louder the voice in her head became. It was screaming for her to run, but her feet felt cemented in place. For some unknown reason she raised her arm and held the silver chain out to him like an olive branch. The horrible smile that played on his lips twisted her gut. He was within an arm's reach when she assured herself that his overconfidence would be his own demise. He took the chain from her hand and absent-mindedly handed her the silver bracelet.

She kept her eyes on him, watching as he gingerly fingered the chain. He appeared lost in cherished memories as he wound the chain through his fingers. She wondered if he was reliving each murder he had ever committed as he studied the necklace. In turn, she glanced at the silver bracelet, slid it on her arm and read the inscription engraved around its outside edge: "And ye shall know the truth, and the truth shall make you free."

The truth will make you free? How many times had she heard that from one or both of her parents? Cat couldn't know for certain, but somewhere in the hundreds, if not thousands. She thought of her parents. Her eyes filled with tears as she thought about never seeing them again. No matter what happened, she would see them again. Her faith would see her through.

Warren's arms grabbed her before she finished the thought. He was putting the necklace back around her neck as she struggled against him. His body weight pinned her against the wall as he clasped the chain at the nape of her neck. She was thinking how rank he smelled, as he buried his face in her hair. Every inch of her body repelled his touch.

She held her breath and forced the involuntary gagging sensation to stop as he whispered in her ear, "I love what you have done with your hair and you smell so good, baby."

She struggled to get free. "Stop it, Warren!" she yelled. She tried pushing him away, but he was too strong. "Get off me," she said, but Warren didn't budge.

"Tell me you love me. Tell me you'll never leave me," Warren demanded.

When she didn't answer, he tightened his grip on her neck and slid his fingers through the chain on her neck. He twisted the chain mercilessly as it cinched tightly against her skin. She began to choke and struggled to get her fingers under the chain.

Panic slammed her mind into action. She bent her knees and lowered her body slightly, as she had learned in her self-defense class. Warren meanwhile, continued twisting the chain, cutting off her air as it bit into the tender flesh of her neck. Cat quickly drew her right leg back and then brought her knee up rapidly into Warren's crotch. Immediately his grip loosened, and she worked the fingers of both hands between her neck and the chain.

As Warren dropped to the ground groaning in pain, Cat jumped clear of him and darted away. She stretched a shaking hand out to the door handle of the roof door just as Warren grabbed a handful of her hair and yanked her back viciously. The pain seared her senses and had her seeing stars.

"Trying to leave me again?" he yelled.

His body was sticky with sweat as he pressed himself against her back. The revolt that Cat's stomach had staged earlier came back with a full vengeance. Dry heaves wracked her body as the tiny flashes of light performed a floating dance before her watering eyes. He forced her to her knees with one torturous jerk of her hair.

"Now I'm going to teach you some respect, slut." He screamed.

Without waiting to see what he had in mind, Cat let go of his hand that held her hair and felt for the blade she had hidden in the sole of her shoe. She wrapped her fingers around the woven handle and moved with deadly stealth as she plunged the knife blade deep into his inner thigh. She knew she had hit her target when massive spurts of bright red blood sprang into view on his slacks and then began pouring down his leg.

She ran back across the rooftop to the ledge. She would jump if she had to, she decided.

Warren realized he was bleeding to death. He screamed a list of obscenities that had Cat turning back around to face him. They stood there staring at each other, accepting their own fates.

Warren ran with incredible speed towards her. Cat didn't know how or why she did what she did next. She crouched down in a fighter's stance, preparing for his attack. When Warren reached her, he was running full blast. With agility she didn't know she had, she side-stepped out of his way and pushed him all at once.

He hit the low wall and toppled over, disappearing out of sight.

Cat stood, feeling nothing for a few seconds before realizing what had happened. Slowly she took a step, then another, as she neared the edge of the building. She peeked over the side of the ledge. She had to see this through to the end, she told herself. Once she saw Warren's mangled body on the concrete below, she could breathe normally again.

Warren wasn't dead, though. He hadn't fallen to the ground. He was hanging onto a bronzed antique light fixture that was mounted to the building. He hung a few feet from the top of the ledge.

"Help me," he pleaded. "Help!"

Instinct told her to help him. She started to give him her hand, but stopped and pulled her hand back before he grabbed it. She stood there staring at him afraid he would pull her over the edge with him.

"Give me your hand. Please, Cat, help me," he pleaded.

"I'll help you, Warren, but don't try to pull me over with you. Let me help you. I can help you."

She didn't know why she did it, but she held her hand out to him. In that split second she saw the transformation in his eyes. The fear of dying, of pleading for help, turned to hatred and malevolence. He smiled as he yanked hard on her arm. The smile faded instantly, though, as he came away with nothing but the silver bracelet as he fell two stories to his death.

Chapter 34

When Sullivan saw the body drop from the building in front of him, he felt his heart stop in his chest. The tires of his patrol car screeched to a stop as the figure fell from the sky. Running to the crumpled form with terror ripping at his throat, Sullivan cast an eye to the top of the building, but failed to see anyone else on the rooftop.

Sullivan nearly cried when he discovered it wasn't Cat on the ground. It was Warren. Kneeling beside the crumpled form, Sullivan placed two fingers on Warren's neck and felt for a pulse, but didn't find one. He pulled his cell phone out of his pocket, his mind wracked with fear over the condition he would find Cat in.

"Send me an ambulance and a supervisor to Northeast 25th and Santa Fe," he demanded. "We have a deceased subject on the west side of the building, and I'll be going in the building at that location to look for others."

He waiting long enough for the dispatcher to repeat the information before he hit the end button and dropped his phone back in the front pocket of his jeans. That's when he saw Cat's silver bracelet. Warren had gotten close enough to Cat to put his hands on her and he still had her bracelet in his dead, bloody fingers.

"Cat! Cat, where are you?" Sullivan screamed frantically as he ran through the radio station.

He followed the blood trail to the stairs that led to the roof and sprinted up them two at a time yelling her name. With every absent reply, his hope sank. He ran out onto the rooftop, out of breath, convinced she was gone forever. That's where he found her, sitting on the roof, her back against the wall that Warren had tumbled over. Her knees were drawn up, her head laying on her arms, and she was sobbing.

Gently he touched her head and knelt down next to her, drawing her into his arms. Lifting her onto his lap, he cradled her against his heaving chest. He kissed her cheeks, her lips, her eyelids as he rocked her back and forth.

"Thank God you are all right." He squeezed her tighter. "I love you, Catherine."

Cat stared into the tear-filled, coffee-colored eyes she had come to adore. She nearly choked on her words as she asked him to repeat that last part again. Sullivan brushed her hair out of her eyes and tenderly held her face in both of his hands and professed his love for her again. But this time, he added, "Marry me," before Cat collapsed against him.

****

The room was filled with everyone Cat cared about. They sat at her parents' oak dining room table and drank the most delicious raspberry-apricot tea she had ever tasted. She glanced from face to face and silently thanked God that she was still there to love them and be loved by them. Phillip, Linda, Susan and Sullivan sat around the table. Delicate little blue and white floral cups sat on matching saucers in front of each of them. Hannah rested in Cat's lap. Occasionally a shiver would run through her little fur-covered body making her cropped ears shake.

Miriam was the only one missing from Cat's circle of loved ones. Miriam's funeral was scheduled for the following Monday. With no family to speak of, Phillip and Linda were handling the arrangements. Miriam would be buried beside her husband in the Rose Garden of the Summit View Cemetery in Guthrie.

Petting the shivering body of her littlest friend, Cat rested her hand on Hannah's tiny head and asked Sullivan to continue. He had come to tell them that they had found Rick's body.

Sullivan said that Rick likely had been killed sometime over the last couple of weeks, stuffed into a large plastic barrel and placed into a rented storage unit on the city's south side. Without any live witnesses to talk to, it was impossible to know for sure Rick's exact role in the murders.

"We are working on the theory that Warren was a serial rapist and killer. Rick just happened to get suckered into the plot by being willing to cover for Warren one time, not knowing what a monster Warren was."

Sullivan glanced around as he spoke. The group hung on every word he said. They watched him intently, waiting to hear what else he would say.

"When Warren murdered Juan Diaz, he was hoping to kill you, too," Sullivan said, as he turned dazzling brown eyes toward Cat. "From what he told you, he was planning to kill you with the necklace after he got it back from Diaz. Unfortunately for Diaz, Warren was going to kill him whether he retrieved the necklace from you or not."

Sullivan's skin looked pale, Cat observed. She watched him intently as he outlined his theories. She watched his lips as they formed words. The gravelly sound his voice made quickened her pulse. His deep voice radiated against her like a drum.

"He must not have expected you so early," Sullivan continued. "I'm guessing that when you screamed, it startled him. He must have grabbed you, searched for the necklace and then ran away when he heard someone coming." He paused as he watched Cat's eyes. She was so beautiful, he thought. "Warren was evil. He knew he had to kill every witness or risk getting caught," Sullivan said.

Cat nodded in agreement. She looked Sullivan straight in the eyes as she spoke, "When I was a little girl, my parents told me about people who don't know the truth from a lie. They called them, the lying kind. Ultimately, that's what Warren was, among other things," Cat concluded.

"This is a token of friendship, a token of truth." She said as she lowered her eyes to her wrist where her new silver bracelet rested. Susan and Cat exchanged smiles as Cat continued.

Betsy Randolph

"I realize now that Warren's necklace was a token of death. It was a token of lies from a liar. I'm glad I gave it back to him."

About the Author

Betsy Randolph worked in radio broadcasting for several years in four states before settling in Oklahoma. She received an Associates degree in Journalism from Northern Oklahoma College, where she wrote for the College paper *The Maverick*. Betsy also obtained an Associate's degree in Horticulture from Oklahoma State University and a Bachelor's degree in Organizational Leadership from South-

 ern Nazarene University. Betsy served twelve years in the U. S. Army Reserves as a military policeman and drill sergeant. She has worked as a police officer and is currently an Oklahoma State trooper. She is a member of the Red Dirt Writers Society and the Oklahoma Writers'

Federation. She is a Master Gardener and writes a gardening column for the *Guthrie News Leader*. She lives in Guthrie, Oklahoma, with her husband, George, and son, Bronson. Her stepdaughter, Whitney, and her husband, Gus, live in New Jersey.

Betsy's literary website is at www.RedDirtWriters.org/betsy .
Betsy's blog "Pistols and Pruners" is at
                                 www.BetsyRandolph.blogspot.com .